Nice, kind...special!

He hated every one of those labels Emily pinned on him. And then she'd kiss his cheek as if he were a good little boy.

Sean didn't believe she was immune to him, quite the contrary. In his gut he felt that she was protecting herself from something, and the something was him. Why? Was she afraid he'd disappoint her, hurt her? Had she heard the stories about his life and believed them? "Sean Townsend, playboy." It was so laughable and so infuriating.

He would not be beaten, had never been beaten in anything that really mattered to him. Emily Smith didn't know it yet, but she was about to find out that this nice, kind, special man could be just as devious as he needed to be to make sure he got what he wanted.

ABOUT THE AUTHOR

Before turning to writing full-time six years ago, Stella Cameron edited medical texts. Her dream then, and even as a child, was to write. Stella has an active imagination and is always plotting; in her head, strangers on the street act out scenarios. Along with her husband and three children, she lives in the state of Washington.

Books by Stella Cameron

HARLEQUIN AMERICAN ROMANCE
153—SHADOWS
195—NO STRANGER
226—SECOND TO NONE

HARLEQUIN SUPERROMANCE
185—MOONTIDE

HARLEQUIN INTRIGUE
50—ALL THAT SPARKLES
83—SOME DIE TELLING

A Party of Two
Stella Cameron

Harlequin Books

TORONTO • NEW YORK • LONDON
AMSTERDAM • PARIS • SYDNEY • HAMBURG
STOCKHOLM • ATHENS • TOKYO • MILAN

For our daughter,
Kirsten Cameron
Gentle and wise,
but best of all a dreamer

Published April 1988

First printing February 1988

ISBN 0-373-16243-X

Chapter One

Sweat soaked her headband. The nylon running suit she wore, now damp and icy, stuck to her arms, the middle of her back, her thighs. Emily lengthened her stride, determined she wouldn't look back again. The steady thud-thudding of her Reeboks comforted her. Then she heard that other sound again. Other pounding footsteps.

He was still there and he was running faster, too.

The nasty sensation in her chest swelled. Why couldn't a woman take a late-night run in a built-up area of Los Angeles without some kook deciding to come along? She knew the answer to her own questions. This was her fault. The rule she'd made never to be out after the night scene quieted down had been the right one. Breaking it, even though she couldn't sleep until she'd exercised, was a risk not worth taking.

She had to look. As she did so, Emily kept moving, sidestepping toward the curb. A blond man again. Now she was sure she hadn't imagined being followed by a blond man while she was running a few nights before—or that time in the parking lot of a grocery store. On both occasions, and perhaps one or two others, she'd credited a creative imagination with working overtime, and blocked out the anxiety.

Imagination hadn't been the problem. Santa Monica Boulevard was well lit and she saw the light glint on his hair an instant before he slipped behind a clump of oleander and disappeared. Two o'clock in the morning was full of mixed blessings. There was no traffic to stop her wild flight across the boulevard—but also no people. Not another human being around, except for the fleet-footed dodging expert behind her.

There were two choices: try to get home on foot, which would mean crossing his path and running through dark, tree-lined streets, or find a taxi.

The taxi won out.

She continued on, scanning the street and fumbling for the money she kept in her pocket. The warm air she breathed seared her throat now. She paused, blinking as stinging sweat drizzled into the corners of her eyes. *Hell.* She'd used the money to pay the paper carrier earlier in the evening. All she had was the credit card she always carried. That and her door key. No taxi driver was going to be thrilled at the sight of a Visa card.

Emily had to have money. Skirting a row of newspaper vending machines, she broke into a mad dash down Benecia to Missouri Street. There was a cash machine in the ABC Entertainment Center. If she could just make it that far she'd be okay; she knew she would.

Two more turns and she saw the street sign for Constellation Boulevard. Ahead lay Avenue of the Stars and her destination.

She stopped for a sleek and vaguely sinister black limousine that slid too slowly past her. Again she glanced over her shoulder but saw only shadows and spears of yellow glow, making angular patterns on the buildings and pavement. Relief brought a kind of light-headedness and the urge to laugh. She'd lost him. Emily considered and immediately discarded the idea of continuing her run.

The ABC Center was a soaring edifice of white marble and chrome. Mannequins, their lifeless faces ghastly beneath layers of paint, stared sightlessly from store windows. Emily ran across the main terrace of the complex, leaped on the nearest outdoor escalator to the lower level and almost fell. Of course the escalators weren't working. She stumbled down the unmoving steps and crossed a wide atrium, her shoes squeaking on the glittering tiles. Just as she'd remembered, there was the dear, wonderful bank machine. She'd get some money, hail a cab and go home to her safe little house.

Please insert your card and wait for instructions read the display on the machine. Emily reached beneath her sweatpants for the card she'd put in the back pocket of her shorts. Which way should she put it in? She couldn't seem to think logically. In the direction of the arrow printed on one side, she finally decided.

She waited, staring back the way she'd come. If her pursuer hadn't given up, if he'd seen her come in here and followed, she'd be trapped.

A little beep sounded, followed by a whirring noise. *Please insert your card and wait for instructions.* Her hands shook. She'd already inserted her card. Maybe it was upside down. She tried again.

Beep. Whir. *Please insert...* "Come on!" She pulled out her card and stared at it, then at the message that flashed on the tiny screen every few seconds. If she'd been the crying type, she'd be bawling by now. Instead she felt the tall glass walls closing in around her. Above, the black sky looked like a distant square held up by the surrounding buildings. The breeze turned her moist skin cold. She'd try the card again.

The clip-clip of a man's dress shoes keeping time with a piercing, whistled rendition of the "Colonel Bogey March" from *The Bridge on the River Kwai*, drained the last vestiges of strength from her limbs and made her heart pound wildly.

She retreated into the alcove beside the machine and waited. The footsteps came closer and Emily held her breath.

The whistling subsided to a hum, and there he was, standing just a few feet from her. She heard the sound of coins rattling in pockets. Then her sole exit was blocked by a solid figure she saw only in outline.

"What the—" The man recoiled slightly, then came in for a closer look. "Sorry, ma'am," he said and appeared to hesitate. "Didn't realize anyone was here."

Emily mustered a little composure and drew up to her full height. She was slender, but her almost six-foot usually brought respect from any man. "I won't be a minute," she said with more assurance than she felt. Please let her get the money this time.

"No problem," he replied and moved back a step. His black tie hung loose and his white shirt glistened against dark evening clothes. Emily thought she caught the faint scent of alcohol. Just what she needed, a drunk to keep her company.

She avoided looking at his face. "Just need to get some money," she said and shook her head slightly. Brilliant observation on her part. Very deliberately, she inserted her card, sliding it in slowly until she felt it grabbed by a feeder.

Please wait. A rush of blood to her head made her lean on the wall. Thank God, she was going to get out of here. She tried not to consider that the man behind her might pose an obstacle to that plan.

Enter your secret code.

Now she was really getting somewhere. She'd deliberately made up a little word trigger to remind her of the password. Something to do with being funny. Joke, that was it. She punched in the letters.

The man was whistling again, and bracing a shoulder on the corner of the wall, the corner that allowed him to face her.

Incorrect code. Please try again.

Emily glanced at the man and laughed tightly. "Do you ever have trouble with these things?" She immediately regretted saying anything at all. She should know better than to encourage the inebriated, particularly in these circumstances.

He straightened, and she was able to see his face and his ruffled, straight blond hair. She couldn't tell what color his eyes were, but they weren't dark, and he was smiling, showing teeth that had either started out perfect, or cost someone a mint. "Can't say I ever have," he said.

She frowned, then remembered her question. Of course he'd never had a problem like this. Men never had trouble with simple operations, or never admitted they did. Emily breathed slowly through her nose. She was a capable woman, a woman who helped run a growing business that required organization and a cool head, and she did the job very well. The bankcard was something she rarely used, but that was no excuse for forgetting the password. Fear must be scrambling her brain. How about jest, or pun? *Calm down,* she told herself, *stay calm and go through this thing until you hit the right word.*

Jest didn't work, neither did pun. "Look—" she stepped from the alcove "—why don't you go first? I may have to run through the entire dictionary to find my code word."

He spread his hands expansively. "Wouldn't hear of it. I'll just wait till you're safely on your way. You shouldn't be here alone at this time of night. It's too dangerous."

Emily swallowed the urge to tell him he was the only potentially dangerous element in sight right now. She hesitated the two seconds it took to figure he was only a couple of inches taller than she but very well built—and very good-looking—then she faced the mechanical beast again.

She tapped the card against her thumbnail. Her business partner, Joe Moreno, who was one of the two people who shared the rented house where she lived, had come up with the perfect way to remember the code word. What had he said?

"Not coming to you?" the waiting man asked pleasantly. Too pleasantly.

"It will," Emily said. She wished he'd go away.

"Sounds like?"

"I beg your pardon?"

"Sounds like?" He came to stand beside her, pushed back his black coat and put his hands in his pockets. "You know, charades. Maybe you need a few hints. You must have some sort of idea what it is."

She could smell his after-shave as well as the alcohol, which was more distinct now. Charades in the middle of the night in the basement atrium of the ABC building. Wonderful. If Joe ever heard this story, he'd really have ammunition against her penchant for late-night jogging.

"Come on," the man said, bantering, and tapped her shoulder. "Give it a try. Little word?"

Emily flinched from the touch. "I've got it, thank you. But really, I'd feel more comfortable if you went first."

"But I insist."

"No, I insist." Feeling very alone, Emily walked past him and sat on the edge of a planter. There was no point in telephoning her house for help. Joe wouldn't be back from his date yet, and Larry Young, the third member of their household, didn't own a car.

Seconds later the man turned toward her, tucking bills into his wallet. "There," he said. "All yours."

"Thanks." She had it, oh, she had it. Quickly, Emily inserted her card into the appropriate slot, paused for the prompt and tapped in *glee*. She should have remembered it at once. Joe had said, "Remember glee club."

The light on the machine went out. Emily reached up slowly and pulled off her headband, staring at the minute screen.

"What's the matter?"

He was still there. "How should I...nothing. I guess it's taking a little time to process."

"It doesn't take any time at all."

Thanks. "Please, don't worry yourself. I can manage."

"It's not working."

The guy was also very observant. "I noticed."

"Take your card back out."

"I can't."

"Why?"

"It—" A loud grinding noise interrupted her, followed by what sounded distinctly like a gulp, then the display came up with good old faithful: *Insert your card* . . . Emily ran her fingers through her short hair. "It ate my card," she muttered disbelievingly. She pointed at the mean black slot. "I don't believe it. The thing ate my card." She thumped the machine with both fists, but nothing happened.

A muffled sound, sounding suspiciously like a thinly disguised laugh, infuriated her further. "Don't let me delay you," Emily said. "I'll have to find a phone and report this."

"At this time of night—or morning?" He coughed, then sniffed. Obviously, he found her little mishap entertaining. "You'll have to wait until business hours, and even then I wish you luck."

She really didn't care anymore. "Excuse me. I must be getting on." She slid through the narrow space between the man and the wall and started for the motionless escalator again.

"Hey, hey, hold up. Wait a minute." He fell into step beside her. "Let me help you. What do you need money for?"

Emily hesitated in midstride. "I don't think that's any of your business." Good grief, the situation was getting more bizarre by the minute.

"No, of course it's not my business. I'm sorry. But it is a bit off the wall to be running around alone in the night and doing battle with a cash machine."

"Why is it off the wall for me to be here and not for you? Please excuse me."

She sprinted, but despite his street clothes he was just as fast. They arrived at the escalator in a dead heat and collided on the bottom step.

Emily turned and tried to squeeze past, but he moved above her and smiled down. She could see his face clearly now, and it was not at all hard on the eye. Mid-thirties. He had a wonderful mouth. "Look," he said, "I'm sorry if I said the wrong thing, but you're a bit of a surprise. I didn't expect to find a gorgeous redhead skulking down here."

"I wasn't skulking." Emily took a deep breath, feeling a mixture of irritation, a sense of the ridiculous and a very slight warming to this green-eyed charmer.

"No, no, you weren't skulking. Just sort of hiding in a corner. And your hair's more auburn than red, isn't it?"

This couldn't be happening to her. Emily wasn't too humble to acknowledge that she was a very attractive woman. After living virtually alone in Los Angeles for four years, few come-on lines were new to her, but the present scene was a first.

"I really should start for home."

"Would you say your hair was auburn?"

She propped an elbow on her other forearm and rubbed her eyes. "Auburn, yes. And my eyes are dark blue. I'm five-foot eleven and 130 pounds. Anything else you need to know before I leave?"

He laughed and bowed his head. His well-cut hair gleamed. "That'll do for a start. You are beautiful, you know. Do you make a habit of running around alone in the early hours of the morning?"

Emily scanned the area. The sick sense of threat was returning. There had to be another way out. She stepped backward.

"Now I've frightened you. I'm sorry. Really, I'd like to help you." He produced his wallet. "Let me lend you what you need."

"Oh, no," Emily said, horrified. "I couldn't possibly. Anyway," she added, "I've decided I don't need it after all."

"But you wouldn't have come down here if you didn't need money."

The whole thing had gone far enough. "Good night." She moved up deliberately and he stood aside.

By the time she reached the top he was right behind her and continued to walk in her tracks all the way to the street.

"Can I give you a lift somewhere?"

Emily cast him a withering look over her shoulder and started to run, away from her home on Overland Avenue. One blond stranger in the night was as threatening as another, and she had no intention of leading either of them to her house.

She set a steady pace, not too fast, not too slow. If she could circle the block without incident, then it might be all right to get back on her original route.

A low purring noise interrupted her planning. A silvery gray Jensen drew level and crawled along the curb beside her. Emily knew without looking who was behind the wheel. From the corner of her eye she saw the nearest window slide down.

Emily ran on, keeping her eyes ahead.

"Please, will you let me help you?" he called to her. His voice was warm and a little gravelly. Under any other circumstances she would have found it appealing.

"If you want to help me," Emily said, puffing now, not from exertion but from stress, "go on your way and let me go on mine."

"Just tell me *why* you needed money if all you want to do is run?"

She slowed down but kept enough distance from the car to give herself room to elude him if he decided to come after her. "I wanted to take a taxi," she said finally.

"A taxi?" His tires hissed against the curb—he must have steered toward her slightly. "Why? Are you tired?"

Emily felt like crying from frustration. "I was being followed by some nut. I think I lost him, but—"

"But you've picked up another nut?" He laughed shortly.

"I haven't *picked up* anyone. All I want to do is mind my own business."

The abrupt turn of the car's front wheels in her direction and the passenger door swinging open brought Emily to a jarring halt, her pulse singing in her ears.

"Get in," he said. "Only a damned fool does what you're doing. You could get yourself murdered out here."

"Get in?" Emily's voice rose to a squeak. "This is crazy. I don't get into strange men's cars."

"I'll take you home, you little idiot."

"Idiot? You're unbelievable. I don't let strange men take me home. Good night, Mr.—"

"Townsend, Sean Townsend. Townsend Industrial Alarm Systems. I'm well known in Los Angeles. Pillar of society. Look me up in *Who's Who* or the phone book."

"Sure," Emily said and moved closer to the buildings before continuing her run.

Sean, or whatever his name was, resumed his snail-paced progress along the street. Every few yards the still-open door of the fantastically expensive vehicle scraped the sidewalk and every time it did Emily winced.

"Listen," he yelled. "if you won't let me take you to your place, come to mine. Then I won't know where you live and you can call someone if you like, call a taxi, anything, only I can't leave you here."

Emily skidded to a stop and bent until she could see his face, illuminated by the lit dashboard. He looked absolutely serious. She began to laugh, holding her sides and bending double to catch her breath.

"What's so funny?"

"You," she said. "I must really come off like a flake. If I won't take you to my house, will I come to yours? I don't know what you mixed with your soda pop tonight but it must have been potent stuff."

Without another word, she broke into a full run, praying he'd give up and go away.

No such luck. Almost immediately the gray Jensen was beside her again, its door still open and scraping the ground in a way that hurt Emily's teeth. Money meant nothing to this guy, or he wouldn't be abusing a priceless car that way.

She passed the 20th-Century Fox Building, crossed a narrow street and plodded on, getting farther and farther away from home. Still the engine purred beside her. Later she might learn to laugh about the ridiculous picture they must make. Much later.

Sean winced as he heard his car door scrape against the sidewalk yet again. He must be out of his mind to do this, but she was something. He *felt* something about her. And she was just about the loveliest woman he remembered seeing in a long time, perhaps ever seeing. He hadn't made a hit with her... yet. But persistence, he'd learned during at least the past twenty of his thirty-seven years, almost always paid off in the end. With women anyway.

He searched for another approach. Getting out of the car and confronting her would undoubtedly be disastrous. And if he continued on this way the result was unlikely to be any better. But he had to have a chance to see her in normal circumstances and that would never happen if he let her get away.

"Hey," he called, fumbling in the breast pocket of his dinner jacket for his wallet, "why not wait here till we see a taxi? You over there and me in here. And then I'll lend you the fare."

She turned her face to him, and he saw she was pale, her high cheekbones clearly defined and shiny, her dark eyes strained wide open. She was scared, but he was damned if he was going away until he was sure she was okay. One way he didn't want to learn her name was to read about her as a murder or rape victim in the morning paper.

A slight check in her stride, a tensing in her body, made him look ahead. A hundred yards away a taxi drew to a stop to let out a fare.

He made up his mind. "Lady," he called, "please humor me. Take this and grab that cab. My gift to you."

She looked from him to the cab, and he could almost feel her struggle to make up her mind.

He crumpled a fifty-dollar bill into a ball and tossed it to her. She caught it and looked at him, panic clear in her eyes. "I can't."

"Yes, you can. Go. Before you lose the thing."

"I can't take this."

He pulled on the emergency break and got out of the car. The taxi driver had turned on his light and begun to pick up speed. Sean ran into the middle of the street and flagged the car to a stop. "Come on, come on!" he shouted to the woman.

She didn't move.

"Come on," he ordered and she ran, slowly at first, then faster until she was beside him. Oh, man, this was one spectacular female. Up close she glistened, every fine feature delicately drawn, a soft shimmer of reddish tint catching her damp curly hair. She opened the palm that held the bill, and for an instant he thought she'd throw the money back at him. Instead, she reached down inside her sweat jacket and produced a card.

"Take that," she said breathlessly, pressing it into his hand, and allowed him to open the taxi door for her.

Sean read the card: *Moreno and Co. The Occasion People.* There were two telephone numbers at the bottom. "What's this?" he asked.

"My business card," she said and murmured something he couldn't hear to the taxi driver.

"Just a minute? What's your—"

But the car was in motion. "Call my office," she said to him through the open window. "I'll get the money to you."

"Okay. But who shall I ask for?"

"Emily."

Chapter Two

Sean was bone-tired, drained. His body felt like an old punching bag. He yawned and walked slowly down the steps from his terrace to the side of the pool.

The usual early-morning pall stretched across Hollywood and the valley to the east, over the Beverly Hills houses below his own. Above the blue-gray smog, a smudge of bronze suggested the sun had risen.

If he had an hour, or even half an hour before Mrs. Sekowsky found him, it would be a miracle. He positioned a chaise so that his housekeeper might not immediately spot him from one of the windows, then he stretched out, sinking down until his head was lower than the top of the chairback. Any minute now Sekowsky would go to his suite with coffee and discover his bed hadn't been touched. Next she'd descend on his study, expecting to find him asleep on the couch and prepared to make a few acerbic comments about his nocturnal schedule. With luck she might then assume he hadn't come home at all and he'd be free to continue with his battle plans until it was time to call the office.

"Moreno and Co.," he said aloud. The card was in his pocket, but he had memorized everything on it, including the telephone numbers. One was a business number, the other a residence. Sean checked his watch as he had done every few minutes since he'd arrived home. Six o'clock.

He'd wait another hour, then call the residence. Moreno. Emily Moreno? Or was she Co.?

Emily was a nice name, a little old-fashioned and sweet. He realized he was smiling and glanced around guiltily. She was it. The one. He felt it in his blood and bones. Love at first sight was supposed to be a myth, but he'd felt the same way the moment he'd met Margaret, and they'd had the best marriage a man could ask for. He smiled again, remembering the woman who had been his wife for eight years. Even when they'd both known she was dying she'd given him the strength to bear it and carry on. And she'd reminded him so often that he should marry again as soon as possible because he was "good at it." That had been almost four years ago, and he hadn't had the heart to even think about another woman as a wife until recently. Now he was really thinking about it. Margaret would have approved of Emily; she'd always been attracted to people with style and guts, and Emily, whatever her last name was, certainly had both.

The sky brightened noticeably. Down there the city was stirring. Frank Horton, his senior vice president, didn't get into the offices on Wilshire Boulevard until eight. Sean would let him know he might be unavailable for at least part of the day. The first priority was to contact Emily and be sure he knew where and how to find her. Then he could decide how to proceed.

A steady sucking noise startled him.

"Morning, Mr. Townsend."

Sean peered through eyes that felt gritty at a small man who was dragging a hose along the edge of the pool.

"Pssst, Dan," he whispered urgently to his groundskeeper.

The wizened little man paused, the hose clasped in both darkly tanned hands. "Yes, sir, Mr. Townsend?"

"No, no," Sean said in a stage whisper, "not so loud. Pretend I'm not here, Dan. Carry on and don't look this way, you understand?"

Dan ran gnarled fingers through wiry white hair that stood straight up from his skull. Slowly, a knowing smile spread over his thin face, deepening the wrinkles of his lined skin. "Hiding out from her?" He nodded toward the house.

Sean grinned back. "You know how it is, Dan. A man needs a little time to himself."

Every member of the household respected Sekowsky—and was mildly intimidated by her. Also, they all knew Sekowsky was the one who had kept this impressive household together since Margaret's death.

The groundskeeper went about his work without another word, and Sean allowed his eyes to close. Townsend Alarms was going well, fantastically well. The business had been smaller but already highly lucrative when he'd taken over from his father. Industrial security needs had steadily become larger and more sophisticated since then and he'd grown with the trends. What he now controlled was a solid gold operation. He was a success story, one of Los Angeles's most eligible single males according to the local and national rags. Too bad his man-about-town, love-'em-and-leave-'em act, which he evidently pulled off so well, went only skin-deep. Walking into the basement of the ABC building and meeting Emily last night had been the most exciting personal event of his life in far too long.

He toed his shoes off, then winced as they clattered to the ground. Earlier he'd been partially convinced that his fascination with Emily must lie in the circumstances of their meeting and that when he was totally sober, in the harsh early light of a September morning, the fascination would fade and quickly be forgotten.

But the attraction he felt for her was as strong now as it had been when he'd stood at her side by the taxi. Lazily, he dwelled on Emily. She looked like a model, but the card suggested she had some sort of business. Her age was difficult to pinpoint. She could be in her mid-twenties, younger than he preferred, but ten or so years' difference in age, either way, didn't matter if two people were right for each other.

She was probably only a couple of inches shorter than he was, if that, so she must be about six foot. And her coloring, the pale skin and auburn hair, the deep blue eyes, intrigued him. Her face had that delicate quality he liked: pointed chin, slender, slightly tilted nose and eyebrows that fanned upward. He could hardly wait to see her in daylight.

In the running outfit her figure had been hard to assess closely, but it was obvious she was slim and graceful, and he liked those things, too.

Sean decided that he was definitely suffering from infatuation. Maybe the next time he saw Emily, she'd prove to be just a nice, ordinary woman who'd struck him as exotic on a night that had been a bore.

The familiar squish of sensible lace-up shoes interrupted his reverie. Too late, he tried to straighten his collar and run a hand through his hair.

"There you are, Mr. Sean." Sekowsky had been calling him Mr. Sean since he was fourteen and she'd first started working in this same house. Margaret had been Mrs. Margaret. After Sean's father died and his mother moved to Miami, Sekowsky stayed on.

With his most winning smile, Sean said, "Morning, Mrs. S. You're looking ravishing today. Is that a new hairdo?"

One worn hand moved instinctively toward tightly permed blue hair. Then the woman pursed her lips and crossed her arms. "You must have been up early this morning, Mr. Sean." She looked significantly at his rumpled evening clothes. "If you'd let me know your plans, I'd have arranged breakfast for you ahead of schedule. Will you have time to eat before you leave for the office?"

Sean's features took on a serious expression. "Probably not, unfortunately. I got involved in an encounter that kept me up half the night." He didn't meet Sekowsky's penetrating brown eyes. "But I could use some coffee, if that wouldn't be too much trouble."

The sniff was almost imperceptible. "Will you take it in the breakfast room? Or should I set it beside your bed?" Her meaning was implicit: he looked the way he deserved to look, as if he hadn't slept all night.

He rallied. Occasionally he exerted his authority with his housekeeper. "I'll take my coffee right here, thank you, Mrs. Sekowsky. And I'll have a croissant, and the morning papers, if they've arrived." He took a long breath. "And be good enough to bring me a phone." There, he'd let her know who was boss. So why did he still feel like a teenaged upstart?

"As you wish." She walked away, but not before Sean saw the disdainful set of her face.

His plan was taking a clearer shape in his mind. He would make as many calls as it took to reach Emily at either one of her numbers. If the mood seemed right, he'd ask her to have lunch. The money she'd want to return could be the excuse for their getting together. If, on the other hand, she refused to meet with him and insisted on mailing the money, he'd resort to overt action—he'd go to wherever she lived and wait until she showed up.

The arrival of Beatrice, the girl who helped in the kitchen, with his coffee and papers was Sekowsky's statement that she felt affronted. She always attended to him herself in the morning. Beatrice returned with a phone and set it on the small wrought-iron table beside him. He smiled at her, and she managed a little upward quirk of the lips before withdrawing quickly. Sean had often heard the plump young woman chattering volubly in the kitchen, but she invariably became silent in his presence.

Ten minutes to seven. The timing could be crucial. A little too early and he might awaken her, starting them off on the wrong foot again. A little too late and she might be gone, and then he'd have to try her office where there could be some telephone watchdog to shield her from him.

Sean took a giant gulp of coffee, held it in his mouth the way his mother hated, the way that had made Margaret laugh, then he swallowed several times.

Now. He'd call now.

He dialed the number and waited, listening to the rings while staring at turquoise pool water and orange trees along the whitewashed brick wall.

"Yeah?"

A man's voice. Sean started to cough and held the receiver away from his face.

"Good morning," he managed when the cough subsided. "Is Emily at home?"

"Who wants to know?"

He felt both foolish and furious. That she could be married had never occurred to him. Now he had to be sure. "This is Sean Townsend." Caution was the key to pulling off this exchange painlessly. "Is Emily in, Mr.—"

"Moreno. Joe Moreno. Why don't you give me your number and I'll have her call you back? She's in the shower."

Chapter Three

They would have to break down and buy a new toaster. Emily pulled the plug from its outlet and pried a burnt slice of bread loose with a knife. She could hear Joe's voice in the living room. He must have gone to answer the phone and forgotten his toast. Larry had already left. He was an employed actor—employed as a set hand, makeup assistant, anything to keep him near his only evident passion, theater, and to provide money for rent and food while he waited for the big break. He rarely talked about his endless auditions, but Emily knew that this morning he was trying out for a part he desperately hoped to get.

She rewound the towel on her head and hitched a second one more securely around her body. Holding Joe's blackened breakfast between finger and thumb, she followed the sound of his voice, leaving a damp trail through the kitchen and hall.

"No, she's not Mrs. Moreno. There isn't a Mrs. Moreno. Her name's Emily Smith," she heard him utter into the phone, followed by his characteristic, "Oh, yeah?" Then, "Sean Townsend, huh? Last night? She never mentioned meeting you. Maybe you can tell me what you need. I'm her business partner. She's the brains and the artsy-craftsy stuff. I'm the muscle and food."

Emily paused just long enough to picture blond hair, green eyes and that marvelous smile. Then she purposefully walked toward Joe who stood with his back to her. He didn't hear her footsteps on the new gray carpet they'd finally managed to buy for the tiny living room. She walked around to face him, shaking her head frantically.

"Hi," Joe said and raised dark brows at her towel ensemble. "I guess she's out of the—"

Emily pressed two long fingers against his lips, still shaking her head—until the towel flew from her sopping hair.

Joe's arched brows rose a fraction higher, and he gently removed her fingers. "Sorry, Sean. I thought she was out of the shower, but I guess I was wrong." His soft brown eyes, the softest things about an otherwise big, tough man, asked unspoken questions. "Anyway, Sean, why don't you tell me what we can do to help you?"

Short of grabbing the phone, she had no way to stop Joe from talking to Sean. Emily couldn't believe Sean would call at seven in the morning when she'd only left him at two-thirty or so.

"Yeah," Joe continued after much too long a silence, "we're into occasions, any kind of occasion. Weddings, funerals—after the funeral, that is. Graduations, promotions, bar mitzvahs, campaign bashes. Nothing too big. Almost nothing too small. Put it in our hands and forget it. Name your needs."

There was a short pause during which Joe propped the phone between his ear and one heavily muscled shoulder while he grabbed pen and paper. "What kind of an affair?" he repeated slowly and glanced up at Emily. "You want to arrange an affair with Emily?" His grin was wicked. He covered the mouthpiece. "Emily, Emily, have you been misbehaving? The guy says he wants to set up an affair with you."

She narrowed her eyes at him, took a pencil and wrote quickly on the pad: *Do not tell him I'm here.*

He gave her a thumbs-up sign and sat on the edge of a refinished cherrywood table. "Okay, Sean. Why don't you

give me as much info as possible?'' There was a short
pause.

"Ahah. Mmm. You'd rather speak to Emily?'' Another
wide grin showed strong, very white teeth. He stuck the pen
behind his ear and studied the fingernails on one broad
hand. "I'm not sure when you can do that, but I'll ask her
to get back to you some time later—tomorrow maybe.''

He eyed Emily, clearly enjoying himself, and she
mouthed, *"No."*

"You need to talk to her now? Well, that's a problem.
Maybe I can just help you with some of the preliminary
stuff and the two of you can get together when you can
both find time.'' He swung a jean-clad leg back and forth,
the bare foot jiggling up and down. "Let's start at the beginning. An affair, you said?'' He laughed that man-to-
man laugh Emily detested. "Yeah, knowing Emily I
guessed you didn't mean that kind of affair.'' A pause.
More laughter. "Yeah, she's a classy lady. Where did you
say you met?'' Joe listened again. "Another runner, huh?
You can have it. I stick to weights myself.''

Emily picked up the towel that had dropped from her
hair, then she perched on the edge of a Victorian gentle-
man's chair that had stuffing popping through worn blue
damask. Obviously Sean hadn't said exactly when and
where he'd met her *running*, or Joe would be on his feet and
ready to go into his protective father act. She tapped her
teeth and kept anxious watch on his handsome, expressive
face.

"Well, could you at least give me a rough idea? Then I'll
get together with Emily and we'll set up an appointment.... You're sure she'll want to talk to you on her own?
Really?''

Good grief, she'd forgotten about the money she owed
him. Not that Sean Townsend looked like a man who would
starve for want of fifty bucks. She wrote on the pad once
more: *Just set up an appointment.* Joe could take the

money for her. She'd simply have to tell the truth about last night and ask Joe to help out.

"Okay, Sean, this is what we'll do," Joe said. "I'll set the meeting up myself and we can sweat the small stuff later."

He retrieved the pen from behind his ear and began to write. "Sunset Plaza Drive? Small world. We're almost neighbors. Our office is just off Sunset Boulevard. Up by Curson Avenue."

Emily waved at Joe, shaking her head. Next he'd be giving their home address, which was deliberately omitted from their business card.

"What kind of affair did you have in mind, Sean? Just so I can give Emily a hint." Joe bowed his head, and Emily could only see the top of his curly black hair. "Only a little party? Fifty or so people?" He scribbled furiously. "Relaxed but sleek. Do you have a location in mind, or will you want us to attend to that?"

The bottom had dropped out of Emily's stomach. A relaxed but sleek little party for fifty? The terms alone spelled money, and Joe never passed up solid revenue.

"Sounds nice," he said, looking at Emily, the expressive brows working toward his hairline again. "So we'll have to see your house and work with some of your staff. But you won't have difficulty accommodating the number if we take care of all the arrangements, will you? I'll tell Emily and we'll meet you there at . . . say, ten in the morning? Seven? Isn't that a bit early?" Joe, twenty-eight and a virile powerhouse, worked hard, but he played hard and he started slowly in the morning. "Yeah, eight's better. See you then."

As he hung up, he continued jotting notes.

"Joe," Emily began tentatively, "can I talk to you about this?"

"Sounds great, huh? You should meet more guys like Townsend when you do your crazy running. We can make a bundle on a few numbers like the one he wants. Big, fancy houses. Lots of money and not enough to do with it." His every word oozed enthusiasm, Emily noted, the kind of enthusiasm not easily thwarted.

"Joe, I don't want to work for Sean Townsend."

"What?"

"I don't want to work for him."

"Did he put the make on you or something?"

"No."

"What then?"

She held the towels tightly against her breast. If she told him the whole truth about last night, there would be the same old lecture on danger. She didn't need a lecture right now. "Joe, I don't ask you too many favors, do I?"

"No-o-o," he said, "but you're going to ask me one now, right?"

There was no need to lie. A straightforward request for help would put things right. Sean probably hadn't had any idea what they did until Joe had spelled it out, so the "little party" was an excuse to see her. The chance for another look at Sean wasn't without appeal, but he was the kind of man she'd decided to avoid—a long time ago—and she wasn't about to go back on that decision.

"Emily? Earth calling Emily. The favor, my lovely partner? What does your little heart desire of this poor man you refuse to see as more than a strong back and a mean connoisseur of canapés?"

"I see you as a wonderful, funny, very attractive man, Joe, and you know it. You're the best friend I've ever had and the best I'm ever likely to have." She and Joe had a rare relationship. They lived in the same house, ran a business together, were aware of each other's sexuality, but there had never been any serious intimacy between them.

He looked at her thoughtfully. "There's something you don't want to tell me, right?"

"No big deal, Joe. But would you mind keeping the appointment with Townsend on your own?"

"We-ell..."

"Please, Joe?"

"But I can't make all the arrangements for his party on my own, Em. I don't lie when I explain how we operate. We have the classic marriage of talents, my dear, and I don't do so well in your areas."

If she told him there wouldn't be a party, the cat would start crawling out of the bag. "I can do whatever I have to do without meeting him."

"You really don't like this guy, do you?"

"I didn't say that."

"You don't have to. Okay, I'll do it. You sure I shouldn't punch him in the nose for something or other?"

The vision of Joe putting his powerful 190-pound, six-foot-tall frame behind a punch to Sean Townsend's straight nose made Emily wince. "No, thanks, Joe. Just go see him, and while you're there give him an envelope from me. Okay?"

"Envelope?" Now he would start again with the questions.

"I don't want to explain anymore. Do you think you could let it go?"

"But..." Joe closed his mouth firmly and shrugged. "If you say so."

She let out a relieved sigh and pecked his cheek. "You're a gem. I owe you one."

"Yeah," Joe agreed and sighted the crunched burned bread Emily held in her hands. "What the hell is that?"

"Oh, nothing, nothing." She smiled sweetly at him. "Why don't you take it easy? I know you didn't get much sleep last night." She'd heard him come home at three-thirty. "We don't have to get busy on the Williamette wedding for another hour. I'll dress and get you some breakfast."

"I already started toast."

"It'll be cold by now," Emily replied, surreptitiously hiding the remnants of his efforts in her towels. "I'll make us both something special. Eggs Benedict?"

Joe moved from the table to a green check sofa and spread his body along its length. "Sure. Eggs are fine." He waited until she was at the door before he added, "I'm not fooled, partner. There's something important you're not telling me about Sean Townsend and, knowing you, you won't be able to keep it to yourself forever."

Important? Emily returned to the kitchen and dumped the toast. Yes, there was something important about the man. He appealed to her more than she ever intended to let Joe know, but regardless of how attracted she was to him, Sean Townsend represented the kind of risk she must never take.

THE OCCASION PEOPLE had been in business a year, since the month after Emily had answered Joe's advertisement for housemates. The Williamette wedding was their biggest assignment to date, and they were pulling it off beautifully, she thought, feeling elated. She drove the van into the drive-through at the Century Plaza Hotel. A parking attendant took over the van, and she ran through the sumptuous foyer to the grounds behind the building. The wedding would be held on a raised platform between oblong lily ponds. Four hundred guests would sit flanking the ponds, each with an unobstructed view of the ceremony. Afterward, an elaborate reception was slated to take place in an elegant basement ballroom.

Emily had coordinated the menu, and now Joe was meeting with hotel chefs and an outside catering firm to go over final details. Checking the public address system and the video setup that were to immortalize the union of Douglas Williamette, Jr. and Azalea DeMuth was Emily's next task. Then flowers. The formal photographs had already been taken and arrangements for the candid shots made.

Evening weddings were Emily's favorite. Many of the out-of-town guests were staying at the hotel and would start coming down to their seats by six. Formal attire was required. Once Emily had hated the glitz and pomp that attended great wealth. Removed from it on a personal level, she now observed, with detached fascination, the grace money could create.

The pressing chores of the day slipped away, and for once Emily made no attempt to stop the rush of memories. On a September afternoon four years ago, she was to have donned white lace and satin and gone, trembling, to meet her bridegroom. Emily's own wedding, the one that never took place, would have been similar to Azalea DeMuth's. By now she and Charles Hennessy III might have had cosseted children tucked away in his sumptuous Boston home. Each day would have brought the calls, from Charles's mother and her own. There would have been visits and dinner parties and expeditions to Cape Cod for sailing, and more parties and empty chatter...and in the brief, quiet times between, there would have been the two of them, she and Charles, alone.

Emily looked at the sky. How many lives had she turned upside down because as a twenty-one-year-old college student she'd made an impetuous mistake and because, although she liked Charles, she couldn't love him? The sadness swept in, as it always did when she thought of her parents. She hadn't seen them since she'd left home a few days after her twenty-second birthday four years ago. They had no way of knowing where she was; Emily had made sure of that. Sporadic calls to her aunt, her mother's sister, were her only remaining link to the family. The short conversations were to let her mother and father know she was safe and well, nothing more. Would there ever be a healing between them all?

Now was the wrong time to wrestle with her old problems. She walked to an aisle between rows of seats and surveyed the area. The bride's mother had insisted on a white carpet instead of red, and Emily disliked its starkness. It seemed to stretch for a mile, from the platform, down the steps and along the length of the pools to the door where the bride would appear.

"Oh, no!" She clamped her hands on her hips, then glanced at her watch. Four-thirty. "Hey," she called to a man she saw behind a bank of amplifiers. "Hey, can you get me some strong backs, quickly?" The man only moved farther behind the equipment. Emily hurried toward him, muttering. The aisle she'd been standing in was the *only* aisle. Instead of arranging the chairs in four blocks as she had requested, they had made two vast sets of rows, which would force people to struggle past one another if they had to leave their seats. She broke into a run until she reached a huge speaker. "Excuse me," she said, looking behind.

The man was gone. She scanned the area. No sign of him. But he couldn't have left without her seeing him.

A sudden breeze gusted, whipping her hair forward over her face. Satin ribbons on flower stands and the corners of the ceremonial table rustled sharply, then became very still when the breeze abruptly subsided.

Emily's face and scalp tingled. She felt more than she saw...no, she saw it now, the slow movement of something dark behind a row of potted trees. Her mouth was dry, but she tried to swallow. What was the matter with her? For weeks she'd had the sensation of another presence, a shadow just outside her field of vision following her. Then, last night...

She shook her head and turned away. She knew she didn't want to confront whoever was behind the trees.

Three hotel employees came into the courtyard carrying more flower arrangements. Baby-white orchids imported from Hawaii mixed with larger, frilly-edged orchids, also white, and delicate sprays of stephanotis. All beautiful but slightly chilly. Emily had prevailed in the color scheme for the ballroom, where she'd persuaded the bride's mother to introduce touches of rose pink and lavender.

As soon as the flower stands were positioned, Emily instructed the men to rearrange the seating and made her way back toward the foyer.

This time there was no mistaking the furtive movement of a figure in dark clothing. He—and she was certain it was a man—had backed away from the trees and now crouched in a shaded corner.

Rage overcame fear, and Emily changed direction, walking rapidly toward him. But he was too fast. Before she could draw close, he leaped up and ran. Emily could see that he was tall but slightly built. A black woolen cap covered his hair except for a few blond curls that showed above a black turtleneck sweater.

Blond. Emily stopped. She'd never catch up with him and she didn't have time anyway. But she hadn't been wrong. A blond man was following her, had been following her for weeks. He had to know her movements and where she lived. A sick feeling swept through her. This man had marked her. True, she'd been lucky enough to elude him every time, but was that by his design? He seemed to be only watching so far, closing in slowly, playing a taunting, cat-and-mouse game. Sooner or later he was bound to make a different kind of move.

In the doorway she saw Joe, good old solid Joe, talking, laughing and waving his arms expressively as he led an entourage of men in overalls in Emily's direction.

Should she tell Joe about the man? She knew the answer before she finished forming the question. There was no one she could tell, not Joe, or Larry, or the police. Especially not the police. Making a new place for herself in the world, breaking ties with the past, had been tough. But disappearing had been her only choice then. Staying hidden was still her only choice...until she was sure her old world had lost its power to gobble her up again.

Emily stared unseeingly at the clipboard she held. A shred of publicity could ruin the new life she'd built. One photo in a newspaper, a snippet on television, and the woman she used to be might be sucked back into a scene she wasn't ready to reenter.

No, she'd cope with her blond shadow on her own, if that's what it took to remain Emily Smith of Los Angeles and keep Sidonie James of Boston where she belonged—lost.

Chapter Four

"Yes, Mr. Townsend?"

Sean hesitated, leaning toward the intercom on the desk in his study.

"Mr. Townsend?"

"Nothing, nothing, Zig. I was going to send for Sekowsky but I've changed my mind. Forget it."

He leaned back in his chair and propped his feet on the desk. He'd been about to order coffee for Moreno and Emily and have it waiting when they arrived. But it would have been a mistake, made it look as if this was a big deal. Sean laced his fingers behind his neck and stared at the vaulted ceiling. This *was* a big deal to him.

Any minute now they'd arrive. The uncomfortable sensation in his stomach surprised him. Sean Townsend was the man everyone said was always in control, always on top of any situation. He didn't feel in control now. He didn't know what to expect. Twice he'd come close to canceling the appointment and now he wished he had, only it was too late. Damn. Why did Moreno have to come, too?

The intercom buzzed raucously, setting his teeth on edge. His palms were wet. He wiped them on the fine fabric of his dark suit pants. Dressing for the office and giving the impression he was fitting in this meeting before a normal busy day had seemed the best approach. Now he wasn't so sure. He knew the navy pin-striped suit, white shirt and yellow silk tie looked good on him. Enough women had told him his clothes fitted him like a second skin, but maybe Emily wasn't like other women.

Another buzz galvanized him. He swung his feet to the floor and answered, "Yes, Zig." Zig Yolande, an elegant blond woman of indeterminate age, spent several hours a day keeping his social calendar in order and coordinating it with his busy professional schedule. Zig did some of the things Margaret had once done so well. Sean glanced at Margaret's photo and immediately looked away. The unfamiliar roll hit his belly again.

"Your eight o'clock appointment is here, Mr. Townsend," Zig said in her warm, clear voice. "Shall I send him in?"

Margaret *would* have liked Emily. He was sure of it. "Yes, yes. Send them in."

He stood up and put his left hand in his pants pocket. Women shook hands as much as men these days. Cool, professional, that was the approach to take. And somehow he'd figure out a way to see her on her own later.

"Morning, Sean." The door swung open to admit a big dark-haired man who filled enough of the entrance to obliterate all of Zig but one slender hand resting on the gilt doorknob. Sean heard her murmur something before she closed the door.

"Moreno, Joe Moreno." The man grasped his hand over the desk and pumped it. Sean smiled mechanically into very dark eyes.

"Uh, hi, Joe." Emily must be parking the car. Parking the car? And he must be losing his mind. He cleared his throat. "Where's Emily?"

Moreno had stopped squeezing Sean's hand and was now looking around the room, smiling, nodding. "Nice place, Sean. Jeez. Emily would go for this. She's into antiques." He wandered across Aubusson rugs and polished oak floors and ran his fingers over an ancient black-lacquered armoire. Then he touched the wall paneling. "Very nice," he murmured. "I've got a place in the San Gabriel Mountains. Just a cabin. But it's paneled. I've always liked wood."

"Where is Emily?" Sean repeated.

"She couldn't make it." Joe turned the full force of a wide smile on him and came back to sit in one of two wing-backed leather chairs facing Sean. "We can go over your plans, and Emily and I will get together on the details later. Then—"

"I don't think so." Disappointment and irritation flattened his voice.

"You don't think so?"

The guy had such an honest face. Sean would have to be careful or his entire hand would be out in the open, if it wasn't already. Emily was obviously a bright lady, and she would have figured out immediately that his offer of work couldn't be anything but an excuse to see her again. He didn't mind her knowing. But Joe Moreno was another matter. Sean had hoped Emily hadn't told Joe that she was sure the appointment was just a ruse to get her here.

"Everyone likes Emily," Joe commented. He was examining a Baccarat paperweight. "I don't blame you for wanting to do business with her direct, but we're a team and she'll be in on everything you need, believe me."

Sean sat down abruptly on the edge of his chair. A team? What kind of a team exactly? Emily wasn't Joe's wife, but that didn't mean she wasn't his lover. Joe had certainly been comfortable answering the phone at her home early in the morning, announcing that she was in the shower. He clasped his hands in his lap. He was being irrational. He'd met the woman only once and now he was getting into a sweat because there could be another man in her life.

"Sean," Joe said persuasively, pulling a notebook from his back pocket, "trust me, okay? You said fifty?"

"Fifty?" Emily was so different from Joe. She was everything he wasn't, cultured, subtle, elegant . . .

"People. Guests. You did say there would be fifty guests at your party?"

Sean regarded the other man narrowly. Stubbornness was a flaw he'd had to overcome, but traces of the old determination to have his own way remained. He wouldn't be diverted from what he'd set out to do—to see Emily Smith face-to-face, on his own turf, in broad daylight.

"Joe," he said levelly, "why couldn't Emily be here this morning? We made a date and I'm a busy man."

The Fabergé egg his father had given his mother for their twenty-fifth wedding anniversary was now the focus of Joe's attention. "She didn't say. We don't keep tabs on each other all the time. If Emily says she has something to do, she has something to do. It's that simple."

Sean pulled in a long breath. One small, bright glimmer of hope: they didn't keep tabs on each other. But that didn't have to mean much. A lot of couples had a so-called open arrangement. "Do you think she'll be through with whatever she had to do pretty soon?"

Joe balanced the fragile egg on the palm of one hand, evidently much more interested in its fine gold and jeweled design than in anything Sean had to say.

"Joe—" his patience was slipping "—that's an old piece. Look at it, but be careful, please. It belongs to my mother."

"Fabergé, isn't it?" Joe commented, apparently oblivious to the mounting tension in the room. "Must be worth a fortune."

"It is." Sean took the egg and set it back on his desk. "Do you want to do this job for me?"

Joe's eyes met his instantly. The guileless smile slipped a little. "That's why I'm here."

"How badly do you want the job?"

"I...we want it. We're small but we're growing and we're good. You won't be sorry you hired us."

Sean had the man's full attention now. Suddenly he'd decided that an elegant party for fifty was exactly what he wanted, and he wanted the Occasion People to arrange it for him, almost as much as Joe did. "Yes," he said slowly, "I'm sure I won't be sorry. *If* I hire you."

Joe bristled slightly and jabbed the point of a pen into a blank notebook page. "From what you said yesterday, I thought you'd already made up your mind on that."

"I'd made up my mind Emily was someone I could work with."

"But you can't work with me?"

"I didn't say that. What I am saying is that if Emily can't spare me the time, and since she's at least half of your operation, maybe I should find another firm, one that'll give me the full attention I expect."

"So—"

"So," Sean broke in, "if you want to work for me, get Emily here, now." He looked at his watch. "We don't have a lot of time if things are going to go off smoothly on Saturday." Where had he pulled Saturday from? He'd better pray he could come up with fifty people who would come to a party on three and a half days' notice.

"*This* Saturday?" Joe asked faintly. "That's not much time, Sean."

"No, it's not. Do you think Emily could be persuaded to get over here so we can put things together? The invitations will probably have to go out by phone. I'll expect her to make the calls." Zig would be insulted by that one, but he'd find a way to soothe her ego.

The sweat forming over Joe's brow suggested he was feeling the tension around him at last. "I don't know if I can reach Emily," he began, an uncertain edge in his voice. "She asked me to deal with—"

"Evidently." Sean tried to keep sarcasm out of his tone. He lifted the telephone receiver and handed it to Joe. "But give it a try anyway. I'll start writing down names."

JOE TOOK ADVANTAGE of her sometimes. "You take advantage," Emily fumed aloud, turning the van onto the steep rise of Sunset Plaza Drive.

And Sean Townsend was determined, she'd give him that. Well, he was about to discover she could be just as determined. Businesslike, that would be her approach. He'd invented his party and she'd make it very real for him, and very expensive. From his address and the car he drove she knew he could afford the best and the best was what he'd get. Then she'd bow out gracefully. Then would come their bill, a nice, fat bill that would raise even his eyebrows. It might just wipe the laughter out of his green eyes, too.... He did have spectacular eyes. Emily shook her head and turned the wheel again. Joe had borrowed her little black Fiat, leaving her with the unwieldy company vehicle, and hill-climbing wasn't its forte.

She looked again at the address scribbled on a gummed memo sheet stuck to the dash. Almost there. On the phone, Joe had appealed to her briefly and in words only she could truly understand. "I think I need you here, Em." Whenever he wanted to win her over, she was *Em*, and he *needed* her. He knew she was a pushover for anyone in need. For a moment she thought about that. Trying to help the needy had got her into a lot of trouble in the past, trouble that had left a scar she'd always have.

A sweeping bend, then another. Townsend lived on top of this hill. The air up here was pretty rarefied. It cost to breathe anywhere so high in Beverly Hills. One more curve and she saw the address, black numerals on a sweeping white stucco wall broken by high wrought-iron gates and overhung with billowing masses of purple and magenta bougainvillea.

The gate was shut.

Emily pulled off the road and got out, leaving the engine idling. A button beside the gate brought a crackly response from a recessed grille, a voice asking her name.

"Emily Smith," she said, some of her annoyance with Joe dissipating beneath curiosity. Through the gates she could see a short driveway leading to a large, Spanish-style house.

After a short silence, the voice said, "Please come in Ms. Smith. Park to the right of the front door."

The gates swung silently open on well-oiled hinges. Emily hesitated a moment before going back to the van and driving into the grounds. Dense plantings covered the wide but shallow area in front of the house. Emily did as instructed, parking on a strip of pale crushed rock.

For several seconds she sat, immobile, staring at tinted windows flanked by black shutters. So this was where Sean Townsend of Townsend Alarms lived. She had looked him up in the telephone book and the man hadn't lied about who he was. Again the little twist of recollection came. She had lied about her identity, over and over again. Most of the time she forgot how she'd slipped so carefully into her new life, but not all of the time, and less frequently lately— since she'd acquired her blond shadow.

She gathered her small briefcase and hopped from the van, the gravel crunching beneath her low-heeled pumps. For Sean's benefit, she'd quickly discarded jeans and sweatshirt and donned a bright blue linen skirt and a white silk blouse with short sleeves. All business.

A tall blond woman ushered her into the house. She said she was Zig Yolande, Mr. Townsend's at-home assistant, whatever that meant. Emily followed her through halls lined with paintings she'd love to be able to examine, across rugs she recognized as priceless and past antique chests, tables and étagères, strategically placed to avoid overexposure to light from high windows.

"Here we are." Zig led the way into a small room dominated by a carved rosewood desk, its glistening surface broken by two phones, a single open book on a leather desk pad and a silver pen stand. "Mr. Townsend said for you to go straight in." She indicated a door in the center of the wall behind the desk.

Emily squared her shoulders, walked toward the door and firmly knocked on a smooth wooden panel.

The door opened immediately.

"Hi there, Em. Come on in." The anxiety in Joe's voice startled her. No one rattled Joe. He must have been standing silently by the door, waiting for her, and worrying.

"Hello, Emily." Sean Townsend rose from a chair behind a desk and came around to shake her hand. "I'm glad you could make it. Joe agrees with me that we need a woman's touch to make the best of what I want to do." He smiled. But there was no laughter in those eyes, only a deep, searching gaze that made it impossible for Emily to look away.

He held her hand for several seconds before releasing it reluctantly. And Emily's resolve slipped, along with a few layers of the shield she'd built against Sean Townsend.

"Good morning," she said finally and managed a thin smile. Oh, boy, she should have stuck to her resolution and avoided this meeting. Temptation could be tough to turn your back on and Sean was one tempting male.

He was returning her smile, touching the back of her elbow lightly, guiding her toward one of two leather chairs. She sat down, her briefcase cradled on her lap. "You wanted to see me?" she asked and immediately took a deep breath. She sounded as unsure as she suddenly felt. "Joe is a very capable man, Mr. Townsend. There's nothing he can't do as well as I can. But of course—" she spread her hands, satisfied with the return of her usual firm projection "—whatever our customer wants, he gets."

"Thank you." He sat on the edge of his desk and put his hands in his pants pockets. The flexing of muscle in powerful thighs distracted Emily for a moment. Sean continued, "I was surprised not to see you, that's all. Our conversation last night led me to believe you would be the one I'd deal with."

Emily felt Joe behind her but didn't turn around. Sean Townsend was cool. *From their conversation last night?* She raised her brows at him. "Quite." He'd read the situation correctly, figuring out from whatever Joe had said that he didn't know the circumstances of *their conversa-*

tion. "I'm sorry if my not showing up surprised you. Joe and I have to divide our energies between clients sometimes. Fortunately, our other client this morning was understanding and agreed to put off meeting with me until this afternoon."

Sean lowered his eyelids. "Good. I shall need your *undivided* attention in the next day or so. As I told Joe, this affair was a spur-of-the-moment inspiration and we don't have much time."

Oh, his affair was spur of the moment all right. And he was also used to getting his own way. He simply assumed she could drop everything to accommodate his whim. Emily rubbed her bottom lip with a forefinger, keeping her eyes on Sean's face. His mouth was even more sensitive than she'd thought last night, the nose even straighter. His hair, not ruffled this morning, shone, thick and smooth. A hint of a wry grin made dimples beneath his cheekbones. Tiny waves of heat somewhere deep inside her made her sit straighter. She must not get involved with this man—and he definitely wanted to get involved with her in a more personal way.

"Em—" Joe was still outside her line of vision "—Sean wants this party on Saturday. The invitations will have to go out by phone and he'd like you to attend to that."

"Why?" She watched the green, slightly upslanting eyes subtly darken.

"Because I would regard that as part of your service if you take on the job. That's the way I always have things done. A woman's voice gives that warm feeling I like to put forward in my private as well as my professional life."

Emily glanced at the photo she'd already noticed on his desk. An ethereal, blue-eyed woman with short dark curls had smiled humorously at the photographer.

"My wife."

Sean's voice made Emily jump. She blushed. "She's very lovely." There was no mistaking what she instantly felt— extreme disappointment.

"And of course you're wondering why she doesn't make my personal calls."

That was exactly what she was wondering. "Well..."

"Margaret died four years ago."

Emily folded her arms and almost knocked her briefcase from her lap. "I'm sorry." She put the case carefully on the floor, using the moment to recover her composure.

"So am I," Sean said with no trace of awkwardness. "I still miss her. Anyway—" he adjusted the angle of the photograph, then centered his attention on Emily again "—we have plans to make for Saturday. I've started a list of guests. We'll use the rooms opening onto the pool. I'll show them to you in a while. You see, the time comes for a few changes, and I've decided I want to develop a new image in my private life, something...well...you can imagine it isn't easy to get away from the stereotyped label of single-male-about-town. But I intend to do that, to let people know I'm a serious man...in every way...and that I'm not interested in casual encounters with...with people who don't matter to me. And I think the Occasion People could be just what I need to help me do that."

Emily took several seconds to realize her mouth was open. She closed it and swallowed. This was her week for firsts. No man had ever tried an approach remotely like the one Sean had just laid on her. "I see," she said slowly. "And how exactly can we help you to, ah, change your image? Isn't that something only you can do? Or a public relations outfit?"

He appeared to fall into deep thought.

"Em," Joe almost whispered, "why don't we let Sean show us the rooms we'll be using?"

She leaned to look at him. He was flashing his eye signal that said: *Don't rock the boat, partner.*

For Joe's sake she should go along. She could get through this one party at least and bring in more of the money they so badly needed for expansion. "You're right," she said brightly, facing Sean again. "Let's look at the rooms we'll be using and then you can turn everything over to us, once you give us some basic guidelines and your guest list...." Her voice slipped away.

Sean had covered his mouth with one well-shaped hand, and he was studying her intently from the toes upward. When his eyes met hers they didn't waver or show any trace of embarrassment. He was utterly certain of himself.

"Sean," Joe began, "why don't you—"

"Yes," Sean interrupted. "I'll take Emily to see the house and meet the staff."

"But I thought—"

"Oh, I know," Sean interjected smoothly, "I made you think I was the kind of man who expects the world to stop for him. I'm a bit preoccupied sometimes, but I understand how busy you must be. And, as Emily said, you're spread pretty thin. So why don't you go and take care of other clients, and we'll carry on without you. Right now I need the artsy craftsy stuff. The muscle and food can come later. Is that okay?" He bestowed a charming smile on Joe.

Emily looked from one man to the other, fascinated. Sean had simply slipped into an apologetic, understanding role without missing a beat and Joe was completely won over by the performance. And it had been *her* comments about having more than one appointment that had opened the door for Sean to step in and improvise.

There came the time to acknowledge defeat and move on. "Joe," Emily said, "Mrs. DeMuth called and said how pleased she was with everything we did for the wedding. Now she'd like to start planning a homecoming celebration for the newlyweds."

"Yeah? Is that usual? I don't remember—"

"Anything's usual if it works, Joe," Emily said shortly. Joe still had a lot to learn about curbing his tongue in some circumstances. He hadn't figured out that showing surprise at anything a customer asked for, no matter how offbeat, was amateurish. "Will you call her housekeeper back and tell her I contacted Jimmy's and they're sure they can accommodate us?''

''Will do, boss.'' Joe saluted, stuffing his notebook into his jeans pocket. Then he frowned and looked from Emily to Sean. ''Are you sure you can manage without me?''

''Quite sure,'' Sean said before Emily could respond. ''Zig will show you out.''

After Joe left, silence fell on the room. Sean remained seated on the desk, his fingers laced, thumbs circling each other slowly.

''So.'' He stood abruptly, smoothing his yellow tie over an immaculate shirtfront. ''Shall we begin?''

Emily hesitated. His hand was spread wide over a very solid-looking chest. ''Mmm? Oh, yes, yes. Lead on.'' She picked up her briefcase and passed him when he opened the door for her.

An hour later she sat with him beside the pool, a tall glass of iced tea at her elbow, her legs stretched out on the chaise he'd insisted she use. The impression of room after room, beautifully furnished with antique furniture and breathtaking objets d'art stayed with her. So did the faces of staff members she'd met, from kitchen help to an imposing blue-haired woman who had treated her with what Emily felt was thinly disguised suspicion. Sean Townsend was an extremely wealthy man, or, if he wasn't, he lived like one. Emily instinctively felt he was the former—he wore the wealth with the unconscious comfort of one never accustomed to anything less.

Sean lifted his glass. He'd positioned his own chair where he could see Emily clearly. She was sipping her tea slowly, holding the rim of the glass between her lips, she was thinking hard, he decided. He looked at her mouth. A sigh started somewhere low in his lungs. Watching her tightened every muscle in his body. He hadn't been wrong last night, hadn't imagined the effect she had on him. She was marvelous. And she wasn't one damn bit interested in him.

''What do you think of the house?''

She started, spilling the tea on her white blouse.

Sean set down his own glass and leaped up, fishing a handkerchief from his pocket. "Sorry," he said dabbing at the stains, "I didn't mean to surprise you."

"That's all right. My fault." Gently, she removed his hand from where it rested lightly on her firm breast, and took the handkerchief from him.

He felt faint color rise to his cheeks. His hand still hovered inches from her chest. "I..." His voice cracked and he laughed and bowed his head. "Sorry again. Reflex action. I wasn't getting fresh."

She continued wiping at her blouse. "Of course not. I was clumsy. The house is lovely. Putting on a party here will be something I'll enjoy."

The heat in his face didn't subside. He sank back onto his chair. "You obviously know how to deal with staff."

"I'm not sure your Mrs. Sekowsky was thrilled with me. I got the impression she's accustomed to managing your parties herself."

He avoided her eyes. They both knew she was right. "She is," he said honestly. "But, as I told you, the time has come for some changes in my life." How long would it take him to break through her reserve? How long would it be before he got to kiss her?

"Yes, well, we'll do our best. Can you get your guest list to me this afternoon?"

Her legs were so long, so narrow at the ankle. "Ah, yes. I'll send someone over with it." The sweat suit she'd worn last night hadn't done her justice. Full breasts and a narrow waist had been covered by the baggy clothes. Her silk shirt settled enticingly in all the right places, and the simple skirt she wore fitted smoothly over a flat stomach and small, but rounded hips. And those legs...

She added notes to the sheet on her lap before glancing at him. "I'd like to suggest a dramatic theme. A scatter of circular tables in those two reception rooms—" she turned and pointed back toward the house, "—and then several more out here. Dark silk arrangements to pick up the colors of some of your wooden pieces, the black particularly, with touches of dusky blue and gray. We could use orange carp, hollowed and iced, to grab attention. What do you think?''

He thought his mind would explode if he didn't think of some way to tell her that all he wanted was to be alone with her . . . really alone. He wanted to know her.

''You don't like it? We could always—''

''I love it. I love it. It's fantastic.'' *You're fantastic*. ''And I'm going to leave everything in your hands.''

''Yes. About the food, though—''

''I'll leave that to you as well. Emily, I . . . I certainly am glad I ran into you last night.'' He laughed and so did she. The husky sound delighted, excited him. For a moment he considered telling her the truth, that he had the sense they'd been destined to meet, but instinct warned him to be careful. ''Can you believe my luck?'' he said, rapidly dissembling. ''Walking, or should I say *running*, into you when you were just what I needed?'' If only she knew just how much she could turn out to be what he needed.

''Perhaps you've always been a lucky man, Sean.'' She stood up and he joined her, a sense of loss sweeping over him even before she left. He couldn't keep her much longer.

''Not always. How long have you and Joe been together?'' Immediately, he held his breath, praying she wouldn't read his question too accurately.

''A little over a year,'' she said evenly.

''You, ah, complement each other's talents, Joe said.''

''We do. And we get along very well, which is just as important.''

Was she saying everything, or nothing? ''Did you meet through your work?'' His heart beat a little faster.

''No.''

She picked up her briefcase and made her way slowly through the chairs surrounding the pool. *Are you having an affair with Joe Moreno?* Sean stuffed his hands in his pockets and followed her. All he'd have to do to completely wreck his chances of seeing her again would be to ask her about her love life.

"Sean!" Emily faced him and put a hand on his arm. "Forgive me, please. I almost forgot, but I really am grateful to you for helping me last night. I know I was a bit standoffish, but I'm sure you can understand why. Joe did give you the envelope, didn't he?"

He frowned. "Joe didn't give me anything."

"Darn. He must have forgotten. Look, I'll have him run it up this afternoon. Or, better yet, I'll give it to whoever brings me your list."

She didn't intend to come back if she could help it. "Don't bother. When you organize the setup—when will that be, on Saturday morning, I guess?—bring it then." Saturday was too far away but it was better than nothing.

"I don't really think it's necessary for me to be here on Saturday."

"Oh, I do, Emily. I'd feel better if you were here during preparations. At least part of them, anyway. And I want you to get a feeling for the way I entertain, for my type of crowd. I know it may be late by then, but I'd also like to talk to you immediately after the party, if you don't mind. Then in the future you'll really know my needs."

"In the future?" Emily echoed before she could stop herself. He was absolutely impossible to deflect. No matter how little interest she showed in him as a man, he would pursue until he got what he wanted. She couldn't believe he didn't have enough women flocking to his slightest call not to need one more. But maybe that was the answer. Any woman he wanted usually capitulated without resistance and she'd challenged his ego by not babbling ecstatically at his feet the instant he came on to her. And he had come on to her in a dozen not particularly subtle ways.

They'd reached the house and entered the cool interior through French doors. "You're right for me, Emily," Sean said, resting a hand at her waist. "I know you haven't had a chance to show exactly what you're capable of yet. But I'm sure you'll do a fantastic job for me.''

His hand was warm and firm. And he had spread his fingers, pressed her side a little harder while he spoke.

She hadn't forgotten the next sensation that came. Hadn't forgotten or ceased to be capable of response. The trembly heat in her thighs and low in her womb was purely sexual and completely wrong right now. Emily moved away, turned, smiled into his face, which was closer than it should be.

''We'll make sure things get started bright and early on Saturday. I'll call Mrs. Sekowsky about the other arrangements. Are you sure she'll be receptive to our taking over?''

He tilted his head up slightly and looked directly down into her eyes. ''Sekowsky is receptive to whatever pleases me.''

Yes, Emily thought, *and you expect everyone else to be receptive to what you want.* ''In that case, we'll be in touch.''

He was right behind her all the way to the front door and to the van. When she was seated in the van his hand, resting on the rim of the window, stopped her from driving away. ''If I need to talk to you about anything I take it I can use either of your numbers.''

She hesitated, knowing he'd use whatever number he pleased, regardless of what she said. ''Certainly. There's an answering machine at the office. And if I'm not at home, leave a message.''

''You have an answering machine there, too?''

Emily thought for a moment, suppressing a smile. Finally she was getting the full drift of some of his questions. ''It'll only be on if neither of us are in.'' No need to muddy the waters for the man even further by mentioning Larry.

''Neither of you?''

''If I'm not there, Joe probably will be.''

"NOT RUNNING TONIGHT, Emily?" Larry asked. He didn't look up from the script he was reading.

Emily, walking behind his chair, ruffled his pale hair fondly. "Nope. Taking a break. I'm in such fantastic shape I can afford it."

Larry laughed and raised his rather long nose from the thick wad of pages. He took off his wire-rimmed glasses and screwed up his gray eyes. "We'll have to arrange a course in ego-building for you, Emily. You're much too humble."

"I know I am, Larry. I'll work on it."

He went back to studying his lines for the small part he'd landed in a low-budget movie, and Emily settled into her favorite spot on the old green couch. Larry was so often the balm she needed when she was troubled. When she'd answered Joe's advertisement for housemates she'd expected to be greeted by a woman. Joe's ebullience and the clear impression he gave that she wasn't the type he was likely to be romantically attracted to put her enough at ease to move in. Larry had arrived a few days later and he created the perfect balance in their little household, possessing the calm and the patience she and Joe lacked.

Looking at him now, with his tall body hunched over, his lips moving, his bony hand making an occasional sweeping motion, Emily felt a rush of affection, and powerlessness. She longed to help him. And in theory she could do it. But she didn't dare give Larry what he needed—the money for formal theatrical training—because the fact that she had access to considerable funds was another part of the truth about herself that couldn't be revealed if she hoped to hang on to her privacy. Sometimes she put small sums into the business account, but only when she was certain Joe wouldn't realize what she'd done. Suddenly offering to pay tuition for Larry would raise too many questions.

Anyway, he wouldn't accept the offer. He didn't talk much about himself, but she knew a few things, that he was thirty-one, had parents and a brother and a sister in Wyoming and that, like her, he was escaping a confining background to prove he was his own person. The main difference between them was that Larry had grown up without any of the advantages that had been showered on Sidonie James.

Emily glanced at Larry, almost expecting him to have heard her real name as she had thought it. He was standing now, completely engrossed, pacing back and forth. She closed her eyes for a moment then picked up a book and leafed aimlessly through the pages. Must be one of Joe's library-fund-raising-sales purchases. His latest thing was "getting less crass" as he put it. Apparently he was studying Chinese porcelain, the subject of this book.

Emily sighed and tucked her feet beneath her. She did miss her run.

"Joe said you got a new job today." Larry had paused in front of her.

"Yes. He's excited about it."

"But you're not?" A deep crease formed between his eyes. "Something's really bothering you. What is it?" Larry always picked up on her moods.

"Nothing I can put my finger on." She sighed again. She wasn't being entirely truthful. Sean Townsend and the very definite impact he'd had upon her was bothering her a lot. He had made her realize just how much she'd lost four years ago and how far-reaching the effects of one action could be. Celebrity gossip on a viciously grand scale had turned her into a fugitive and would probably keep her a fugitive. Being around a man like Sean very often could make anonymity almost impossible to maintain.

Larry was regarding her silently, waiting, as he always did when he sensed she might have something more to say but wasn't sure.

"Would you like me to help you with your lines?" she asked and smiled as cheerfully as she could. "I'm so glad you got the part." He was a good actor, but he never seemed to get more than little nibbles at what he really wanted, the big time.

"Yes, I would, please. But first, Emily, *is* there anything at all I can help you with?" His thin face and gentle mouth took on a pinched look. "Is there anything?"

She patted the seat beside her. Sean Townsend was only one of two unsettling subjects that crowded her brain. She couldn't talk about Sean, but the other was beginning to be more than she could keep to herself. "Come and sit with me, Larry. You always make me feel better. There is something on my mind and I'd like to tell you about it—if you promise not to tell Joe."

He swallowed audibly. "Not unless you say I can."

"Someone's following me." She'd said it. Her shoulders sagged and she rested her brow on one fist. "Don't ask me why, but there's a man following me. I've seen him several times now...or not really *seen* him, not up close, but he's there. And I'm scared, Larry."

Larry stared at her for a long time. "Are you sure that someone's following you?" He slowly lowered himself beside her.

Emily told him every incident she could remember and Larry listened without interrupting. When she finished, she rested both hands on his wrist. "So you see why I'm afraid to go running."

He nodded slowly, sucking in one corner of his wide mouth. "Emily," he began tentatively, "how closely have you seen this guy? Are you sure it's been the same man every time?"

"I've never seen his face, but I know he's blond. And I'm sure it's always the same man."

"Could be a coincidence, you know." He patted her hands then smiled at her. "But just the same, even though I want you to stop worrying, I'd feel a whole lot better if you stayed close to home for a while. At night, I mean."

"What about the daytime? He was at the Century Plaza in broad daylight."

"But that was the only time you thought you saw him during the day?"

She thought for a moment. "Yes."

"You could be a bit jumpy, Emily. That time could have been some sort of fluke."

"I suppose so," she said doubtfully. Maybe she was letting her imagination get away from her.

"I'm pretty sure of it. No sane man would try to do anything to you in broad daylight."

Emily couldn't seem to inhale properly. "No," she agreed, "a sane man wouldn't do that."

Chapter Five

Late Saturday evening Emily arrived, panting, at the gates of Sean's house. Leaving her Fiat at the bottom of the hill and jogging up Sunset Plaza Drive had seemed like a good idea. Now, fit as she was, her legs were rubbery and she half expected the next breath she took to be the one that would kill her. She leaned on the wall, allowing her heart to settle down. In a minute she'd ring the bell. Dressed in a baggy sweatshirt and jeans, she'd been here earlier to check everything out before the party. And Sean had been at her shoulder every inch of the way. Even as she'd climbed into her car to leave, he'd repeated his earlier plea for her to stay, to be one of his guests. And she'd refused. Staying would have been nice, if she had been dressed, and if she could have been sure no one would recognize her. But she could never be completely sure of that, particularly with the kind of people Sean counted among his friends. One day it wouldn't matter anymore. She'd know when that day came but it hadn't yet.

Her breathing had calmed and she lifted her hand to the bell, but she didn't have to ring. The gates opened and a red Maserati purred past her. Through its open windows Emily heard music and high female laughter. A tinge of nostalgia swept over her. Sometimes she missed the glamor of the old life, just a little bit, anyway.

She watched the car turn left onto the highway then trudged up the driveway and toward the side of the house, wanting to take a quick look at what was left of her careful outdoor setups before going into the kitchen.

Only one car was still parked in front of the house, a silver Mercedes coupe with a personalized license plate that read *Red One*. Emily reached a corner of the pool and peered around. The owner of the Mercedes was easy to spot. Seated with legs crossed Red One wore a silver dress, which was split from its narrow hem all the way up to the suggestion of black lace at her hip, revealing her almost impossibly long, smooth thighs clad in sheer, also silver, hose. And her hair was the reddest Emily had ever seen, flaming, setting-sun red.

Red was the only remaining guest and her attentive listener, seated at one of the buffet tables, was her host, Sean Townsend, who regarded her intently over the tortured shape of the bulging-eyed carcass of an orange carp. Emily's jaw tightened. She shouldn't care that Sean appeared to lean a little farther over the table with each passing second, but she did. She hated it. Yet she knew that that kind of reaction was way out of line. What he did, or who his friends were, had nothing to do with her. It struck her that if this was Sean's idea of changing his image, then she'd definitely misunderstood what he'd meant. In the tableau before her he looked very much the eligible man-about-town on the hunt.

With a muffled sniff, Emily set off purposefully for the door closest to the kitchen.

She didn't reach it.

"Emily! There you are. Come and meet Red."

There was nothing she wanted to do less at this moment than meet Red. She waved at him, taking slow steps backward. "I'd love to, Sean, but I'd better check in with the staff."

"Nonsense." He was on his feet. "I promised Red she'd get to meet you. I've spent the evening bragging about how wonderful you are, not that I had to. Everything was a smash, sweetheart. Wasn't it, Red?''

Emily cringed, but she also noticed the nonchalant way he'd called her sweetheart and warmth quickly softened her irritation. Red looked as if she reciprocated Emily's less than enthusiastic feelings about a meeting, but she stood up, slowly, gracefully, her marvelous legs very visible. She smiled lazily, bowing her head to let that wonderful hair cascade over an enviable décolletage. Emily advanced toward an extended silver-taloned hand, her navy sweats feeling like rather damp Salvation Army specials, and clasped Red's cool fingers in her own hot palm.

''Hi. Red VanEpson,'' the woman said and her smile seemed genuine. ''Sean tells me you do all this—'' she swept out her other arm, indicating the tables, ''—for a living. Sounds like too much work to me, but you certainly do it very well.''

''Thank you.'' Emily withdrew her hand. ''I enjoy it.''

''She does all kind of affairs, Red. Anything you need she can cope with. Can you believe that? Not that it'll do you any good because I intend to keep her too busy to work for anyone else.'' At Sean's show of innocent enthusiasm, which curled Emily's toes, the woman eyed her from beneath slightly lowered lids.

''I'll have to remember you the next time I'm putting on a little get-together,'' Red commented, then to Sean she said, ''What were we talking about, darling?''

Sean didn't bow his head in time to hide his smile completely. ''The diamond you just bought from Van Cleef? Or was it the new sable? Emily,'' he gave her his full attention, ''as soon as I see Red out we'll go over things. If you wouldn't mind telling Sekowsky what a fantastic job she's done, I'd appreciate it.'' He winked broadly and the dimples formed beneath his cheekbones. ''I think you're already winning her over and that takes a lot of talent. Okay?''

''Okay,'' she agreed and quickly went into the house.

In the kitchen, Sekowsky was holding court, ordering the staff to perform clean-up duties with the precision of a sergeant-major drilling troops. "Len, take inventory of the wines please; we might need to replace stock. Susan, as you clear the floral arrangements, put them in the boxes they were brought in. Don't knock anything loose. Beatrice, you've done very well tonight, but next time remember this isn't a fast food restaurant. *Our* guests *don't* use the same silverware—for anything. Seafood forks are removed as they are set down and immediately replaced. And china, Beatrice, china. Our guests do not get left holding a plate covered with toothpicks and sauce when they're about to select a *choux* pastry. Is that clear?"

"Yes, Mrs. Sekowsky." Beatrice gave what looked like an abbreviated curtsy and Emily smothered a cough.

Sekowsky spun around and saw her. "Ah, Miss Smith. Mr. Sean said you would be stopping by." She folded her hands over her stomach. "Will you need some sort of written report of the evening, what was used and so on? Of course, I'll want to know at once if there's something you don't approve of. Mr. Sean made it clear you would be in charge of all social events in this house in future. And he said he expected me to give you as much help as you need."

Emily was glad she'd missed that discussion. Sekowsky's dark eyes glittered and her mouth was drawn into a tight line. Suddenly, Emily felt sorry for the woman. That she was efficient was obvious and the unexpected appearance of an apparent usurper must be infuriating.

"Mrs. Sekowsky," Emily began, smiling, "I don't know how often my firm will be working with you and Mr. Townsend, but he's right in assuming that when and if we do we'll need your expertise. I imagine you've been here for some time?"

There was a slight untensing of Sekowsky's raised shoulders. "Twenty-three years," she stated and lifted her chin a fraction. "I worked for Mr. Sean's parents first."

"Ah. I'm not surprised. I thought everything ran like a well-oiled machine around here. Thank you for helping us so much this evening. Did we seem to make the right calculations, on quantities and so on?"

"I . . . well, yes, I'd say so."

"Good, good. And the sushi bar, did that go over well? I didn't see it in operation. Although I have elsewhere, of course."

Sekowsky sniffed and Emily thought the corners of her mouth turned up a little. "I heard some of the guests saying how much they liked it," she said. Then she added, "You're very good at what you do," and Emily felt she had scored a small victory.

"Thank you. I hope Mr. Townsend was just as pleased." And she did truthfully hope he was satisfied. In her head, the figures she'd planned for his bill were starting to lower. After all, he was a . . . nice man? Who was she kidding? She didn't think of Sean as a *nice* man. There were a lot of adjectives that came to mind, but nice wasn't among them. "Tell Mr. Townsend I'm well pleased with the whole evening, particularly with the help I received from you and your staff. And that I hope he is too. I'll be in touch with him within a few days." Getting away, going home, seemed very important.

"Oh, but I'm sure he wants to talk to you himself before you go," Sekowsky said in a rush. "He said so."

Emily hitched up her sweatpants and smoothed a hand over her disheveled hair, remembering the sexy Red VanEpson. "I think he's busy and I should go home. Anyway, I can't imagine he really wants to waste time with the help at this time of night."

Sekowsky picked up a sponge and vigorously wiped a butcher block island in the middle of the huge, white-tiled kitchen. "I think he really does want to see you." She didn't meet Emily's eyes; instead she glanced around at the rest of the staff who were all too busy to be listening. "In fact, I think he's been waiting all evening to see you. He must have been in here a dozen times to remind me you were coming. And he *never* comes into the kitchen.''

A furious blush burst into Emily's face. The rest of the blood in her body seemed to drain to her feet. She wasn't a fool. That Sean Townsend had a minor case of infatuation for her didn't take much figuring out, but for him to be so obvious that Sekowsky noticed meant he could be more difficult to discourage than Emily had thought. *If* she wanted to discourage him. She pressed her back against a wall, her arms crossed. It had happened, what she'd always been afraid might occur—a man, the kind of man who could reach the heart she'd tried to protect, had come along. And he was also the kind of man who would probably be able to cope with discovering that she'd once decorated the front page of every major newspaper in the country—and not only because she had been one of society's most sought-after singles.

''There you are, Emily.'' Sean strode into the kitchen, effectively stopping every worker in his or her tracks. ''Have you and Sekowsky been congratulating each other? You certainly have a right to. This was the best party I ever gave and it's all because of you two.''

He was hearty, too hearty, his smile wide, his eyes flashing such enthusiasm that Emily shrank a little. She glanced at Sekowsky and saw that she wasn't fooled by his flattery, but, Emily was relieved to see, neither did Sekowsky appear antagonistic toward her.

The rest of the staff gradually returned to their tasks, while Sean stood, rocking back onto the heels of his Gucci loafers, the sleeves of his taupe—probably Giorgio Armani—suit jacket pushed up to his elbows. Emily knew the labels, and the cost. She also knew that many men could afford to dress as Sean did but that few could manage even a hint of the style he brought to whatever he wore.

''Mrs. S.,'' Sean said softly, going to stand close beside her, ''do you have everything under control now?''

She raised surprised eyes to his. ''Of course.''

"Well," he cleared his throat, "if you don't need Emily or me anymore, I'd like to discuss another couple of ideas with her. You two worked so well together this evening I think we should make sure you do it a lot more."

"Whatever you say, Mr. Sean." Sekowsky nodded and turned away to talk to Beatrice.

Sean had been dismissed by his housekeeper and Emily was amused to see how he backed away several steps before he turned his smile on her and offered her a hand. Without thinking, she slipped her fingers into his, and they walked back to the grounds.

Once outside, he released her. Emily watched him as he hesitated at the top of the three steps leading down from the terrace. She still felt the pressure of his fingers on hers. Low lights, focused on exotic paintings, cast a soft glow over the area and picked up his face in profile. Emily noted the slightly tense set of his mouth, the limpid quality of his green eyes looking steadily ahead.

Emily was uncomfortable, breathless again. She wanted to leave, yet, at the same time, she wanted to stay with him.

"Would you like to see the rest of the gardens?" he asked suddenly. "They aren't big. None of them are up here. But we have more ground than most people and my father did some interesting things."

Still he didn't look at her.

She took in a silent breath of warm air filled with the heavy scent of roses. "Thank you," she said, "but shouldn't we get our business out of the way? It's late."

He was already walking slowly down the steps. "We can talk business just as well while I show you around." He had reached the pool.

Arguing seemed pointless, so Emily silently followed keeping a few paces behind. The faint clatter of noise reminded her that a small army of waiters was clearing away party debris. Sean continued on, skirting the pool until he was on a path between the straight trunks of a dense group of date palms.

"Watch your step," he said over his shoulder. "The ground isn't too even in places. Let's go a bit higher where we can see the lights in the valley."

She followed in his tracks, peering down and trying to judge where to plant her feet. All she could make out clearly in the darkness were her white Reeboks.

"Will this do? The view's great from here."

He'd stopped and she slammed into his back, grabbing his jacket when the soles of her shoes began to slide. "Yes," she managed and felt his arm go around her.

"Sorry about that." He laughed, still holding her firmly to his side. "I forgot there's a little waterfall up higher and the runoff makes the grass and fallen leaves pretty slimy. You okay?"

"Fine." She nodded, trying to pull away from his grasp. But he kept his hand around her, his fingertips just barely resting, on the side of her breast.

"I like to come out here," he said, and the fingertips stroked, so very slightly.

Emily was afraid to move. Overreaction would make her look a fool. Not doing anything could give him the wrong impression. And as she stood, pressed to him, a burning ache started in her breast. Beneath the tight cotton T-shirt she sometimes wore instead of a bra when she ran, her nipples hardened and she gritted her teeth.

"Where did you say your offices were?" Her voice had just the right politely interested note, she thought gratefully. "On Wilshire?" And as she spoke, she took a step forward, out of his encircling arm.

Sean laughed softly, a teasing laugh that said he was aware of his affect on her. "Yes, on Wilshire. Our main plant's out by the airport."

"Industrial alarms."

"Uh-hmm. Alarms. My father started the business back when electronics was still looked on as some form of black magic."

"Times change."

"They sure do. Watch it here again. Come on. When I was a kid I put cinder blocks against the wall so I could look down over the city." Again he took her hand and steered her ahead of him. "Feel the blocks?"

Emily held on tightly until she felt them with one toe. Then she stepped up and rested her elbows on top of the wall. Sean came up behind her, put an arm around her and held her while they both looked out on the Los Angeles night.

Neither spoke for what seemed to Emily a very long time. She heard Sean's breath, felt it ruffle her hair. His aftershave was light, musky, and against her back his chest made an unyielding shield. She closed her eyes for a moment, absorbing him, giving in to the irresistible temptation to be overwhelmed by his subtle masculinity and the blatantly female responses he evoked. A strong man, a confident man who was also not afraid to show gentleness, that was the man she took Sean to be and if he turned her in his arms now, kissed her... Emily opened her eyes. She stiffened her body and concentrated on the skyline.

"Pretty, huh?" Sean asked.

Far below, lights from the city cast a blue-gold wash into the sky. The hillsides were undulating waves of glittering pinpricks. "Very pretty." She lifted her chin, ever more aware of his shoulders behind hers, the arm around her, his hands close enough on the wall to warm her fingers. "Is Red VanEpson an old friend?"

She snapped her mouth shut. Of all the things she might have said, that had to have been the worst choice.

"Mmm," Sean murmured and she heard the laughter in the sound. He was laughing at her. She'd given him the only signal he needed to prove she was interested enough in him to be jealous.

Emily recovered. She managed to put a little gap between them by pressing slightly forward and gripping the far side of the top of the wall. "She seems nice. And she is absolutely gorgeous, Sean. A knockout."

"She sure is."

It was Emily's turn to smile into the night. Sean was interested in her and he knew she wasn't immune to him. But they were both so civilized, so adult. And they were both being so careful about being honest. Her smile faded. He was probably being honest. She wasn't. But then, she didn't need to be, and she didn't intend to get to a point where she'd have to tell him about herself and then, possibly, watch him walk away from her. Protection was the name of her game, as it had been for four years now. She mustn't let herself get involved with Sean on more than a professional level, as much as she longed to at this moment.

"Red's real name is Nellie," Sean said suddenly. "She decided Red was more glamorous. She'd like to be an actress."

"Wouldn't just about everyone in this town?" Emily said, thinking of Larry. "Does she have any talent?"

"Only what you saw, I think. And, like you said, she sure does look something."

Jealousy hit again and Emily pursed her lips, not liking herself. "It's got to be tough trying to make it here—or anywhere in the theater. But you'd think her looks would make it easier."

"Or harder. Men in the industry tend to look at her face and body and forget she may also have a mind, which she does."

Emily expelled a long breath. He sounded as if he cared about Red VanEpson. "And that bothers you?"

"Yes. My wife was her sister and I guess I feel a sense of responsibility. Not that she'd appreciate that if she knew. I think she has it in her head that I'm the one who needs looking after with Margaret gone. Red's a good sort."

Emily's stomach slowly turned. He'd never mentioned his wife's name before. "You're a kind man, Sean," she said without thinking. But she didn't regret it afterward.

"Thank you, ma'am. Coming from you that means a lot." His right hand moved to rest on her shoulder.

It was time to finish this conversation and move on. "What did you want to discuss with me, Sean?"

His fingers at her temple, brushing back tangled curls, froze her in place. "Several things. You're wearing sweats. Were you running before you came here?"

He would avoid and avoid if she allowed him. "Yes. I parked just off Sunset and ran up. I need to get back, Sean. If you like, you could call the office and we'll see if we can help you with whatever else you need."

"You ran up Sunset Plaza Drive?"

"Yes. It's steeper than I realized. You could call us tomorrow."

"You ran up here at midnight?"

"I guess. Sekowsky seems very easy to get along with and she said the sushi bar went over well."

"When are you going to learn?" He spun her around and they both almost fell from the cinder block ladder. Sean pulled her against him and she clutched the front of his cotton shirt. "Didn't you say someone was following you?" he asked sharply. "That night when we met in the ABC building?"

"Well . . ."

"Have you given any thought to why that might have been?"

"Well . . ."

His arms tightened. His face was so close she could see the intensity in his eyes, the whiteness of his teeth as his lips moved. "Young women, particularly young women who look like you, don't run around the streets of Los Angeles alone at night. Not if they don't want to end up . . . raped—" he swallowed "—or dead."

Emily felt as if she were suffocating. "You sound like Joe."

He paused for a long time. She could feel his heart beating against her breast. "And Joe's right," he said finally. "I'm surprised he lets you do this."

Defiance flared inside Emily. She'd worked too long and hard for her independence to have one man after another telling her how to live her life.

"Joe's my partner, not my keeper. He doesn't know where I am or what I do on my own time."

Sean moved his fingers up her arms, his touch gentle. "So he didn't know you came up here alone tonight? I kind of expected him to come with you since he is supposed to be your partner."

"This job was my responsibility," she said, fury still sweeping her along, "and anyway, Joe had a date."

As soon as she'd spoken she closed her mouth firmly. Maybe Sean wouldn't pick up on what she'd said. Joe made a useful excuse whenever a man started to get too interested. And she'd been so careful not to give Sean any direct answers about her personal relationships.

"Does Joe date a lot?" Sean asked softly.

He hadn't missed a word. "Quite a lot."

"How about you?"

"Oh," she said, trying to organize her thoughts rapidly, "not too much. Work keeps me pretty busy." She couldn't remember the last time she'd gone out on a date.

"Good," Sean said.

Good that she was busy, or good that she didn't date? He could have meant either or both, but Emily knew exactly what he meant. She had a lot of thinking to do, all of it relating to Sean Townsend and whether or not she could work for him and not get emotionally involved, whether she might want to get emotionally involved with him anyway and if so, how she would cope with what that might mean.

"Sean," Emily said clearly. "Regardless of what you think about my habits, I do have to run back down that hill and it is time I got going. So if there's something you want me to be thinking about, could you give me a few details and I'll get back to you when I've thought about them."

"Yes, I can do that. Only you won't be running down the hill. I'll be driving you."

"No—"

"Yes. There are two things I'd like your help on."

"Sean, I'll call you—"

"It's been years since I gave an after-theater party. Do you think that would be a good idea?"

He was like a steamroller. He plowed down everything in his path. "They can be lovely. They're also very simple to arrange. I'm sure Mrs. Sekowsky can cope perfectly well."

"Not the way you can."

Emily bowed her head for a second, then met his eyes. "When is the show and what are you seeing?" she said tiredly.

"Show?"

She couldn't help smiling again. "The show you're going to go to before you have your party. Did you already reserve seats?"

He chuckled. "I completely forgot. I guess I really am a bit out of the swing of things."

"You do know who'll be going with you, though?"

"Of course, of course. Small group. Ten or twelve. I can let you know that tomorrow."

"And will you want us to make the reservations for you?" She was making this too easy for him but she was also enjoying herself.

He nodded and she noticed for the first time how deep the cleft in his chin was. "Yes, I'd definitely like that."

"And you'll be seeing . . . ?"

His lips had remained sightly parted and she could almost see him searching his brain for the name of some show, any show currently in town.

"I don't want to intrude upon your thoughts," she said demurely, "and you've probably seen it already, but if you're into costume and choreography, *Cats* is spectacular. Just an idea, of course."

"*Cats!*" He wagged a finger. "Exactly what I had in mind. I couldn't think of the name for a moment. That's what I wanted."

"And for ten, or twelve?"

Sean looked down into Emily's face. What would she say if he asked her to make reservations for two, the two of them? He already knew. No, Townsend, he warned himself, patience. He had to build her trust and her attraction to him before he came totally into the open. Not that she wasn't already attracted and perfectly aware that her professional skills weren't all that interested him about her.

"How many people?" she repeated.

"Let's say ten. Keep it small."

"And you'll give us the guests' names tomorrow."

"I will." He certainly would. One more excuse to talk to her. So far he wasn't doing badly at keeping her within reach, and with practice he'd get better.

"Great. I'll be going then."

She'd leaped from the blocks before he could move. Silently cursing the slippery soles of his shoes, he quickly followed, ducking tree limbs as they snapped back in her wake.

He caught up with her in the driveway. "Hold on, Emily. I'll get Len to bring the Jensen around."

"No need," she insisted. "This hill is so steep, I'll go down so fast no one could catch me even on skates."

"But I'd feel better if I saw you to your car."

"I'm not your concern."

A cold feeling slipped over his skin. His scalp tightened. It was there again, the distance she was determined to put between them. And he couldn't stop himself from caring, dammit. "I'll walk you down."

She'd arrived at the gates. "Thanks. But I really do want to run."

"Okay. So I'll run."

Emily looked at his feet. "In those shoes? You'd break both your legs. Please, Sean. I'm okay, really I am."

He wasn't going to make any more progress tonight, no matter how hard he tried. She released the lock on the gates and they swung open.

"Listen," he said, suddenly inspired. "You have a real flair for color and design."

She paused. "Thank you."

"Well, I'm going to do some redecorating in my wing of the house and I thought I'd go to an antique auction Zig told me about. There's a George II games table I'm interested in."

"Sounds fascinating."

"Would you like to come?"

The darkness closed in while she seemed to consider her answer. Somewhere nearby a band of frogs set up a jam session.

"Emily, I'd like your opinion on the table."

"I don't know much about antiques. It's been a long..." She turned her head away. "I can't come. But I appreciate the invitation."

He knew better than to push farther. There had been a slight hesitation before she'd refused. Maybe next time the decision would take her longer, and maybe, in the end, she'd agree.

"I understand," he said, although he didn't. "If I get the table, will you come and see? And help me decide on some colors and so on?"

His hands were on her arms again. Emily looked up in frustration. He needed an interior decorator, not a social dropout. "I'd love to see it," she said. *And now would you let me go, Sean, please?*

"Thanks," he whispered, lowering his mouth to her cheek.

She turned her head and his lips missed her face, passing lightly over her mouth. She became very still, holding her breath, her body rigid.

"Thank you, Emily," Sean repeated, letting her go and stepping back. "Now, run, sweetheart. You'd better run... fast."

Chapter Six

The steady thud of hard rock music in Cassie's Place carried through the thin wall between the bar and the Occasion People's office. Although Joe and Emily always referred to the bar as being next door, the two small rooms they rented from Cassie herself were actually behind Cassie's Place.

Joe slammed his pen on the desk and covered his ears. Emily knew she was supposed to react. Instead she sat down on the linoleum-covered floor in front of a battered metal file cabinet and started filing brochures.

An ear-splitting boom made the lone picture on the wall vibrate. The picture was a photograph of Joe, smiling from behind a table at the restaurant where he'd been assistant manager prior to the brainwave that started him and Emily in business. When Emily had moved into the house and he'd discovered that she had an eye for color, an aptitude for math and a lot of style, he'd tentatively told her about the party business he'd always wanted to start. Unemployed at the time, Emily had enthusiastically encouraged him, then accepted his invitation to join in the operation. He never questioned how she knew so much about etiquette and protocol and exactly what every occasion needed to be a success, and she never told him, beyond remarking that she'd always enjoyed reading about how the famous and the wealthy lived.

The wail of a trombone pierced the air and even Emily winced.

"That does it," Joe thundered, leaping from his seat with enough force to tip it over. "We've got to get out of this place. We've got to have the kind of front this business needs if we're going to be taken seriously, really seriously."

"We're already being taken pretty seriously," Emily remarked placatingly.

"Yeah. As long as we can meet the customers on their own turf." He waved his arms and marched back and forth across the small room. "We need to be able to invite people here to show them pictures and price lists, and discuss plans and ideas. We need to interview the clients instead of creeping into their places with our tails between our legs, begging them to hire us. Damn it all," he roared, "I want to *be* someone and I can't as long as we have to go through a sleazy hole full of weirdos to get to our so-called office."

Emily fought against laughing; laughter now would just send Joe into a worse tantrum. He rarely lost his temper but she hated it when he did. "Partner," she said quietly, "cool it, huh? Cassie's isn't full of *weirdos* as you put it. And that term went out with the last century. It's an okay place if you like a lot of noise and happy people. That's all it is, noise and happy people, and it fills a need."

"Oh, yeah? So now you're a philosopher, too. Sometimes you're so damned reasonable you drive me nuts."

She bounced quickly to her feet and stood face to face with him. "Joe," Emily began, keeping her voice as level as she could, "don't vent your frustration on me. We're different, aren't we? You're the volatile one and ..." She pressed her lips together for an instant. She'd once been all too volatile and she'd paid the price for her lack of control, but Joe didn't have to be concerned with her history. "I guess I'm the steadying influence. Didn't you tell me that once?" She sat on top of another file cabinet and crossed her arms, suddenly drained.

Joe expelled a noisy breath and raked his curly hair with both hands. "Yeah, I guess I did. I'm sorry if I ran off at the mouth." His dark eyes met hers and the corners of his full mouth turned up in a pleading smile. "Sorry, okay? I want too much too fast. I know that but I can't seem to help it."

"Joe," Emily said gently, "we're doing very well. Sometimes I want to shake you and make you take a long look at how far we've come."

"Why don't you then?"

"Because you're too damned big."

They both laughed.

"You're right, you know," he said. "We have made a lot of progress. I was thinking the other day that we probably ought to hire someone to do some of the running around for us."

Emily relaxed. "Me, too. And I even had an idea who that could be."

"Oh, yeah? Who?"

"Larry, who else? He's always hungry and he's been cheering us on from the beginning."

Joe frowned. "Yeah. I like that idea. Maybe I'm way off base, but I worry about the guy sometimes, you know, about whether or not he's making it as well as he says he is. I'm not even sure he ever gets a decent meal if one or the other of us isn't cooking and invites him to eat."

"Oh, Joe." Emily stood and flung her arms around him, hugged him tight. "You are so special, so good."

Joe slowly put his arms around her and squeezed her in a breath-destroying grip. Emily closed her eyes, feeling, as she had felt before, that she'd never had a friend like this big, rough, incredibly kind man.

The soft clearing of a throat fractured the moment and she raised her head from Joe's chest. Over his shoulder she saw that the door was open, and the eyes that met hers were deep green and expressionless, despite the smile on their owner's lips.

"Sean! Hi!" She put her hands on Joe's bulging biceps and took a step backward. "We didn't hear you come in."

"I should have knocked louder. That's some wild joint out there," he said, and when Joe looked over his shoulder he added, "Hi, Joe. You said we were almost neighbors so I decided to come and look you up." He glanced at his watch. "It's lunchtime and I thought I might be able to lure at least one of you to a little place I know on Sunset. Trattoria Italia. Some of the best Italian food in town. I'm becoming a celebrity, party-giver *extraordinaire*, and it's all your doing. I thought if I fed you you might have one or two more ideas to help put me even more prominently on the social map."

Emily couldn't return his smile. She felt him, saw every tiny movement of muscle and nerve in his handsome face and the way his shoulders shrugged inside the immaculate jacket of his dark gray suit, but she felt a huge distance between them. And she watched his eyes, tried to read his reaction to the scene he'd walked in on. Perhaps he was indifferent after all. Just as she had no right to be concerned over his romantic involvements, he had no right to care who she was involved with. But he did care. His questions about her living arrangements—which he still didn't fully know about—and his reaction to her comment that Joe was involved with someone else had indicated more than a casual interest in her private life. She put several feet between herself and Joe.

"Well," Sean said and Emily heard a false note of cheerfulness in his voice, "any takers?"

Joe set his chair back on its feet and sank into it. He put his feet up on the desk and laced his fingers behind his neck. "You bet," he said with enough enthusiasm to cause Emily's eyes to open wide. "Emily here has been giving me a hard time all morning. I just got through trying to calm her down. Take her out, for God's sake. Turn on her creative juices and while you're at it, persuade her to go easy on me. Her ambition is going to be the end of me."

Emily opened her mouth and closed it quickly. Joe was impossible, but that had always been part of his charm for her. She'd never known anyone like him.

"Sounds like an emergency," Sean said and laughed. "I'd better get to work on the problem immediately. By the way—" he concentrated his attention on Joe "—the theater party was a knockout. For two days I've had calls from people who want to be included in my next 'event'."

Joe spread his hands. "All Emily's doing. All I did was contact the right chef."

"I know, I know," Sean said enthusiastically, "but the crêpes did it. Everyone loved *Cats*, but the French *crêperie* on my patio swept 'em away and I guess I have you to thank for that, Joe."

Joe bowed his head but Emily could see his smile. "Glad it went over okay," he said. "But Emily's the real idea factory. In fact, she was talking about you earlier. She's got another brainwave cooking."

"She does?"

There was no way she could flash a warning at Joe. She'd deal with him later and he wouldn't like it.

"Yeah. A terrific idea. But she'll tell you about it. Over lunch. Emily loves Italian food, don't you, Em?"

She turned around and screwed her face at Joe. "Oh, yes, I love Italian food."

"So enjoy," he said with a smirk. "And don't hurry back, Em. I've got the Shilletto picnic in hand. Our gourmet hot dogs and treasure hunt routine sent Mrs. Shilletto into ecstasy. It'll be a breeze. Give Sean all the time he needs."

"Thanks," Emily said grimly. He'd dropped the lure and she knew Sean would bite, only she had no idea what brilliant plan she was supposed to lay on him.

"Off we go then," Sean said. He took her hand and put it around his elbow. "They do a marvelous calamari. Lightly breaded and smothered in a tomato sauce with something I can't quite identify. You eat outside and today's the perfect day for it. Great location."

She quelled the impulse to retort that he'd missed his calling. Instead she smiled sweetly into his face, said, "Lead on," and vowed she would come up with something for Sean Townsend that would tax even Joe Moreno's overdeveloped ambition.

Today Sean drove a new white Jaguar. Emily made no comment. He probably owned several expensive cars, or he changed his wheels to suit his mood, or he was having scratches on the door of the Jensen repaired. That reminded her of her blond shadow, so she pushed the thought away and enjoyed the opulence of supple black leather and the excitement of sitting beside the sexiest, most interesting man she'd ever met.

Trattoria Italia was nestled between two boutiques on the Boulevard displaying figures encased in black leather studded with brilliant stones. Sean parked the Jaguar and led her to the café. Other customers went inside to place their orders, then returned to the outdoor seating area. But Sean simply waited until a slight, dark-haired man rushed toward him, welcoming Mr. Townsend and being grateful for the honor of having him at his restaurant again. Sean accepted the proprietor's greeting with a slight nod of the head and asked for a table in the narrow area between the café and one of the boutiques. "Less frenetic," he remarked as they followed the man. "You don't mind, do you?"

She didn't mind. What she would prefer, unreasonably, would be to go with Sean to some place where they could be completely alone. She'd like to sit with him in silence, to watch the rapid change of expression that was part of him and to touch him. He'd taken off his jacket and slung it over his shoulder and she couldn't help noticing the ripple of muscle in his back and chest as he turned and gestured.

"If you'd rather sit at a sidewalk table..." His voice had become uncertain and Emily was pulled back to the moment.

"No. No, Sean. I don't like crowds and noise." When the owner pulled out a chair for her, she ignored it and slipped into the one facing away from the street. A habit she'd developed.

Sean murmured several words in Italian and sat in the chair the man held. "Thanks, Giovanni," he said. "Something to drink?" He addressed Emily.

Her composure had fled. "Order for me. No..." She slapped both palms on the table. "I know what I want. Cinzano Bianco. Do you have it?" She looked at Giovanni who smiled and bowed from the waist in assent. "Good. Cinzano Bianco. It will remind me of my first visit to Italy."

Giovanni left and she sank back into her white metal chair.

"So you were in Italy?" Sean asked. "How long ago?"

Warnings of caution flashed in her mind more sharply than they had ever before. "I don't remember. A long time ago."

"But you went more than once?"

She studied her hands in her lap. "Twice. I don't remember anything about it."

"Except that Cinzano Bianco reminds you of the place."

She met his eyes. "Yes. It makes me think of stalls heaped with oranges with shiny leaves on them. And pink plastered buildings that were peeling and some of the most beautiful views I've ever seen."

He was quiet for a moment. "You feel everything intensely, don't you?"

"Perhaps," she responded and felt defensive. "Or I did. That's common with the young."

"You're still young."

"Twenty-six. Hardly a baby."

"I'm thirty-seven and most of the time that doesn't feel so old to me."

"It shouldn't. You're a very attractive—" *Oh, her loose, loose tongue.*

"Don't stop, Emily. A very attractive what?"

The waiter brought two glasses of Cinzano and she realized Sean hadn't said what he wanted to drink.

She opened her mouth to comment but he shook his head and raised his glass, waited until she did the same, and clinked it to hers.

"Very attractive what?" he persisted when they'd both taken a sip of the pale aromatic vermouth.

Emily met his eyes squarely. "Man. But you knew that, didn't you?"

"Not from you. And for the record, I don't think I ever feel as young as I do when I'm with you." He rested his fingers on the backs of her hands.

"You hardly know me," Emily said. She looked at their hands, hers beneath his.

"I'd like to know you very well, Emily. But I can't read you. I don't know how you feel about me."

"I can see and feel what happens when we're together, but it isn't a good idea to push it any farther. Please believe that."

"I don't want to."

And neither did she. But they hadn't known each other long and she couldn't judge yet whether he would ever be able to accept her once he found out that everything he thought her to be was a lie, that Emily Smith didn't really exist.

"Emily?"

"Let it go for now, Sean." She withdrew her hands and lightly stroked his outstretched fingers upward, feeling the texture of fine brown hair as far as the cuffs of his immaculate gray-and-white striped shirt. He wore a slender white-gold Patek Phillippe watch with a black face. Emily laid a finger on the lizard strap where it rode low beneath the prominent bone in his left wrist. Every tiny detail of the man enthralled her.

"I'm not sure I can let it go," he said, and when she looked at his face the corners of his mouth twitched.

She must stop this, now, make time and space for them both to think. "I know having us work for you was an excuse, Sean."

"It was at first. Now it's only partly an excuse . . . to be near you."

"You do like what we've done so far, don't you?"

"You know I do."

"Sean, I'm not sure I'll ever be ready for more than a business relationship with you. And perhaps, if you want it too, a friendship. Can you go with that? Do you still want us to work for you? I'll understand if you don't. Joe may not, but I can make an excuse and he won't push. He never pushes me."

Sean looked at her for a long time, then made a fist against his mouth. "Don't go away altogether, Emily," he said, so low she leaned closer to hear. "And don't shut out the idea of us being something other than employer and employee, not completely."

"I can't work for you if—"

"No, not if I make things tough for you. I understand that and I won't." He smiled suddenly, brilliantly. "I bought the table."

It took Emily a while to remember the games table he'd wanted. "Congratulations. I'm glad."

"Will you come and see it?"

He hadn't given up, but then, she didn't really want him to. "Yes," she said. "Next time I'm at your house I'll see it."

"How about after lunch?"

"I can't."

"Why? Joe said he didn't need you for the rest of the day. He said you were to concentrate on me, or something like that, so come and see my beautiful table." He tipped up his chin and sat back in his chair. "Beautiful things don't mean as much when you don't have anyone to share them with."

He missed his wife. He'd said so. "Okay," Emily agreed. "After lunch. But we'd better make it short. I'm sure you have plenty to do and something tells me Joe will have come up with a new project by the time I get back."

"Thank you, Emily," Sean said. "You're different, you know that? You're real. It's a long time since I was around someone as real as you . . . or as honest."

A feeling of dread took Emily's appetite away. She pushed her glass back and forth on the table making damp rings on the coarsely woven fabric of the tablecloth. Her mind scrambled for a way out of the present line of conversation. Joe had promised some great innovation for Sean's social life. She'd think about that, get Sean thinking about it. She gazed at the sun-drenched walls along Sunset Boulevard.

"Emily," Sean said very quietly, "did you hear what I said?"

"Hmmm? Yes. Thank you. A costume party. What do you think?"

"What?"

"A costume party. Remember Joe said I had an idea for you and that was it, only it would be a costume party with a difference."

Sean's elbows rested on the table. "Go on." The tolerant expression on his face told her he wasn't enthusiastic or even particularly interested.

Emily cast around wildly, then, slowly her mind settled and began forming the patterns the last year of business had trained it to make. "You've heard of mystery parties, Sean?"

He glanced upward for a moment, then nodded.

"Whodunit events," Emily rushed on. "Everyone has a part to play. They come in costume to fit their fictional characters and know as much of their history as they're given on the invitation. Then a crime unfolds and the guests learn more and more, not just about themselves, but about each other.''

"I've heard of them," Sean said dubiously. "But I'm not sure how that would fit into my serious image."

She thought fast. "Actually, I was thinking more of Red. If we gave her a really dramatic, important part, and you invited some of the right people, it might give her the showcase she needs."

Sean regarded her narrowly. "You surprise me. I didn't think you were particularly taken with Red."

"Well, it's just an idea. You don't have to like it."

"I do. I do like it. On one condition."

"Yes."

"That kind of thing makes me nervous. If we do it, will you help me with my costume?"

She relaxed. "I'd love to."

"And can we fix it so we can have a lot of people there. These things are usually pretty small, aren't they?"

"Yes. But we can adapt. We'll have celebrity extras. How's that?"

"Great. But there's one more thing. I'm not as confident as you think. Could you find a way to be there, Emily, as much on the outskirts as you like, but just to give me a high sign when I get uptight?"

"Well . . ."

Before she could continue a waiter came for their order and Sean, after nodding at Emily, said that they would both have the calamari.

She waited until they were alone again before she said, "I could be there, I suppose. But I don't think you need me." She knew he didn't need her. He wanted her, and that started a rising, burning excitement Emily reveled in. After all, she'd be in costume too, and could easily make sure she was totally unrecognizable. She should steer clear of Sean, but she didn't want to, and she told herself that in time, if fate smiled on her, she'd be able to tell him exactly who she was. Afterward, more explanation would be unnecessary. Anyone who was anyone knew that Sidonie James had been accused of bringing about the downfall of a famous man. What Emily had to believe was that Sean would listen to and accept her side of the story . . . when the time was right.

THE SPANISH-STYLE HOUSE was even bigger than Emily had thought. Sean used one wing as a kind of hideaway. Glass doors, covered on the outside with black metal grills, opened from the huge master suite onto an enclosed terrace. Sean's bathroom was roughly the same dimensions as the entire lower floor of the house Emily shared with Joe and Larry. Emily touched the shimmering black tiles along the edge of a tub the size of a small pool, then peered into a doorless shower with dual gold heads. Black and white towels were stacked in piles on a black wicker hamper and hung in rows over gold rods. There were no plants, pictures or ornaments of any kind. But on a shelf mounted beside double sinks were men's toiletries, and a razor and comb. Emily smelled the subtle, clean scent that would remind her of Sean even in twenty years, in some place far away from here.

She glanced up and their eyes met in the mirror. She smiled. Sean didn't.

"You have a beautiful home," she said and swallowed. Yes, she'd remember him always.

"I wanted you to like it. All of it."

"I didn't have any idea how big it is. You keep all the rooms in this wing just for you?" The question sounded vapid.

"Yes. Closed off as much as possible. My parents did the same thing. The house belonged to them before it came to me. Actually my mother inherited it from my father but she didn't want to live here after he died, so she gave it to me. She lives in Miami now. I'd like you to meet her. You'd get along very well."

How had Sean felt about being here after his Margaret died? Emily had seen a shadow cross his features when he'd spoken of his mother preferring to be elsewhere after she was widowed, the same shadow she'd noticed when he'd talked about needing someone to share special things with.

She didn't respond to his remark about his mother. "Show me the rest of your domain. And the table! That's what I'm here for, isn't it?"

He stood back in the doorway to let her pass. Besides the bedroom with its massive four-poster Jacobean bed there was a sitting room furnished with big, comfortable couches and chairs in shades of cream and gold with touches of blue. Sean urged Emily toward a white marble fireplace.

"Do you know what this is?" He held the frame of a needleworked pole screen.

Emily shook her head. "I'm really not very good with antiques. If you hadn't said the bed was Jacobean I might have said something dumb, like is it Chippendale?"

He laughed. "I doubt that, but I'll teach you. Tell me what you think of the screen."

She looked at it closely. "It's lovely. Must have taken someone forever to make all those tiny stitches. I like pastoral scenes. I know it's very old, how about that for an acute observation?"

"Wrong." His lips parted in a delighted smile. "It's a fake oldie made by my mother. When you do meet her she'll love you for getting the right wrong impression."

Emily grimaced. "You set me up."

"Yup. In there—" he pointed to a door she hadn't noticed before "—is a tiny study I rarely use. Across the hall there's a breakfast room where I eat all my meals if I'm alone and there are two more, smaller bedrooms with their own bathrooms. One of them was mine when I was a boy."

And you and Margaret intended for them to be filled with your children one day, Emily thought, an overwhelming sadness making her turn away from him. "I'd like to see it all, but I think we'd better make do with the table for now."

Sean shoved his hands in his pockets and started back the way they had come. The table was set against a wall in his bedroom with four circular eighteenth-century portraits of children grouped above.

"Lovely," Emily whispered, her hand hovering inches from the flawless walnut surfaces. "It opens out, doesn't it?"

"Yes." He pulled the table away from the wall and spread the top. "And this is where candleholders can be put and these are places for chips. What do you think?"

"It's marvelous." Her own father would covet this if he saw it. Their Boston home had often reminded Emily of a museum. Sean clearly had tastes similar to her parents' but with a flair for creating warmth that the Jameses didn't have.

She was marvelous, Sean thought, and elusive and infuriatingly desirable. "Sit down," he offered and dropped into one of a pair of Victorian upholstered chairs. She hesitated for a moment but he'd made a refusal difficult. So she sat in the other chair, facing him.

"You never talk about yourself," he said. "For me you began in the middle of the night in a deserted building complex. You know a lot about me, now it's your turn. Where are you from?"

His attention was instantly pulled to the way she crossed her legs tightly and folded her hands over her knees. She dug her fingernails into the seams at the sides of her jeans and when he looked at her eyes again they darted away.

"I'm from the East," she said. "What time is it, Sean?"

The lady didn't want to talk about herself. "Almost three."

"Would you mind driving me back?"

"Not at all. Emily, can I ask you a very personal question?" His heart contracted while he waited for her response.

She didn't answer.

"Joe Moreno. You mentioned he was on a date the evening of the first party you arranged for me."

"Yes."

"Well, this is none of my business, but does that mean there's nothing between you . . . but business, that is?"

She let out a long breath. "Joe and I are good friends."

"But you aren't lovers." If she got up and walked out he wouldn't blame her.

Emily regarded him steadily. "We aren't lovers, Sean. We never have been. Neither are Larry and I."

"Larry?"

"The other man who shares the house where I live."

"Is there another woman there, too?"

"No."

"Just you and two men?"

"Right."

He knew he wasn't dealing with this very well. "And that doesn't . . . that doesn't present any problems for you?"

"Why should it?"

"Um, no reason, I guess. Except some people might not understand that kind of arrangement."

"Some people like you?"

"I didn't say that."

He didn't have to, Emily thought, getting up. Disapproval sharpened every feature in his face. Well, where and with whom she lived was nobody's business but hers. And she'd just learned something—Sean Townsend was a man who believed in traditional standards. There were things that were just not done, like sharing a house with two men. And having one's name linked with a politician's personal scandal would undoubtedly rank a whole lot higher than that on Sean's list of unacceptable behavior.

He didn't try to stop her from leaving, didn't offer her a drink or make small talk. On the way down to Sunset Boulevard he remarked only on the weather, exceptionally good for late September. Outside Cassie's he got out and came around to open Emily's door.

She joined him on the sidewalk and thanked him before turning to walk into the bar.

"Wait a minute." She had reached the door when Sean hailed her. He still stood on the passenger side of the car but held her purse aloft. "You forgot this."

They met in front of the Jaguar and Emily took her purse. "Dumb of me," she said. "I probably wouldn't have noticed I didn't have it until I got home." She felt empty.

Sean stroked her upper arm. "I enjoyed having you with me this afternoon," he said.

Emily nodded, tracing marks on the hood of the Jaguar.

"Jeez," Sean muttered, "what's that? Looks like I scraped under something and dented the thing." He peered closely at the paintwork on the car. "I'll be damned. Have you got some paper in your purse—and a pencil?"

"I, yes, I think so." She fumbled with the contents of her purse until she found a pencil, then tore a sheet out of a notebook. "What are you going to do?"

He laid the paper on top of the rough area and rubbed the pencil lead back and forth. Then he held the paper up for Emily to see.

"Numbers and letters," she said and shook her head. "What do they mean?"

"They're the license numbers from this car," he said, frowning. "Someone must have put down a piece of paper like I just did and copied the plate. And they were in such a hurry they pressed hard enough to leave an imprint, probably shredded their paper. But why would anyone do that?"

"I don't know." Emily closed her purse and backed away. "Maybe you parked in front of a driveway or something. Look, Sean, I've got to run. Sorry about the car. And thanks again for the good time."

She didn't look back, didn't stop running until she reached the hallway between Cassie's Place and the office.

Someone had written down the number of Sean's car. It could be a coincidence, something as petty as she'd suggested. Or *she* could have been the reason for the unusual interest in the Jaguar. Had the number only become important after she'd been a passenger? For a few days she'd almost forgotten her fear that she was being followed. Was her pursuer still there after all and getting even more determined in his vigil?

Emily covered her face with both hands. Either she was becoming paranoid or she definitely had cause to be very afraid.

Chapter Seven

The brunette on the bar stool to Sean's left swung toward him until her knee dug into his thigh. "Whoops!" She pressed peacock-blue-and-pink-striped nails against pouting, mauve-painted lips and giggled. "Clumsy me." A wide-necked T-shirt, also mauve, slipped from one raised shoulder.

Sean stayed put, the sharp knee still insinuated against his leg, and looked into the pale blue eyes that blinked, attempted to focus on his, then blinked again. One of the world's lost in a sea of the world's lost. "Can I buy you a drink?" he asked and instantly wondered why he had. She nodded and he saw a pathetic hint of gratitude in the black-rimmed eyes. She wasn't as grateful for the drink as she was for his not rejecting her clumsy advance. He signaled the bartender.

On a wall clock half hidden by a shelf of cluttered bottles, a neon palm tree rocked away the seconds. Sean was waiting for Frank Horton, his vice president. Watching the clock through a film of cigarette smoke, he felt himself moving away from the moment, from this place he'd suggested to Frank simply because he'd seen the bar so many times while driving along Sunset. Getting out of the office just to talk, to do what they hadn't done for a long time and mix a little business with personal conversation had been Frank's idea. Sean had selected the place. A bad choice, he decided. When Frank arrived they'd better go somewhere else.

The girl was talking. The din around them drowned her out. Sean shook his head and leaned a little closer. She smelled of nicotine and strong, cheap perfume.

"I said I haven't seen you here before."

"No." He ought to move now. But what would it cost him to wait for Frank and save what was left of her ego by telling her then that he had to go?

"It's a nice place," she said. "You live close?"

"Not too far." He saw Frank. As tall as the man was, at least six and a half skinny feet, he had to stand on tiptoe to peer over heads, his customary frown in place. Sean waved and slid from the stool.

The girl touched his arm and he glanced down at her. "Thanks for the drink." No surprise that he was moving on. Most of the people she met probably moved on.

"You're welcome." Sean smiled and the second before he left her he realized what he hadn't noticed before—she hadn't been a girl for a long time.

He wove his way toward Frank, the familiar old depression setting in with each swing of his shoulders, each "excuse me." He was like these people, alone and hating it. The difference was that he'd finally found the woman, the only woman, the one he wanted to share his life with, and yet he had as much hope of success as most of the men who walked into this place. At least they came to hunt and the possibility of scoring was always there, even if only in their minds.

Frank had seen him and immediately turned away. Sean hurried, but by the time he caught up, Frank was already sliding into a booth in a fairly isolated corner.

"The sides of you are endless, Sean," Frank said after Sean had settled across from him. "I had no idea you were into meat markets."

"Hell, I'm not." Sean rubbed a hand across his jaw, raising his eyebrows at a leather-covered rump almost resting on the edge of their table. "I see this place every time I drive by, you know, a name over a door. Simon's. It sounded okay and what do I know? We should go somewhere else."

"Why?" Frank glanced quickly at the curve of black leather near his elbow. "I lead a sheltered life, thank God, but maybe I should get a little education. I've heard about these places. Now I'll be able to speak about them with authority." He favored Sean with one of his rare grins. Several years Sean's junior, Frank Horton was a very serious man and the best right hand Sean could have hoped for.

A waitress wearing buckskin shorts and a halter top popped gum while Sean ordered a martini and Frank a Perrier.

"So," Sean began, "I bombed out on the choice of a bar, but you're the one who wanted to talk. Get reacquainted, wasn't that what you said? What's up, Frank? I've always felt very well acquainted with you and grateful you came my way. You're very important to me, you know that."

Frank glanced up as the waitress returned and waited for her to leave before he said, "I didn't mean that I think there's anything wrong with our working relationship. That's why I didn't try to talk to you at the office. And you know how much peace we're likely to get at my house with the kids. Anyway, I..." He cleared his throat and swallowed some Perrier. "You can tell me to drop dead and mind my own business, if you like, but you haven't been yourself lately, Sean and, frankly, that has me worried. I was talking to Jean about it and she's worried about you, too. She thinks you haven't let yourself grieve properly about Margaret and now it's starting to hit you."

Sean stared at him. He couldn't think of a thing to say.

Frank bowed his face and swirled his drink. "Out of line, right? Back off and take a walk, Frank." He ran his fingers over thick dark hair that was graying at the temples.

"No, no." Sean took a deep breath and gave the room a sweeping look, seeing only color and movement. "But, hell, Frank, your insight scares me. I'm that transparent, huh? You think I'm slipping at Townsend?"

"I don't," Frank said in a voice louder than Sean had ever heard him use. "That's not what I think. But I can feel you slipping away in every other area. How long is it since you and I played racquetball?"

Sean turned both palms up.

Frank snorted more than laughed. "Not that I was ever any competition for you. But it used to be a good time and you seemed to beat some of the..." his voice trailed off and a faint flush colored his thin cheeks.

"Yeah, I know. I used the games to smash away some of the frustrations and hurt I felt over Margaret. Jean's not far off, but she is off. It took a while, but not the seven years the gurus say it takes to deal with the death of someone you really love. I'm never going to forget Margaret, what man in his right mind would? But, and this is because of her, because of the way *she* prepared me for her death, I made it through and I'm ready to go on."

It was Frank's turn to stare. "You mean," he began slowly, "that you're looking for another wife? Is that why you're so preoccupied these days?" He reached over the table and grabbed both of Sean's wrists. "Good, good," he said and the physical contact with this quiet man told Sean more than he'd ever guessed about the loyalty and deep caring Frank felt for him. "Then we'll get started. Give Jean and me a while to think and we'll come up with some women for you to meet. Nice, suitable women. We'll give some parties—"

"Frank." Sean held up his hand and couldn't help smiling, an amused yet touched smile. "Not necessary, friend. I've found her."

And as soon as he'd said it, in the few seconds it took Frank to gape, recover, then lean back in the booth, a broad grin transforming his lean face, Sean almost wished he could pull back the words. Then he smiled too and downed the rest of his martini. He shouldn't have another since he had to drive, but he hailed the waitress. He could always take a cab home. Frank, ever the moderate, broke down and ordered a spritzer.

When the fresh drinks came, Frank raised his glass. "I can't tell you how happy this makes me. And I know Jean will be over the moon. When's the date? Or I guess I'm getting ahead here. *Who* is she?" Quickly, he put a finger over his mouth, shaking his head. "Let me guess. It's Red. Makes sense. You two didn't used to get along, but you both loved Margaret. It's a natural, sure it is. Wow, will you two make a pair. Jean always says you're the best-looking man she's ever met." He gave a mock grimace. "Great for my ego, but she says she loves the inner me."

Sean laughed. "Frank—"

"Just joking," Frank cut in. "With my brains, who needs to look like a movie star? But you could just have your hands full with Red. I don't think I'd cope too well with a number like that."

"Frank," Sean said gently, "it isn't Red. It isn't anyone you know."

Frank slowly set down his drink. "It isn't? So who? Come on, Sean, spill. Who is it?"

"She isn't anyone." He bowed his head and looked up sharply. "Wrong, she is definitely somebody, but she's nobody anyone knows. Frank, she is a beautiful, honest, fresh human being and I love her."

He immediately planted his elbows on the table and clamped both fists against his forehead. Here he was, professing his love for Emily to his vice president when he had never mentioned love to the woman herself, had never even kissed her, except by accident. And as for making love? He turned his face to the back of the red-and-black, plastic-lined booth and closed his eyes. Oh, he could imagine what making love to Emily *might* be like, but that was as far as any kind of experience in that department went.

When he looked up at Frank, the other man had settled a pleased smile on his lips. "Sounds like the perfect woman

for you, Sean," he said. "Someone quiet. A homebody like
Jean. Honestly, man, you don't want a mouse with no
opinions who doesn't know the Faroes from Mozam-
bique. But one very visible member in a family is enough.
She'll be there when you need backing up and you'll always know you've got a solid base."

A solid base. Sean allowed himself to dream of Emily in
his sitting room. Emily in the breakfast room, in a soft
wrap, sharing morning coffee and discussing the day's news
before he had to leave for the office. Emily waiting for him
when he came home at night . . . He didn't see her as a total
homebody, she was too strong and vital not to be involved
in something challenging. But to have her with him, to
know she was there . . .

"So, who is she?" Frank prodded.

Sean snapped out of his reverie and looked seriously at
Frank. "She's a very special, very private woman. And I'm
a long way from persuading her that I'm the best thing that
ever happened to her."

"Oh," Frank seemed to deflate a little. "But you do
think you'll pull it off?"

"I . . . yes." He knew now what he would do next, the
obvious, yet the last thing he'd thought of. "I'll pull it off,"
he promised. "I may need a little help, but I think I know
where to get it. And, Frank, you know how I hate to be
pushed."

Frank nodded emphatically. "Not another word until
you're ready to discuss it, Sean. You have my word. Is it
okay if I tell Jean?"

"It's okay." Every important facet of his own life had
been shared with Margaret, and it was the same between
Frank and Jean. Statistics said they were part of a rare
breed. Sean preferred to think the statistics weren't repre-
sentative of a broad enough base. He had to believe that
strong relationships between men and women prevailed and
would continue to proliferate.

Frank was getting up. "I'd better get home or I'll face the music." He rolled his eyes then looked around. "Boy, I sure couldn't make this scene a habit. I'd rather shrivel up all on my own."

"Me, too," Sean agreed. "But some people need more than others." He needed, probably just as much as every man and woman in this room, and he was going to do something about it.

As soon as Frank walked away from him in the foyer, Sean went into a phone booth.

"HEY, SEAN!"

At the sound of Joe Moreno's voice, Sean looked up from the aft deck of his ketch and yelled, "Hey, Joe." Sun shimmered on the hulls of pleasure craft moored along the docks at Marina del Rey.

Sean pushed himself out of a chair, shading his eyes. "Come aboard."

The head of every man and woman on the deck of the motor cruiser next to Sean's boat turned as Joe's big, surprisingly graceful body approached. When he was halfway down the gangplank he jumped the rest of the way to the deck. "This is something, man," he said, his smile reminding Sean of a kid in the candy store he'd just discovered belonged to his favorite aunt.

"Thought you'd like it. I don't get down here often enough. Business. You know how it is?"

"Yeah, I know." The almost imperceptible tightening of Joe's mouth, the sober set of his features, seemed out of character. But he relaxed almost at once and the old smile came back. "How big is this tub?"

"Fifty-two feet," Sean said.

"Sea-going then? You could take her anywhere?" Joe sat in a deck chair and accepted the can of beer Sean offered him.

"Just about anywhere. But like I said, I don't have too much time."

"You must need a crew to run the thing."

"Just two. Skipper and a hand. The hand is the skipper's wife and she also does the cooking."

Joe slid forward in his seat and curled the fingers of one hand behind his neck. "Nice," he said on a long, expelled breath. "Very nice."

Sean picked imaginary pieces of lint from his loose khaki shirt, waiting, giving Joe time to completely settle down. The call of the previous evening had been to ask if he and Joe could get together. Suggesting they meet on the boat had been an inspiration. Sean was glad he had thought of it. First, they were completely alone, and second, with Joe's obvious appetite for the expensive, being aboard the *Serena* for a while should soften him enough to make Sean's task a little easier.

"Joe." Joe was gazing up at the naked masts soaring overhead, his expression oddly intent. The breeze whipped his black curls across his forehead. "Joe," Sean repeated, "did you mind my getting you down here this morning? What did you say to Emily?"

The dark eyes met his. Although he wasn't smiling, the skin around them crinkled. "I said I was meeting a friend for a few hours."

Sean thought about that, then said, "And she doesn't mind if you suddenly decide to meet a friend for a few hours in the middle of a morning when you should be working?"

Joe shrugged. "You didn't have much trouble getting away either, did you?"

Sean kept his expression impassive and quelled his irritation. Joe Moreno was fresh. He might go very far, or he might end up on the bottom. His fate would depend on whether he learned to control his mouth.

"So Emily doesn't know you're with me?" Now wouldn't be the time to lose his temper, not if he wanted to get Joe on his side.

"Uh-uh, no way. She thinks I had to get together with a lady. Not that I exactly said that, just kind of hinted. Was that okay?" He frowned, as if asking approval, and Sean felt what he'd felt before, that Joe Moreno wanted the business he'd decided Sean represented, wanted it badly enough to do almost anything to get it.

"That was fine," he said easily. Joe could have his business. He was good at what he did. He could have it even when Emily was no longer a part of the Occasion People. Oh, he could certainly have it then. Sean smiled to himself.

"So, what's the score, Sean?" Joe asked. He sat forward and tipped up the beer can, holding it several inches from his lips to let a thin golden stream pour into his mouth.

Sean watched him a moment, eyes narrowed. "I want to ask you a favor, a big favor. But first, I am right in assuming you and Emily don't have anything going, aren't I? Outside of the housing arrangement and the business, that is?"

The can collapsed between Joe's crushing fingers. "Yeah. You're right. Em and I are purely business. Not that I don't think she's one fantastic lady. But she's not my type, and, even more so, I'm not her type. Why?"

Sean was going to stop playing games. "She's my type, Joe. Exactly my type. I'm not sure how she feels about me, but I'd like to find out. Only I'm not having much success getting to first base with her."

Joe made as if to heave the can over the side, caught Sean's eye and grinned. He wiggled it between finger and thumb instead then set it beneath his chair. "So where do I come in?"

"You tell me what you know about her. I mean the parts of her life when she isn't working with you. Is there someone else? She's very private so I haven't had the guts to ask her, not directly, anyway."

"Nope. There's no one. The field's clear. Go for it."

Sean raised his brows. "Just like that, go for it? Does that mean you think it's a good idea? You think she might be interested if I really pushed it?"

"Emily isn't easy to push. But I do think she's interested in you."

A huge weight seemed to have eased off Sean's chest, leaving him strangely light-headed, euphoric.

"Why do you think she's interested in me?"

Joe shrugged. "You got another beer?"

Sean reached into a cooler and passed a can. "There's chips here, too. And fruit. Want some fruit?"

"I don't *want* fruit, and the gut says I'd better pass on the chips, too." He settled a broad hand on his flat middle. "The beer isn't such a hot idea either, but what's a morning on the water without a beer, huh?"

Sean made a polite noise. Right now he'd get a whole lot more excited about a double martini. "So, back to Emily. Has she said anything about me?"

Joe tipped back his head and laughed, showing strong white teeth. "Yeah. All of it bad."

"Bad?" Sean slammed the lid of the cooler, wondering if he'd heard right. "But you just said you thought she was interested in me."

"Exactly. And that's why she's been trying to avoid you since the night you met. Listen, Sean, women are a science. They always pretend they don't want what they're really dying to get. It's all part of the game, see. She's pining away for you, I tell you. I only have to say your name and she goes off into a silent spell. I can see what she's thinking in her eyes. You know what her eyes are like?"

Sean didn't reply. He gazed at the sky, a deep, clear blue, and saw Emily's eyes.

"Well," Joe went on. "She tries to make sure you don't look directly at them when she doesn't want you to know what she's thinking. Mirrors of the soul, isn't that what they say about eyes?" He laughed a little self-consciously.

"I'll be spouting poetry next. Didn't know I had all that deep thought in me, did you?"

"I wouldn't be surprised at anything you have in you," Sean said honestly, thinking that Joe could turn out to be a much smarter man than he liked to appear. "So, expert, she likes me and I like her. But she insists on keeping everything between us strictly business. So how do I get to know her?"

"You mean get together with her?"

Sean bit back the temptation to retort that getting together with a woman he wanted was what a man usually had in mind. "You've got it. How do I persuade her to spend some time with me?"

Joe whistled, then hummed, then turned toward Sean and jabbed a finger into his chest. "Easy," he said. "You go see her."

"I go see her," Sean repeated slowly. "I don't get it."

"Well, all she does when she's not working is stay home and read, or listen to music—she does that a lot—and run, of course. But that wouldn't help much, unless you want to try running into her." He laughed and quickly cleared his throat. "Unintentional pun."

"Okay. She stays home and listens to music."

A frown raised Joe's brows. "Too much to ask, huh, even for a woman you like? I understand. I don't think I could take sitting around listening to *Porgy and Bess* for anyone."

Sean closed his eyes. There was nothing he'd like better than to sit around listening to music with Emily, endlessly. "She likes opera?"

"Huh?"

"*Porgy and Bess*. Emily likes opera."

"Oh, yeah. Plays it all the time unless I get to the stereo first. She and Larry really go for that stuff. You should see them. Larry practicing lines, waving his arms around in time to all that yelling and Emily lying flat on her back with her eyes closed looking like she just won a million."

Sean would like to see Emily lying there. He'd like to lie there with her. "Okay, so she's home most nights and I should go see her, is that what you're suggesting?"

"You got it."

"I just drop by and sit there with you and this Larry and Emily."

"God, no." Joe set his beer on the deck. "Larry's an actor, see. And at the moment he's in a rare condition." He smiled. "He's employed for once and he's gone all evening. And I can be gone any time you give the word." His smile was expansive and conspiratorial. "I don't have to come home at all if that's what you want. Just let me know when you're coming over and I'll blow."

Sean absorbed what Joe suggested slowly. He felt for him a mixture of gratitude and vague dislike. Keeping Emily involved with Sean probably seemed to Joe the best way to make sure the Occasion People continued to get the fairly lucrative jobs he gave them. He drummed the fingers of one hand against his mouth. But he could take Joe up on his suggestion and drop by Emily's. The worst that could happen was that she'd say she was too busy to see him . . . or simply tell him to get lost.

"What do you think?" Joe was watching him.

"I think you should find yourself a hot date for tomorrow night."

"All right!" Joe held out a palm until Sean slapped it, then reversed the process. "You got it, buddy. Seven o'clock tomorrow night and I'm gone. You want me to stay away all night?"

The guy was pure finesse. "I don't think that'll be necessary. A few hours should do it." And even with that Sean knew he was being an optimist. "You're sure this Larry won't show up?"

"You've got my word. He's playing a pimp in some revue. I thought you had to dance and sing in a revue, but apparently he got the part anyway and he can't sing a note. Not that I've heard, anyway—"

Sean didn't need the life history of Larry. "Well," he interrupted, "I can try anything once. But, Joe, you don't ever repeat this conversation, right?"

"Right. You've got—"

"Your word," Sean finished for him. "I know. Thanks. How about going up to the club for lunch?"

"Terrific."

Sean walked behind Joe up Bali Way toward Admiralty. He wasn't going to be able to eat. His stomach had decided it preferred being in his throat. But tomorrow he would make that visit.

He trained his eyes on Joe's topsiders. Between now and when Emily opened her door, he'd better come up with some good lines.

EMILY FINISHED PUTTING DISHES in the dishwasher, poured in the soap and turned on the machine. The noise was almost a relief. The house was too silent. Usually she liked it that way, but tonight she was jumpy... and lonely.

She poured a glass of white wine and carried it into the living room. Joe had said he'd be late and she knew Larry wouldn't be home until the early hours of the morning. Not that it was their responsibility to worry about what she did with her spare time. If she was alone too much she had no one to blame but herself.

The wineglass made a wet ring on the table beside the couch. Emily started back toward the kitchen for a paper towel, switching on the radio when she passed it. There might be a play. She loved radio plays.

Sean hadn't called for two days, not since he'd gone into his disapproving act over her living arrangements. Emily returned to the living room, wiped the table and used the towel as a coaster. Then she curled up in the corner of the green-and-black checked couch she was beginning to loathe. She didn't want Sean to call anyway, did she?

Yes, she did, darn it.

Tears welled in her eyes and she blinked them away. Self-pity wasn't going to help a thing. Sean had let her know in a dozen ways that he was interested in her and she'd done nothing but turn him off. She sipped the wine and wrinkled her nose. Joe had bought it and it was too sweet for her taste.

If she weren't afraid, she'd go for a long, long run. She'd run Sean Townsend right out of her mind. But she was afraid. The most unpleasant idea to come to her about her shadow so far was that he might be someone hired by good old Charles Hennessy III. Charles had seemed as suspicious of her as the others before she'd decided to drop out of circulation, but she'd always had the feeling he cared for her. No, it couldn't be Charles. Why should it be? He had nothing to gain from having someone follow her around. This was a nut, she felt it in her bones. Yet she wasn't prepared to go to the police and complain. Some of her ID might not hold up so well under their scrutiny, particularly if they decided to run a complete check on her.

Emily pulled up her knees, wrapped her arms around them, and rested her forehead. She could almost hear the seconds ticking by. How many until morning? She was beginning to hate the nights.

SEAN PARKED THE JENSEN on Overland Avenue, across the street from the address Joe had given him. Only one light showed in the gray-painted house with two identical trees, one each side of an arched front door. He turned off the engine and watched the light; it was probably in the living room. That's where Emily must be, listening to her music, trying to unwind from a day's work if she was anything like him after a round of business battles.

He ran his hands around the steering wheel. The Jensen gave him pleasure. Explaining the scrapes and scratches on the bottom of the passenger door to Len, who then had to explain it to the body shop hand, hadn't been easy. But they'd patched it up as if nothing had touched it and he was glad to have its familiar shape around him. The Jag wasn't his favorite although it made a good second car. He winced, remembering that he'd have to have the scratches on the hood of the Jag dealt with. He'd do that later, when Len had forgotten the Jensen's woes.

He unlocked his door and opened it, then shut it again. What the hell was he going to say to her? "I was just in the neighborhood...." The breath he pulled in took up too much space in his chest. How about, "You're driving me out of my mind. I think I'm in love with you and I may want to marry you. What do you think?" He sighed and rested his head on the steering wheel. The immediate blare of the horn made him jerk upright. His heart beat a tattoo against his ribs as he looked again at the light in the small window.

Townsend, he lectured himself, *you are thirty-seven, you are wealthy, confident, good-looking, witty, competent in bed, a real find for any woman. Just go tell Emily Smith how lucky she is you even want to look at her.* With that, he got out of the car, marched across the narrow street to the glass-paneled front door and leaned on the bell. *Authority*, his brain said, *show her you're always in charge.*

Then he shoved his hands into his pockets and took a step backward. What had he done? What was he really going to say? He took another step backward. There was still time to change his mind.

The door opened a crack and one blue eye stared out at him. "Sean!" Emily said. She closed the door again, slid off the chain and then faced him, a long, stretchy terry-cloth sleepsuit in red and white stripes clinging to every inch of her.

He glanced down. Her toes poked through holes in the attached feet. His eyes returned to her face, her hair. A woolen cap, a different shade of red with snowflakes woven in a circle, covered her hair.

"Sean, what are you doing here?" She crossed her arms as if suddenly realizing what she wore.

He swallowed. "Well, I was in the neighborhood..." He bowed his head. "I mean..."

"Do you want to come in?" she asked and he looked at her gratefully.

"Yes, if you don't mind."

Chapter Eight

He looked different tonight. The jeans, the loose cotton shirt tucked into an unbelted waistband, the tennis shoes, were more casual than anything she'd ever seen him wear, but it wasn't the clothes that made the difference. It was something she felt in him. Unease?

"You're sure you don't mind me just dropping by?" The shadow of uncertainty in his eyes was new, too.

"I'm glad you did," she said and sucked in her lower lip. Saying the first thing that came into her head had been getting her in trouble as long as she could remember.

Sean crossed the threshold and waited until she'd closed the door. "I'm not really here by accident," he said.

She smiled. Sometimes honesty paid off if it caused someone else to return the favor. "You mean you came because you wanted to discuss business?"

"Partly." They both leaned against a wall. "That's some hat you're wearing. And the rest of the outfit's something, too."

Emily grimaced and pulled off the cap. "What can I say? I shop in all the best places. This house seems cold at night and...empty. Anyway, I like to be comfortable. My grandmother usually wore some sort of hat. She said you lose more heat through your cranium than through any other part of your body. So..." She was talking too much.

"So sometimes you do what your old granny said you should do."

"Sometimes." What would he think if he knew, had even a dim picture of what Grandmother James had been like? Although the woman had been dead for fifteen years, Emily could still hear the rustle of the black silk she invariably wore, smell her perfume—never anything but Joy—and visualize some of the truly spectacular hats that had been especially made for Charlotte James.

Sean had shrugged and walked tentatively into the living room. Emily hugged herself even tighter and followed him slowly. Compared to his own home, he couldn't possibly see this place as other than a dump.

"You're on your own?" He reached the middle of the room and faced her. She saw him swallow.

"Joe's got a date and Larry's working," she said simply. "And I was going to have a glass of wine and listen to the radio."

"Opera?"

Emily was taken aback. "How do you know I listen to opera?"

Sean blushed and the effect was startling. The high color brightened his eyes and made him look very young. "Just a wild guess," he said. "I like opera, so maybe I was hoping you do, too."

A voice on the radio droned, giving out the latest news, Emily thought. "I do like it. Actually I was hoping for a play tonight but I don't think I'm going to get lucky. Would you like a glass of wine? We don't keep much else."

"Please." He sank to the edge of the worn blue chair and let his hands hang between his knees. "If it's not too much trouble?"

"Not at all." She tossed the hat onto the table, wishing she wasn't wearing the ridiculous overgrown sleeper with its front zipper, button-up seat and holes in the feet...and nothing underneath. "Why don't you see what you can do with the radio."

In the kitchen she hunted for the one decent wineglass she knew they owned, the one she'd gotten in the mail as an introductory offer. The rest of their glassware was strictly grocery-store purchases.

Emily found the glass, poured the wine, then couldn't seem to move. Why would Sean decide to come see her at night? Was he lonely too? She went into the hall. He was lonely and so was she, and they felt that in each other, she knew they did. He might be wealthy and well known, sought after by beautiful women and successful men, but he was lonely. Emily understood. She'd been sought after by the so-called best people once. No party had been planned without her name being on the guest list and without her having a line of escorts to choose from. Yet she'd so often felt alone, even after she'd become engaged to Charles. Maybe especially then, because it meant that she was cut off from the few friends she was moderately close to and increasingly caught up in the empty, high-class society that was to have become her entire life.

Sean would wonder where she was. She entered the living room and found him with his back to her, bending over the radio on its shelf on the wall, turning the tuning knob. She silently set his glass on a table beside his chair. He straightened, apparently satisfied and realized she was there. He raised his brows, inclining his head to the set.

"Good," Emily said. "*Tannhaüser*. Have you ever heard it? Live, I mean?" The Pilgrims' Chorus soared with its tenor sweetness.

"Once. I like Wagner. How about you?"

"Some of it. I'm ashamed to admit that I've slept through a few segments of *The Ring*."

Sean laughed. "Haven't we all? Where did you see it?"

"In San Francisco. How about you?"

"Seattle. Would you like to go to the opera with me sometime?"

"I..." She closed her mouth. Her first impulse had been to say that she'd love to go with him. But it couldn't start.

She mustn't let anything start with Sean that they might come to regret. "I don't think so."

"Well. Maybe you'll change your mind later." The words were easily delivered but the light had gone out of his eyes.

Why does he want me? Emily returned to her seat on the couch and automatically curled her feet beneath her. "The wine's a bit sweet, I'm afraid."

Sean picked up his glass and instead of sitting on the chair he came to take a place at the other end of the couch. "I expect you're wondering why I dropped by like this?"

"Yes, I was."

He drank some wine and while he did, Emily saw his eyes pass over the skin-tight fabric covering her body. She shifted slightly. Sean's face was expressionless but his scrutiny made her feel warm. She should excuse herself right now and get a robe.

"You talked about a costume party," he said.

"And you didn't seem particularly keen."

"Yes, I did. We even talked about you helping with my costume."

And she'd been regretting it ever since, although, with his silence of the past two days, she'd half expected that the subject would never come up again. "You still think it's a good idea? Really good, I mean? If we're going to do it it'll take a lot of preparation and you have to be all for it."

"I think it's a fantastic idea. How long do you think we need for the planning stages?"

Emily relaxed a little. "At least three weeks. And if we're going to make it by then, the invitations should go out immediately."

He looked at his watch. "How about Saturday the twelfth?"

Emily scooted down the couch until she could see the date on his watch. "Cutting it too closely, but we could manage if I could have your list by, say, late tomorrow."

"I'll get Zig right on it."

She started to move away, but Sean settled a hand on her wrist, not holding it but just resting there. He offered her his glass and, after hesitating a second, she took a sip.

"Was it all right for me to come this evening?" he asked quietly.

"Yes." Emily returned the glass and put her hand on top of his. "I was lonely. It gets lonely here sometimes. That must sound funny." She looked into his face, at the blond hair falling over his brow. "Who can be lonely in a city like Los Angeles, right? With all these people and so much going on?"

He turned his hand and laced their fingers together. "I can feel very alone. That's why I came tonight, really. Oh, sure, I need the good work you and Joe do for me, and I do think the costume party will be a smash. But I need those things for my public image. They don't do much for me, the man. I felt you might be the same as I am in some ways and that's why I came. There was no one else to go to. No one else I wanted to go to."

She smiled at him. He did always seem so in control, so on top of the world. But his story of emptiness was no surprise, nothing she hadn't considered many times before. What did surprise her was that he had the courage to admit it and that he'd chosen her as his confidante.

"You can come any time you want to, Sean," she said impulsively. "I do know about being lonely. I don't make friends very easily. If I can be a friend to you, I'd like to be."

Sean felt a mixture of triumph and frustration. All he wanted at this moment was to take her body, her lithe, full-breasted body, into his arms and kiss her lips. And he knew that if he did he'd lose every inch of ground he'd just gained.

"Thank you, Emily." *Tread carefully*, he cautioned himself. "You don't like to be around a lot of people, do you?"

She took a long time to answer, then she said, "No, not usually."

"Is there something we could do together sometimes? Something you wouldn't mind?"

She shrugged. Her head was bowed and the dark auburn curls at the nape of her neck made her skin appear very pale. He lifted his hand to touch the spot, but she looked up at him then, so he rested his arm along the back of the couch instead. "I just don't do much, Sean. You're kind to offer, but I don't know what to suggest. All I really do these days is run."

"I like to run," Sean said. Not strictly true, but with Emily he'd learn to like it a lot. "I could come with you."

"Oh, but I just go around here and pretty late in the evening. You wouldn't want to do that."

Either she was being deliberately obtuse, or he'd lost the ability to communicate his feelings. "I would. I'd love to. And you shouldn't run alone at night anyway, Emily. We've already had that conversation."

"I know. Joe goes on about it too."

Sean felt his nostrils flare. He didn't want to hear about any cozy conversations Emily had with Joe. Jealousy. He fastened his gaze on a picture of children playing on a seashore that had been hung above a table piled high with papers. He didn't want Emily to spend time with anyone but him and that was ridiculous.

"Do you want to go running tomorrow evening?" he asked. "I could bring over the guest list for the party and then we could take a run before I go home. We could talk about the party as we run." The idea was beginning to appeal to him. In fact, there was nothing he could think of that he'd enjoy more than going running with Emily tomorrow night.

"I don't know." She'd crossed her arms again, unconsciously pressing her breasts upward this time rather than covering them. "Are you sure you're not just saying you want to come because you think someone ought to be my watchdog?'' She blushed and laid a hand on his thigh. "I'm sorry, that sounds ungrateful. Only I don't want anyone to feel responsible for me."

He remained very still. Every nerve in his body seemed to have rushed to the few inches beneath her hand. "Why don't you think of it this way? You'll be helping me keep my body in shape. It's time I watched out for flab."

Her gaze swept over him. Sean was glad he didn't need to suck in his gut. Frank had been right, though; he'd better spend more time keeping in shape. The running would be a good start.

Emily's smile was impish. "I don't think there's much wrong with your bod, Sean. But I guess we could run together tomorrow, if you like. I wouldn't want to be responsible for your losing your boyish figure."

THEY'D RUN ON WEDNESDAY NIGHT, and on Thursday. And that's all they'd done, run and talked and said good night over a cup of coffee at a café near Emily's place before Sean saw her home. Each evening they'd discussed the costume party. Tonight was Friday and Sean parked in his usual spot across the street from Emily's and got out. He'd bought a new jogging suit since she'd noticed that his old one was just that, very old, and had suggested it had probably been far too long since he'd exercised. Maybe this would be the night he'd manage to at least kiss her.

He locked the car and went to ring the bell. He was grateful she had yet to register surprise at Joe's repeated absences. But then again, it seemed probable that Joe was usually gone in the evenings.

A light flickered to life on the other side of the door and Emily's face appeared in the crack behind the chain. Immediately, the door swung open.

"Sean, I didn't know you were coming tonight."

He frowned. No, they hadn't exactly made a date the way they had for the two previous evenings. He'd just assumed, and that could turn out to be a great mistake with this lady.

"Sorry," he said and thought fast. "I went out and bought a new torture outfit and I couldn't resist coming to show you," he improvised, and pivoted slowly to show off all sides of the perfectly ordinary green sweats.

"Very nice," Emily said, a smile creeping into her eyes. "Torture suit, huh?"

"Slip of the tongue, you know what I mean."

"I guess. I thought you might be getting to enjoy the torture though."

"I am." *He was, he was.*

"Would you mind if I didn't come running tonight?" she asked. She wore jeans and a voluminous pale blue shirt, spattered with bleach spots. Her feet were bare.

Sean looked at his own feet in the new running shoes he'd also bought. "Of course not. Um..." he glanced up again and frowned. She was pale. "Emily, you don't look so hot. Are you sick?"

A little color returned to her cheeks. "No. Not feeling up to par, that's all."

He regarded her closely. "What's the matter?" His stomach suddenly felt sickly. "Have you seen a doctor?"

Emily's color deepened even more.

"Do you have a fever?"

"No, Sean." She sighed and opened the door wider. "Why don't you come in?"

He followed her inside, slamming the door behind him, almost tripping over her heels in his hurry. She went straight into the living room and sat on the couch.

Another second and he could really get sick. "Emily—" he sat beside her "—please don't hold back with me. I...I care what happens to you. It's foolish not to see a doctor the minute you think there's something wrong with you."

She stared at him, comprehension dawning. Then she felt incredibly insensitive and foolish at the same time. The sweat suit intensified the clear green of his eyes and she saw fear there. He'd lost his wife, she'd never asked how, but she assumed to some illness. He was afraid she was ill, too, really ill.

"Sean, relax, please. There's nothing wrong with me. I feel a bit punk, that's all."

Rather than relaxing, he leaned closer and took both of her hands in one of his. "Are you sure?" With the other hand he brushed back her hair and felt her brow. "You feel a bit warm. Maybe you've got a touch of the flu?" The relief that leapt in his eyes made it hard not to throw her arms around him.

"Maybe."

"Did you take aspirin?"

"Yes."

He frowned again and she saw his chest expand. "You should still see a doctor, though, you know. A lot of things hide themselves as something simple. Low-grade fevers are common with some very serious illnesses."

Emily gently disengaged his hand from hers. "I don't have anything serious." A faint flush started beneath her collar but she went on, "Sometimes I have a problem with the first day or two of a period. That's all it is, honestly." She should feel awkward, but she didn't. She could almost see the muscles in Sean's body relax. "Mostly I don't allow any self-pity but tonight I really am a bit achy and wobbly."

"Now I understand." Sean stood up and swung her feet onto the couch. He took a pillow and put it behind her back. "Allow yourself a little self-pity. If I'd been born a woman I'd probably have myself admitted to a nursing home once a month for total bed rest. And boy, would I complain."

Emily laughed aloud and Sean smirked, clearly pleased with the effect he'd had on her.

"How about a hot drink? Hot milk?"

Emily made a face. "I hate hot milk." She also couldn't imagine Sean in the old-fashioned kitchen trying to make anything. "If you don't have anything else to do you can sit and keep me company for a while. And if I start looking sorry for myself, tell me off."

"You're sure I can't get you anything."

"Sure."

He sat again and pulled her feet onto his lap. He started a slow massage of her toes and Emily closed her eyes. They were beginning to be very comfortable together, too comfortable.

"I probably shouldn't ask this when you aren't feeling good, but did the invitations for the party go out?"

"I'm quite well enough to operate normally. And, yes, they went out this morning. Zig's wonderful and I think she quite likes working with me."

"She does."

Emily looked at him sharply. "How do you know?"

He made an airy gesture. "She just happened to mention it." He paused and grinned. "After I asked her."

Emily thought about that and decided she didn't mind Sean discussing her with Zig. "She and I talked over some of the details," Emily said, settling herself more comfortably on the pillow. Her stomach felt as if it had been kicked but she kept from grimacing. "You know the kind of thing. Should there be a theme? Shouldn't there be a theme?"

"What kind of costumes will we have if we don't have one? I kind of like the really fantastic ones—particularly on the women." He waggled his brows.

"Yes, I'm sure you do. And we can do it that way if we decide to use one idea I had."

Sean's massaging fingers moved to her ankles. "Which was?" he asked.

"Murder among the rich and famous. Fabulous prize for the most fabulous costume and another for whoever guesses the identity of the murderer."

His warm hands were inside the hems of her jeans, on her calves now. "And where do we find the story? Use an old script, or something?"

"No. We'll make it up. If everything else is wild enough the plot won't have to be very complex."

"*We'll* make it up? Sweetheart, I'm into alarm systems, not writing plots."

"I'll make it up, Sean," she said. "Joe will help me. And Larry. Larry's particularly good at that kind of thing."

"Hmmm. If you say so. How much notice are you going to give the guests of the parts they're going to play?

"Enough. We'll do it by phone. It'll add to the tension. And we'll tell them to decide what costume goes with the personality they're playing."

"I just hope they don't all forget what they're supposed to be doing before we get halfway through," Sean said doubtfully.

"It won't matter if they do. We'll just make a grand announcement and hand out the prizes and you can sit back and wait for congratulations."

"And you'll be there?"

"I don't think—"

"You promised."

"I didn't exactly—"

"Yes, you did. And I need you."

Emily gently bent her knees, pulling away from him, and lowered her feet to the floor. "I don't really think you need me at all, Sean. But if it means that much to you, I will be there. On the sidelines. No introductions, no forcing me out of my comfort zone though. Promise?"

"I promise."

The silence that followed went on and on.

"Emily?"

"Yes."

"Is there something about me you can't stand?"

She stared at him, amazed. "Why would you ask a question like that?"

"Just give me an answer. Sometimes I think I have the same effect on you as a snake does on some people."

"Oh, no, Sean." Her teeth couldn't control her shaking bottom lip. "Oh, I can't believe you'd think that. You're just being funny."

"I've never felt less funny." He stood up and reached into his back pocket for his car keys.

Emily jumped up and held his arms. "Sean, look at me." When he did she raised herself to her toes and wrapped her arms around his neck, resting her head on his shoulder. Her insides trembled. "I...I like you so much, Sean. You're the nicest, kindest man I've ever met. And the most unaffected. It means so much to me that you like me, too."

His hands loosely circled her waist. "Thanks," he said against her hair.

"You are special, Sean." She leaned away until she could see his face, then, very gently, kissed his cheek. "So special."

He held her waist for another second, then set her away, almost roughly. His smile had a bitter quality and it didn't reach his eyes.

"Thanks again. Coming from you that's quite a compliment." Sorting through the keys he turned and went into the hall.

Emily took a step after him, "Sean?" He'd looked... angry, no, hurt. "Sean, wait!"

But the next sound she heard was the front door slamming and, seconds later, the violent gunning of a powerful car engine.

Chapter Nine

For one wild moment he considered going to Simon's. He could almost count on finding his friend with the mauve lipstick and airbrushed nails at the bar. Her stool probably had a Reserved sign on it when she wasn't there. She'd talk, he'd listen, buy her some drinks, then walk away. For a few hours in between he might forget how lousy he really felt.

Just as quickly as the thought came, Sean discarded it and pointed the Jensen's nose west. West was as good as north, south or east, he just had to drive, to go somewhere and think.

The streets were all familiar, names he'd seen since he was a boy riding beside his father in the imported black Bentley Charlie Townsend had loved so much. Dunkirk Avenue, then a right onto Midvale. Left, right, left again. He rolled down his window and rested his elbow on the rim. In the heavy, moonless night, the air was thick and stung his eyes and throat.

Wilshire Boulevard lay straight ahead. He could follow it to the coast, be there in half an hour. In what he was wearing he could blend in with the usual crowd on Santa Monica beach, find a quiet spot overlooking the bay and let his mind float free.

By the time he neared the coast the beach no longer appealed to him. Someone might decide he wanted company. He did, but only from one woman and she wasn't available. Definitely, Emily Smith was not available to Sean Townsend, not in the way he needed her to be.

He cruised at a leisurely pace, heading farther north along the Pacific Coast Highway until he saw a small road he didn't recognize. It angled off into the hills overlooking the ocean and he took it, passing one or two isolated houses until he reached a point that jutted, seemingly unsupported, like a finger pointing at the invisible horizon.

He parked and reclined his seat as far as it would go. The air slipping through the window was clean now and markedly cooler. He pulled up the collar on his sweats and hunched farther down.

"The nicest man I ever met. The kindest man. Special."
She was glad he liked her enough to want to be her friend. His clenched hands were icy and he flexed his fingers. She would like to help him out when he felt lonely—as a friend, of course. It was no good, she just didn't feel about him the way he did about her. The only sane way to deal with the situation was to be grateful they'd met because she and Joe were good at what they did and his social image had been in a rut and needed an overhaul. They'd carry on as strictly business acquaintances. Thinking he could have something else with Emily had been a mistake. He really was meant to be a bachelor, probably for the rest of his life. It was a good life, great. He pulled his shoulders up close to his ears. A few stars pierced the sky now and he concentrated on one of them. What man in his right mind would give up his freedom and the chance to play the field, to take his pick of the beautiful women in this town, and tie himself to one?

Damn it all. He sat up, hunched forward over the steering wheel. *He'd* give it up for one woman if she was Emily. They wouldn't be the perfect, picture-book couple at the beginning. He was too strong-minded, and so was she, but they'd come through the growing pains of a new marriage and from there on most of it would be smooth sailing.

But she thought he was *nice, kind, special!* And he hated the sound of every one of those words. He'd never use any of them again unless he intended to be insulting. And she'd kissed his cheek as if he were a good little boy who needed comfort.

Right. Sean turned the key in the ignition. No more hanging back and waiting, or creeping around being Mr. Restraint. He didn't believe she was immune to him, quite the contrary. In his gut he felt that she was protecting herself from something, and the something was him. Why? Was she afraid he'd disappoint her, hurt her? Had she heard the stories about his life since Margaret died and believed them? *Sean Townsend, playboy.* It was so laughable and so infuriating. Infuriating enough to fuel as much determination as he was likely to need in the weeks and months to follow.

He backed up, screeching rubber on loose gravel. He would not be beaten, had never been beaten in anything that really mattered to him. Emily Smith didn't know it yet, but she was about to find out that this nice, kind man could be just as devious as he needed to be to make sure he got what he wanted.

AS A LAST THOUGHT, she grabbed the old red cap that had been on the table in the living room since Sean's first visit.

Outside the front door, she hesitated. The last time she'd chosen to go out this late at night she'd regretted it. Common sense almost made her turn around and go back into the house. Almost. She'd just spent two sleepless hours tossing in her bed, and she wasn't about to continue with that or to sit in the mean, miserable little living room where every corner, every chair, everything she touched, reminded her of Sean.

The last time she'd gone out late had also been the night she and Sean had met. Emily smiled, a small, slightly wobbly smile, and tears came to her eyes. Why couldn't she just accept that she and Sean could not get on together on anything but a professional basis, if that? They couldn't be friends. Tonight had proved that. No, it wasn't that they *couldn't* get together—they most certainly could—but they shouldn't because that would mean she'd have to tell him her so-called history, and afterwards wait to see if he would accept her side of the story and then be able to handle what he'd be getting as a package deal. Would he be able to switch overnight from thinking of her as plain Emily Smith to accepting her as Emily Smith who was really Sidonie James?

Emily placed the sole of one shoe against a wall and gripped her toe, gently pulling, flattening her body to her leg. She straightened and stretched the other leg. Then she did deep side bends and knee bends. She jogged in place, pulling the cap firmly onto her head and set off, steadily but at an easy pace. She really didn't feel terrific tonight but the exercise would do her good once she got into stride.

An hour outside, muggy atmosphere aside, should be the cure she needed for her insomnia.

She ran straight to Santa Monica Boulevard. It wasn't quite as late as it had been that other night. Cars whizzed by regularly. Another jogger passed, a headset clamped over his ears. Emily didn't like to shut out the sounds around her when she ran. Voices approaching, then fading, laughter, sometimes birds, sometimes music from open windows, even the noise of passing engines, they all added texture to being outside and made her feel completely alive.

Sean was hurt. She'd hurt him. Emily raised her chin, swallowing, and her throat burned. This was no whim on his part, some fascination with spending time with someone who lived in a world he had never touched before. He wanted to become part of her life—even if only for a while. Sure, sexual desire was a strong part of what he felt for her, she wasn't a fool or too childish to recognize that and she wanted him sexually, too. But also, he liked her and she liked him.

She was tiring much too quickly. Her shoes didn't seem to absorb the shock of concrete beneath her feet and her shins jarred.

Whether she wanted to or not she was becoming emotionally involved with a man who could have the power to tear apart everything she'd built up in the last four years. And she didn't have the right to consider only herself in this. There was Joe. He trusted her and had taken her at face value. She wished Joe had known the truth about her from the beginning, but that hadn't been possible. When they'd met she'd still been in the process of becoming totally comfortable as Emily Smith and trusting anyone with her secret had been out of the question. Later had been just that, too late.

Her thighs ached almost unbearably and she turned back. If she took a chance, allowed herself to get closer to Sean, the gossip columnists, the press, would pick up on the relationship and they'd start digging. It wouldn't take long to track her. Before they found and exposed all the crummy details that had decorated the papers of a few years ago, she'd have to warn Sean. A pain began somewhere in her chest and it wasn't physical. Her breath came in tortured gasps around the start of dry sobs. All she had to do was appear with Sean a few times socially and she'd be fair game. Before she could do a thing the past would sweep in and drag her away.

Sidonie James, out of hiding and masquerading as a caterer—what would that mean for Joe? She tried to think rationally. At first, it would be pay dirt. Everyone in Hollywood would want to hire them. She could almost see the headlines, and the columns of words reiterating how she'd been cited in a celebrated divorce case, how she'd been the probable cause of a valuable man being lost to the country's government. And the evidence, the candid photos taken at the time, were so very convincing.

Overland Avenue was less than a block away, thank God. She couldn't go on running, or thinking. But the decision had been made. Regardless of what she felt for Sean, regardless of what he did to her every time she as much as saw him, there were too many lives, her own included, that could be ruined if she gave in to her own desires. Particularly when she had no guarantee of Sean's reaction to her little truth package. His family was solid, old money now by American standards; he wouldn't throw away that reputation just for physical longing, no matter how strong.

A breeze must have picked up. The bushes behind her swished. Emily raised her head and took off her cap, waiting for the coolness to sweep over her. Her heart felt like a ball of lead.

Nothing moved her hair. The film of perspiration remained, warm on her face.

She heard the rustle of the bushes again. No breeze. Nothing to move the branches but... No. Her mouth opened and she began to pray. No, not again. Spinning on her heel she ran backward, watching the bushes. A car passed, and another. Arm in arm a couple crossed the street, the man gazing down, the woman with her head craned up. No one would do anything wild here.

Emily turned again and ran on to Overland Avenue. Sometimes she forgot how long the street was with its scraggly trees and the shadowy hulks of parked cars.

A squeak stopped her in her tracks and she stood absolutely still. It was the sound of a soft-soled shoe pivoting on concrete, probably coming around the corner, the same corner she had just turned.

Slowly, she turned.

Nothing.

Now she was really going off her rocker. Hearing things, seeing things, imagining things.

A spear of darkness spread gradually from behind a parked car, slicing the sidewalk, climbing the side of a house.

Someone had hidden behind that car, waiting. And then he had leaned out.

He'd leaned out to look at her, gauging how far away she was, preparing to leap.

Emily clamped both hands over her mouth and turned her head, left and right. There was no one, no one anywhere but the man hiding behind the car.

On legs that no longer seemed to belong to her she leaped, wove from sidewalk to street and back, dodging between cars, ducking, peering out to see where he was.

Nothing.

But she knew he was there. She was also getting closer to home. Ahead, the single light in the little gray house shone out like a beacon calling her home to safety.

Emily halted again, then crouched down behind a small pickup. Was she leading him home? Did he already know where she lived or would this be giving away her final refuge? Reason told her he must already know the address of her home, her only safe place in the world.

She was alone in this. She gritted her teeth. No man was going to drive her away from the place she'd made for herself. Not again.

In a mad dash, she made for the house. The key was already in her hand when she reached the door and she flung it open, dived inside and shot home the chain. Tomorrow, she'd get a dead bolt. There would be questions from Larry and Joe, but she'd make an excuse.

Too weak to take another step, she sank to the floor in the hall and rested her head against the wall. She would never, no matter how much she wanted to, go running alone in the night again.

Lethargy seeped into her, turning her limbs to heavy, lifeless lumps.

The rattling sound entered her brain slowly and she lifted her head. She heard it again, then once more.

Someone was trying to open the door.

Chapter Ten

Emily peered out the window and saw the shadow move and bend forward. The handle rattled again.

She scrambled up and inched along the hall wall. The phone was on the far side of the living room. How long would the police take to get here? *If* she could manage to call them before the man pushed the chain mounting from its screws. The wood was old, it wouldn't hold for long. The lock itself wouldn't take him more than seconds to break. One good shove and it would give.

She took several breaths, preparing to make a run for it.

The door slammed against the chain. Joe had promised and promised to replace that old lock. Emily's heart thundered so loudly she could hear it in her ears.

She pushed away from the wall and ran. In the darkness, she bumped into furniture and tripped over obstacles on the floor as she went. Somewhere she remembered reading that in a situation like this she shouldn't put on any lights because they would make her easier to locate.

"Emily!"

She stopped, one shaking hand coiled over the telephone.

"Emily! Are you home? Joe?" The sound of wood grinding against the chain came again, then loud knocking.

"Oh, Larry," Emily whispered, hardly able to breathe at all anymore. She stumbled back to the hall. "Larry, just a minute."

"You put the chain on, Emily," he said through the crack.

"I know. I know." She opened the door wide and pulled him inside. "I'm so glad to see you. Oh, Larry." She held on to the front of his old jean jacket with both hands and rested her head on his chest. He smelled of greasepaint and backstage dust.

He wrapped his thin arms around her and hugged her tightly. "What is it? What's the matter? Why is it dark in here?"

Weakly, she reached under his arm and turned on the meager overhead light, then stayed where she was, clasping him, feeling the breeze whipping through the open door, cooling the sweat on her face.

Larry rubbed her back awkwardly. "You okay, Emily? Did something happen?"

She looked up into his face. Traces of black clung to the rims of his eyes and a band of dark tan stood out starkly along the line of his jaw. He always waited until he got home from the theater to finish cleaning up.

"Tell me, Emily," he insisted quietly, easing her away.

They went into the kitchen and she poured out her story. When she'd finished speaking, Larry sat still for a while, studying the backs of his hands where they rested on his thighs.

He got up and put the kettle on. "What are we going to do?" he said, lowering the gas flame. "I should have taken you seriously the first time you talked about this guy. Maybe he'd be behind bars by now."

"I doubt it."

Larry looked at her sharply. "Why?"

She shrugged. "Oh, he might be, but only if he'd done something bad enough to get him there. Like beat someone up or commit rape or murder. And the someone would probably have been me.''

"Don't talk like that."

Now it was her turn to ask, "Why? Avoiding an issue never solved anything."

"I don't want to think about it." Larry spooned instant coffee into mugs. "Emily, I know you get mad at Joe for telling you what to do. You know, when he says you shouldn't go out on your own at night?"

"Yes, I do."

"Are you going to get mad at me?"

"If you're going to suggest that I should give up running at night on my own, I don't think I'm going to get mad at you. After what just happened, I don't know if I'll have the courage to go out in the daytime, let alone at night."

"You can't live like that. Perhaps you should call the police."

Emily stuffed her hands beneath her legs to keep them from shaking. She smiled at Larry but her stomach was a squirming thing. "And tell them what?" she said. "That I *think* someone is following me?"

"You know someone is."

"But I don't have any proof. He hasn't touched me."

"But you could give them a pretty good description?"

"No, I couldn't. Tall and blond. How many tall, blond men are there in Los Angeles, do you think? They'll just say, 'Thank you ma'am. We'll keep an eye open. The squad cars in your area will take a run down Overland Avenue now and again.' Larry, the truth is that until this joker *does* something to me, the police aren't going to waste two seconds on me. How can they?"

The kettle sputtered, screaming through boiling water. Larry never failed to overfill the kettle, but he never seemed to notice what he'd done, either. Emily said nothing. She watched the clumsy way he poured water over the coffee, slopping some onto the counter, then smearing the mess around with the clean dry cloth she'd set out earlier. She only shook her head slightly and smiled as he set the mugs on the table.

"Look, Emily—" he sat beside her "—we don't have to worry about the daytime, really. I'll have a word with Joe—"

"No! No, Larry, I'm sorry to shout, but Joe is like a tank sometimes. He's likely to round up a bunch of those guys he pumps iron with to escort me around. Or he'll suddenly punch out some poor man who accidentally glances at me. You know how he is. Please, don't tell Joe." Joe would also be likely to insist on calling the police and now she was calm she knew for sure she didn't want that. "Like you said, the daytime isn't any real problem."

Larry stretched out his long legs. His tennis shoes were old, his socks looked gray and there was a hole over one ankle bone. He needed some financial help. Again Emily longed to be the help he needed. Just a little could mean so much.

"Okay," he said. "The daytime isn't a problem. But will you do something for me?"

"If I can."

"Will you let me know if you're going somewhere unusual, somewhere on your own."

She stared at him. "What do you mean?"

"I don't know." His gray eyes seemed darker with the makeup. "Just that I'd like to know if you suddenly have to go out of the area for some reason. You could check in with me and let me know how long you expect to be gone. Kind of a buddy system, like mountain climbers or something, I guess. I'd just feel better."

It wouldn't help, but what could it hurt if it made him feel useful. "I'll do that. But I don't usually go too far afield."

"Good, that's fine. But there's still this nighttime thing."

"I know. And I won't go running late at night anymore." She thought of Sean, of the two evenings they'd run together. Why hadn't she gone with him tonight, regardless of how she felt? Then she probably wouldn't have ended up insulting him, or whatever she'd done to his feelings, and neither would that man have had the guts to come after her.

When she looked at Larry his eyes were on hers. "If you do really want to go, I'll come with you," he said.

Emily laughed, then coughed. She stood up and wrapped an arm around Larry's neck. For a few seconds she held him, then she ruffled his hair. "You are some friend."

He looked puzzled. "Thanks."

"You just let me know what a neat man you really are. I've heard it suggested that I'm wacky to live in a house with two men. I think I'm the luckiest woman on earth. I couldn't *stand* living with a bunch of temperamental females but somehow fate smiled and I got Joe and you." She bent over him. "Larry, you hate to run. At least, I'm sure you *would* hate to run. Don't worry. Unless I have company of my own choosing or can go early, I'll stay right here. But you're an artist, love. No way will I have you beating the streets with those elegant feet of yours when you should be stretched out in your smoking jacket with a glass of champagne in one hand. That's what you should be doing at this moment. In fact, I just happen to have a bottle of champagne one of my clients gave me."

Larry's hand on her arm stopped her from moving away. "Thanks, Emily, but not tonight, okay?"

His fingers shook slightly and she frowned at him. "Is there something wrong with *you*, too?"

He wiped the greasepaint off his jaw, then looked at his stained fingers. "The show closed."

"Oh, no." Emily sat down slowly. Larry was still looking at the greasepaint, rubbing it between his fingers. Tears sprang in her eyes and she squeezed her lids shut. He looked so lost.

"It happens, kid. There'll be other shows."

"Yes, sure. There'll be other shows." She sniffed and searched her jacket pockets for a Kleenex. "Damn, Larry. I really hoped this would be the start you needed."

"So did I. Hey—" he raised her chin and when she opened her eyes he was giving her one of his sweet, lopsided grins "—we're survivors around here, right? Look at what you and Joe have made from nothing. I'll make it too, Emily, I know I will. One day I'll find a way to get into a good acting school. I really think that'll make the difference." The corners of his mouth jerked, but he presented his profile, pointing his long nose at the ceiling. "Is this the face lightweight pretty-boy parts are made for? No. This is the face of a character actor. And one day—with the right training—I'm going to be the best." He looked at her and slumped again. "I only hope it happens before I'm ninety."

Emily got up and went to the refrigerator. She took out the bottle of champagne she'd been saving for a celebration and opened it. They didn't have the right glasses, but she found Joe's two matching tumblers, artfully decorated with the black-and-silver pirate insignia of the Los Angeles Raiders, and filled each a third full of Moet et Chandon.

"Here," she handed a glass to Larry, "I've been saving this for a special occasion."

He bit his bottom lip. "What's the occasion, Emily? What are we drinking to with this? How much does it cost a bottle? What's the toast—to failure?"

Emily touched her glass to his and held her smile in place. He wasn't coping the way he wanted her to believe. "It doesn't cost that much. And no, Larry, we're not drinking to failure. Here's to success. Determination. You'll make it because you want it badly enough. That's what makes the difference in the end; wanting something badly enough not to give up, and you are never going to give up."

She sipped the pale dry wine and waited for Larry to do the same.

He sighed. "This is wonderful stuff. You're wonderful. And you're right, I'm not giving up, just temporarily stunned, that's all."

"Larry," Emily began hesitantly. "How much does it cost to go to a good acting school?"

"Too much." He took another sip and closed his eyes. "I could fall in love with these magnificent bubbles."

"How much?"

"Thousands. And that doesn't buy you a whole lot in time. Just a series of classes."

Emily held her glass by the base and swirled the champagne. She could have the money tomorrow morning when the banks opened. "I've got a bit of money saved." Already color was sweeping up her neck. She'd never been a good liar.

"You're a sweetheart." Larry was drinking steadily now. "But this is going to take more than a bit of money and you need what you've got."

"I could lend you—"

"No, you couldn't." His vehemence shook Emily. He finished the rest of his champagne and stood up, staring down at her, a disconcerting hardness in his eyes. "I've spent my adult life proving I could go it alone. I don't have anyone else to fall back on and that's okay by me. If and when I do make the grade I'll have done it on my own. Meanwhile, I guess it's back to whatever studio commissary will hire me. I'll do a fix-up job on the front door and wait around till Joe gets home. You go to bed."

Before she could reply he left the room. He had no way of knowing how much his words had stung. The one thing she could never wipe out was the fact that she had been born wealthy, and that she did have someone to fall back on if the bottom suddenly fell out of her world. Her parents would welcome her back, she knew that.

For almost an hour she sat at the kitchen table, thinking. To Larry she'd been saying the man who was following her was a nut. But she wasn't sure. What if some journalist with a long memory had spotted her and was looking for a way to turn her into another big story? And if this was the case, how long would it be before he made a direct approach? Would she then be on the run again, trying to become someone else? Who would she be next? When would she start not even knowing who she was anymore?

On the run again. Leaving.

She crossed her arms on the table and buried her face. If she left she knew it would mean never seeing Sean again.

She wished it weren't so, but that bothered her more than any of the rest.

"WHAT ARE YOU PLOTTING, Sean?" Frank Horton asked, as he entered Sean's Wilshire Boulevard office.

Sean pushed his chair back and stood, extending a hand to Frank. "Morning. Thanks for coming so promptly. I had this little brainwave—" he waved Frank into a chair and sat down again "—a real brainwave. Coffee?"

"No, thanks. You seem to be hot on nifty brainwaves lately. We were wondering why exactly?"

Sean inclined his head, vaguely confused, then decided he and Frank were not understanding each other's words correctly and pressed on. "What do you know about the state's penitentiaries?"

Frank got up, moved his chair closer to the desk, and sat down again. "What is all this? Sean, are you feeling okay?"

"Of course I'm feeling okay," Sean said irritably. "I asked you a straightforward question. How about a straightforward answer? What do you know about penitentiaries?"

"Nothing."

"That's what I thought. Neither do I, but we're going to find out. I want you to put someone on it. I need to know all about routines...yes, particularly about routines—who does what for them and so on. Will you put someone on that? Whelks, maybe? He's a good legman."

"I'll speak to him later," Frank said. "By the way, I got the call this morning."

Sean raised his brows. "Call?"

"Call. I'm the cuckolded husband and she's been having an affair with this Zolinov guy."

Sean leaned forward slowly, realized his mouth was open, and shut it with a snap.

"Jean's a floozy," Frank continued. "She's into flashy jewelry and furs I can't afford to buy and she stays out half the night several times a week and it's good old Prince Zolinov who foots the bill—for a price."

"Frank?" Sean pressed his intercom. But when his secretary answered, he said, "Forget it," and got up. He went to a wall, rosewood paneled as was the rest of the big room, and pushed a small button. Immediately a bar swung into view. "Brandy's what you need. Good God, man, how awful. You don't deserve this kind of trouble. You've always been so good. I can't believe it. Not Jean."

He was pouring Courvoisier into two big snifters when he heard a muffled sound behind him and turned around, horrified. "Please, Frank," he began, "don't—"

Frank was laughing, hunched over in his chair.

"What the hell?" Sean walked toward him, a glass in each hand.

"I'm not the one in trouble, friend," Frank sputtered, "you are. Don't you know you're having one of these murder parties? I thanked you when we got the original invitation and you seemed to know then. This morning we got a call from some Moreno guy. With the Occasion People, does that ring a bell? Anyway, he gave us more information: who we're going to be at your bash, who we know, why we're going to this party given by this Zolinov guy, even though neither of us want to. Hell, Sean, it's your party."

Sean managed a sheepish grin. "I'm sorry, Frank. I just didn't make the connection. They haven't given me the story line yet and I didn't know when they intended to call guests with the final instructions. Oh, boy—" he sat down "—did you ever scare me there, for a moment."

Frank sniffed the brandy and set it down. "Well, you scare me sometimes. More and more often lately. Suddenly you're having more parties in a few weeks than most people give in a year. You come up with this fantastic murder-costume bash. And then you send for me, and the first words out of your mouth are about penitentiaries. I guess I'm having difficulty keeping up with the way your mind works these days."

Sean loosened his tie and undid the top button on his shirt. He moved papers around on his desk. "Is there anything wrong with a man deciding he needs to broaden his social horizon?"

"Oh, no, no, of course not. Will she be there?"

The air-conditioning must be on the fritz. He got up and went to open a window, then remembered they didn't open.

"Quit being so damn cagey, Sean. Is *she* going to be there? I'm popping a gut to see this woman of yours. So's Jean."

He couldn't tell them Emily would be there but that she preferred not to meet anyone. Frank wouldn't understand; neither would Jean. *He* didn't understand. "She won't be there." He hated to lie.

"Oh." Frank raised his shoulders and slid his hands into his pockets. "What happened? Did you give up on her, or what?"

"No, I did not," Sean came back sharply. "She's just not a party type, that's all."

Frank nodded, then shook his head. "I don't understand you at all. We really had it figured out that you were getting geared up for married life again, you know, entertaining at home a lot and so on, and we also decided this would be the time you'd chosen to introduce . . . what's her name?''

"I'm still not ready to tell you that." But, damn it, he was going to change all this. He was ready to put Emily where she belonged, at his side. "Be patient, Frank. She's really something. You'll meet her soon."

"Progress is being made?"

"Loads of progress, believe me." The brandy smelled foul to him but he took a gulp anyway. "Now, back to the penitentiaries."

"You want to know about them."

"Makes sense, doesn't it?"

"Not to me, friend. I don't ever intend to see the inside of one of those places, do you?"

"Probably not."

"*Probably?* Are you planning to really knock someone off at this little shindig of yours?"

"Very funny, Frank. Sometimes I think you exemplify the Peter Principle so well."

"Thanks a lot."

"I want to expand. I'm looking for new markets." He screwed up his eyes at Frank. "And, voilà, I think I've found one."

Comprehension dawned on Frank. "Got it. You want to get into security alarm systems for prison facilities. Why didn't I think of that?"

"You probably did but you were being kind enough to wait for me to catch up so I'd still feel useful around here."

Frank ignored the crack. "It's an interesting idea, but the competition's got to be stiff. Being government, they probably have it worked out so the supplier almost works for the honor of doing the job."

"That's something we've got to go into. We have to start somewhere, and a general study should be the right place. I don't even know if they work with lasers."

"That'll be easy to find out."

"Right."

"Is that all, then?"

"That's all for now, Frank. Tell Jean I'll look forward to seeing her on Saturday night. As a floozy, she should be worth seeing." Jean Horton's dress was always understated, elegant. She knew that a small woman should keep her wardrobe simple.

A light tap came at the door just as Sean and Frank reached it. Sean turned the handle and was confronted by his secretary, her lips hesitantly parted.

"Mr. Townsend, a lady just phoned. She didn't give her name because she said you'd know who she was. I'm to tell you her message. She said to thank you for the candy you sent yesterday, and the violet she got today," Candace Sherman recited her speech uncomfortably. "She said the man who delivered the violet seemed embarrassed but that she had reassured him that she didn't think it was a...a pretty miserable gift from someone with as much money as you have the way the delivery man thought. In fact, she thinks you've got a lot of insight into people and how different they each are." Candace consulted a piece of paper in her hand. "She said she wouldn't have liked the orchids you sent the other lady nearly as much, and you obviously guessed that the violet was more her style."

Sean nodded to Candace, then shut the door and leaned on it.

"Let me guess," Frank said. "This is *the* lady?"

Sean nodded. He felt sick.

"Who'd you send the orchids to?"

"Red. It's her birthday and she loves fancy, flashy stuff."

"I know. And your...friend doesn't?"

"Damn, damn." Sean tilted up his chin. "That's the last time I use that florist. I'll get the delivery man fired. I just thought I was being subtle, that's all. Dark blue violets, the same color as her eyes. And she is simple, quiet. She loves music and reading and lovely things. She likes my antiques. Even though she doesn't have a passion for them yet, the way I do, she will in time ... when the rest of the world stops getting in our way."

Frank patted his arm. "Sure she will, Sean," He moved Sean aside and opened the door. When he was outside, he poked his head back in. "She'll understand a lot of things once you understand her. I don't think you do yet."

SEAN SAT IN ONE OF THE CHAIRS flanking his precious games table and crossed his arms. He'd put on the black-and-white striped pants, held up by narrow suspenders, and the uncomfortable wing-collared shirt, cut so high he'd have to keep his chin elevated all evening. And he'd looked at the old-fashioned tie. But that was as far as he'd go. Emily had promised she'd be here in plenty of time to help him with his outfit and brief him. Then she was going to use one of the spare rooms in his wing to change and he'd promised that although he was to know who she was, he would make no attempt to draw her into the party other than as his prompter.

The main point was that Emily had promised to be there and she wasn't yet, so he'd simply wait.

She'd sent him an outline of the plot for the evening. Sent it. She could have agreed to his suggestion that they get together and go over it together, but she'd been *too busy*. For ten days she'd been too busy. He'd seen her three times when he'd stopped by to ask her out for a run. Once she'd even gone with him. She'd thanked him for the violet that night and apologized for calling his office, explaining she'd been having a bad day and that the delivery man made her feel foolish. Briefly, he'd congratulated himself, taking comfort in the renewed evidence that Emily was just a little jealous of the possibility of another woman in his life. But after they arrived back at her place, she hadn't even invited him in. For the first time in his life a woman was truly getting the best of him, and he hated it.

He heard the door to his sitting room open. When he leaned forward he could see her entering the room, a suitcase in one hand. A twisting inside him hurt, and it hurt fiercely. If he had his way, he'd get her settled in one of the rooms across the hall and later he'd find a way to make sure she didn't go home all night, didn't want to go home.

"In here," he called. He mustn't sound irritated or too anxious.

"Coming. Are you decent?"

Sean smiled. "Absolutely. Just stymied. You'd better get me finished up and make sure I know what I'm doing. I don't want to be the laughingstock of Beverly Hills by morning."

She paused in the doorway to his bedroom, eyeing him critically. "We'll get the tie on, then I'll have to do something about your hair."

He smoothed a hand over his head. "What's wrong with my hair?"

"English butlers are conservative men—"

"I'm a conservative man."

"No, you're not. But that's not the point. For tonight you are Prince Vladimir Zolinov's butler, his ultimate status symbol, also his valet and the only man who knows almost as much about the Prince as the Prince himself. You live vicariously through him. You're a bit of a weasel, a small-minded man who's an observer rather than a doer. You're a moral coward who would like to engage in the wild affairs your employer describes to you in detail, but you don't have what it takes. In your fantasies you, not the Prince, seduce the wives of famous men and go to bed with a string of gorgeous, sexually innovative showgirls and actresses. When you dream, you are the man married to his wife, the Princess Nadia."

Sean watched her animated features. She was tying his tie and he reached up to hold her wrists. "I don't think I like me."

She shook free and continued. "You don't have to, just play the part."

"Did I do it? Did I kill old Zolinov?"

"Wait and see."

"Someone ought to kill the bastard."

"Someone has. Sit still." She went to work on his hair, parting it down the middle and sweeping it back severely. "I need something to grease this down with or it'll fall forward."

He shook his head. "Nothing doing. No grease."

She sighed. "All right. But you've got the biggest part in this thing, except for Nadia, so you'd better get into it."

"Red knows what she has to do?"

"Red will be terrific. As the Princess Nadia, she'll look like she's the real thing and she'll act it. And from the guest list for this evening there should be one or two people who will appreciate her performance."

"Can't you tell me who did it—the murder, I mean?"

"No. And remember, you'll be the one who keeps sweeping in with the silver tray, card on top, to announce each new clue."

"Can you just tell me how he died?"

"Some people never grow up. No, I can't tell you. If it makes you feel better, at this point, apart from our people, you're the only person who knows the host is dead at all. Now, put on the jacket and you're ready. Although I really don't know about your hair, Sean."

"My hair stays the way it is."

She brushed at his shoulders and straightened the tailed jacket. "You're vain."

"And you don't like me?"

"I didn't say that."

"Good, we should go over the rest of the plot. Why don't we do that while you get ready."

He was impossible, she decided, and almost irresistible, darn it. He hadn't let down an inch and, worse, she didn't want him to. "We will not go over anything while I change. Where am I going to change, by the way?"

He grinned. "Well, you can't blame me for trying. I'm putting you in one of the bedrooms across the hall. I think you should spend the night, by the way. This thing is going to go late and you'll be bushed.''

"Not too bushed to go home." Emily didn't smile as she said it. He was teasing, but only barely so. She knew what he wanted—her, in his bed. "Joe will be overseeing kitchen operations and flitting around behind the scenes generally. Watch me for signals. When you feel a lull, look at me and if I nod you'll know it's time for the next clue. The cards will be on the little table just inside this wing."

"You haven't told me what part you're playing. Which of Zolinov's mistresses are you?"

"I'm not. I'm just one of the showgirls he put out of work when he canceled the most recent show he was financing. He couldn't get the leading lady into his bed often enough so he punished her by cutting off the cash."

"Nice guy." He had stood sideways to her and straightened the jacket over his trim middle. "It all sounds good to me. I just look at you from time to time, right?"

"Right. I'll be the one in the gold mask."

His head snapped around. "What do you mean, gold mask?"

"I'll be dressed as a member of a chorus line. Gold mask, gold feathers on my head. You won't have any difficulty locating me."

He frowned. "If you say so. What else are you wearing?"

She hunched her shoulders dismissively. "Regular chorus-girl stuff. Tights and so on. Time's getting short. If you'll show me my room, I'll get ready while you go meet your guests."

"Hmmm." He sounded unsure. "When will the truth come out?"

"At dinner. From your—" she pulled a list from her pocket "—your Carl Freebourg of Freebourg and Associates?" She looked up questioningly.

"He's a producer, small but good."

"Well, tonight he's a plainclothes detective who reveals himself during the proceedings and by dinner he will have worked out the whole plot. He'll drop the truth on everyone while they dine. In theory, this will be someone's last dinner before a trip to the local police station. We decided to knock out the contest for solving the crime. We don't need it."

"You're clever, you know that?"

She pretended to yawn. "If you've got it, you've got it, what can I say? Now, go greet your guests and be prepared for Red. We had a long chat and she really has a feel for this. She'll be a knockout."

Sean showed her to another bedroom and left. She decided this had probably been his room as a boy. All heavy oak and cardinal colors. By the window stood a chipped desk, deeply scarred by carvings not quite filled in with varnish. Among the groups of letters and crude outlines she identified SCT and decided these must be Sean's initials. If she ever had the chance, she'd ask him what the C stood for.

The bathroom was simple but adequate and she noted the ample supply of fresh towels, black and white like those in Sean's bathroom. A bottle of bubble bath had been placed on the rim of the white tub, and when she saw the label she laughed. Joy. Grandmother James would have approved. She didn't laugh when she saw an entire row of little baskets filled with violets on the windowsill. Every one was the same dark blue as the one Sean had sent her and she realized now, as she'd realized *after* her dumb, peevish telephone call, that he'd chosen them to match her eyes. She picked up the Joy, pulled out the stopper and sniffed. Too bad there was no time for a leisurely bath right now.

She put the suitcase on the bed, made sure the door was locked and undressed. Forty minutes later she was ready.

Why had she done this? Shaking a little, she sank to the edge of the bed. Supposedly she was to be almost invisible. She would indeed be unrecognizable, but invisible, no.

She'd deliberately set out to make certain she caught and held Sean's attention all evening, and she was going to do just that. If she'd been reading his signals correctly, the man was likely to have a hard time concentrating on anything else.

In the foyer, Sean kept one eye on the corridor leading to his wing and the other on the constantly arriving stream of guests. The babble and enthusiasm pleased him. He felt terrific. Emily was marvelous. No woman could put on a party the way she could and Joe was pretty good too. He'd even met the third member of their household, a quiet, pale man named Larry Young who was obviously bright and who appeared to be chief gofer for the night.

The army of specialists that had been at work all day were from a variety of firms only Joe and Emily were familiar with, but they all knew their jobs. His house looked like the emporium of a deranged merchant with too much money and zero taste. Scarlet feathered arrangements vied with black velvet hangings. His Austrian chandelier in the dining room had been festooned with strands of extra prisms in various clashing shades that shot colors across the walls. Every bare space between his precious antiques had been carefully filled with gaudy props. Everything from plaster boys urinating happily into shells to plump shepherd girls dropping clusters of cherries into their pouting mouths. It was awful, wonderfully awful.

A woman approached him purposefully, carrying a silver tray. She was swathed in swishing black bombazine and wore a black concoction, with a few spiked protrusions, on her head.

She put her face close to his ear and muttered, "Mr. Sean."

He drew back and stared. "Sekowsky?" He controlled his laughter with difficulty. A few blue curls peeped from the headpiece. She glared at him for a few seconds then, slowly, a smile transformed her features. "What is it?" he asked.

"She's something, that Emily," Sekowsky murmured, then she straightened and held out the tray. "You are to call for order and make the announcement on this card. Afterward, take the tray and return it to the table just inside your wing."

Sean accepted the tray, picked up the card and peered around. No sign of a gold mask.

"Okay, everybody," he tried.

The noise level didn't lessen.

"Everybody—" The resounding boom of a gong shocked him, but he maintained his composure as guests fell silent and pressed around him closely. Could there be a hundred people in this space? It certainly felt like it.

"I have an announcement to make. I am Gieves—" *Oh, original, Emily* "—Prince Zolinov's butler. He has asked me to inform you that he will be late but that he will join you as soon as possible."

Immediately Red, and he knew she was Red despite the diamond-studded veil that covered her face and her flowing scarlet gown, pressed forward. "My husband will be here soon, darlings. A little business matter. You know how it is with these *important* men. Follow me to the terrace and we will break open the champagne ordered especially for this special evening." She started away then halted and turned back, raising a black-gloved hand. "The pool is full, darlings, and sooo warm. Anyone fancying a little swim has only to take a little jump. We have plenty of extra suits, or..." Her fading laugh was silver and then she swept away, a laughing entourage in tow.

Sean watched them go and prepared to follow. People crushed past him, coming from the rooms behind.

Then he saw the gong. And, at the same time, the gold mask, the soaring golden feathers and the flesh-toned body stocking spangled over thrusting breasts and below the navel with gold sequins. He lowered the tray slowly to his side. Around her hips a puff of feathers were fanned to match those on her head and her feet were shod in incredibly high-heeled gold sandals. Emily had the most beautiful legs he had ever seen.

Invisible, huh? He stood still. So did she. Her eyes were impossible to see behind the mask, but he smiled at her, saluted, covered his heart with one hand and bowed from the waist in silent homage. What man would fail to notice her?

His eyes passed over her body. Absolute perfection. Only a perfect body could carry off that outfit. He felt the stirrings of arousal but made no attempt to turn away. Instead he came toward her until they stood only a few feet apart.

"Still want me to believe you aren't interested in me as more than a friend?"

The gold mask didn't move.

"You are the most spectacular thing I've ever seen. I knew you were before and tonight you decided to prove it, didn't you?"

Still she didn't reply.

"Okay," he said quietly. "Play your game, but later we talk. And Emily—" he saw the flash of the blue eyes now "—I'm sorry about the violets. You aren't simple, are you? I'll know better next time. Only I'm not sure if there are flowers exotic enough for you."

Emily's heart did flip-flops as she watched him walk into the hallway, open the door and take the next card she'd left for him. In a way, she'd probably hurt him more. She'd flaunted what she knew she could be, devastatingly attractive. She'd given him the ultimate come-on by making sure only he would know who she was and then dressing in a way guaranteed to make him want her physically, no matter what his emotional feelings toward her were. And now she'd have to deal with what she'd started. She owed him that.

Her breasts hardened, her stomach grew tight and the ache pressed downward into her thighs. She truly desired this man. But it hadn't been the physical part of her that had fallen for him first. If she went to him, made love to him, she'd still have to cope with her mind and heart and what he already meant to her, even if all she could do afterward was leave him. But at least she'd have the knowledge that she'd cared for him, been with him. No matter what happened with the rest of her life, she'd always have that part of Sean.

The evening progressed, stage by stage, just as she'd planned. She heard the applause, the murmurs of surprise with each revelation.

Prince Vladimir Zolinov was found, drowned, in a bath shallowly filled with Dom Perignon. Female garments were strewn around the bathroom. A famed private detective on vacation had stepped forward in this time of need, and prime suspects were identified: a jealous first wife, spurned actresses, a woman he had promised to marry before the glamorous Nadia arrived on the scene, Nadia, who had been the bereaved widow of another wealthy man, already well endowed financially and running a world-renowned club in Zurich when she met Zolinov.

The new young prince, his father's successor, came under suspicion. He was a spender, a gambler, a womanizer who argued constantly with his father over a too-meager allowance. Now he would inherit all. But, there was the cuckolded husband. Frank Horton performed his part beautifully, as did his wife Jean, from frothy blond hair to floating organza dress and doleful expression. And then there was the producer and cast of the show from which the Prince had withdrawn funds.

And throughout, Emily gave Sean the nod at the correct time. And each time his eyes lingered. At first he didn't smile, for hours it seemed, but slowly she saw the softening in his features, the way he hesitated much too long, looking at her, before he turned back to his guests. One tall man, who was playing the husband of the woman who had supposedly betrayed him with Zolinov, also looked at her often, a different look, always followed by a glance at Sean.

Once Emily saw the man look at her and go directly to talk
to Sean who took the man aside and said something. After
that the man did no more than glance at her. Sean had told
him who she was, she could sense it, or at least he'd told
him something to stop him from pressing further.

Dinner started. It was, Emily acknowledged with pride,
a masterpiece crowned with the most perfect caribou
wrapped in a pâté shell and rolled in spinach and delicately
garnished with baby glazed carrots and small red potatoes.

For dessert the guests had many choices, but few passed
up a cake of layered crispy meringue and chocolate mousse
with huge curls of minted chocolate on top. Sean bowed
and smiled at the compliments and Emily found herself almost aping him from her spot at the end of another table.
He caught her eye and laughed aloud. Her mouth was the
one part of her face not covered by the mask and she smiled
broadly before popping another forkful of the confection
into her mouth.

Sekowsky, magnificent in her bombazine, came behind
the phony investigator and he shushed loudly. Emily rose
and hit the gong gently.

"Ladies and gentlemen," the man announced with just
the right intonation, "I have received a most disturbing and
incriminating piece of evidence."

Silence was total.

Emily took several steps toward the doorway. She would
make sure all was well and make a run for it. What she had
done this evening was indefensible. She didn't like herself
for it and neither would Sean. Later she'd apologize, but
not tonight.

"This announcement will shock you all as it does me,"
the producer-cum-detective continued. He bowed his head
for a moment. "Princess Nadia, do you have anything
you'd like to say?"

"I?" Red let her hand flutter over her breast and Emily
couldn't help grinning. She might have liked Red if she'd
ever had a chance to get to know her.

"Yes, you," the man thundered. "This is medical evidence."

Red let her eyelashes flutter downward. "My poor husband is dead, drowned in...drowned by some thug who was strong enough to throw him into a bath of champagne and pretend my honest Vladimir was part of some assignation. My dear, faithful husband who wanted to do nothing but love me and do good for others."

This was perfect. What better group to pull off a Hollywood murder party than a Hollywood group?

"Not so, my dear," the producer intoned like a mortician reciting the benefits of a metal over a wooden casket. "Vladimir had a problem. A soft spot behind his ear—"

"No!" Red shrieked.

"Yes. And you were the only one, apart from his doctor in Zurich, who knew that pressure on this point would render him unconscious, would make him pitch forward and thus allow you to *help* him into the bath where he would drown in the champagne. You summoned all these people here, all these people with reasons to want him dead, and thought you could pull off your heinous crime and go undetected."

"No! No!" Red cried, covering her face. "Why should I when Uri inherits everything? Why would I do this?"

The facts poured forth. The princess was, in fact, Pearl Slumsky, originally a dancer from Liverpool in England. Behind her lay a trail of men she'd used, one of whom had given her the money to start her club in Zurich. He had died before she met Zolinov. And Zolinov had wanted her to give up the club, to become more respectable. He'd cut off the funds that kept her enterprise alive. And the final proof of her guilt: a few weeks before this party and Zolinov's death, she had persuaded him to cut Uri out of his will. The boy, who was nothing but a useless gambler, she'd insisted, should never get his hands on the fortune. She, Nadia, was pregnant and would bear the prince another child to carry on the name. All the Zolinov fortune would go to Nadia and her child.

The revelations continued. Nadia was, of course, guilty of murdering Prince Vladimir Zolinov to gain control of the money she coveted.

Applause broke out. People crowded around Sean, slapping him on the back. And Emily walked slowly backward until she could turn and run into his private wing.

She checked the clock on the bedside table. Almost midnight. But the party would go on for at least an hour or two more. Plenty of time for her to change and make her getaway. Joe had left as soon as the food was served. He said he would drop Larry off before he went to meet a friend. Emily never asked about Joe's friends.

The skullcap holding the feathers in place made her head ache. She pulled it off and threw it on the bed. The mask followed.

Quickly, she grabbed her jeans, sweater and underclothes and ran into the bathroom. The mask had meant she needed no makeup, but it had dug into her face, painfully making lines.

A slim zipper closed the bodysuit. She reached back to loosen it just enough to ease the transparent fabric from her shoulders. Then she turned on the cold water and bent over the sink to wash her face.

Cool hands on her back stopped her. They didn't make her jump. She knew Sean stood behind her.

Chapter Eleven

"You expected me to come, didn't you, Emily?"

She shuddered from head to foot. "No," she said, honestly. "I thought you'd be tied up with your guests for hours. But I knew you'd want to come. I made sure of it and I'm—I'm sorry I was a tease. I really didn't set out to be."

"Did you really intend to get away before I came? I find that hard to believe."

"I don't blame you." She faced him, aware of the weight of her breasts, unsupported now. "I did do it deliberately, Sean. We both know why, though, don't we?"

"Why don't you tell me?"

"We're attracted to each other. Initial attraction is always mostly physical, but it grew to something else, for me, anyway. I . . . I really . . ."

"*Don't* say how much you like me again, Emily, please. Don't say how nice I am. I may be a nice, kind guy, but I'm also normal, and I much more than like you, lady. I might even . . . oh, hell, Emily, come here."

She came. He pulled her into his arms, and the brass buttons on his jacket dug into her barely covered breasts. In her high, high heels she was a fraction taller than he.

"You are gorgeous," he muttered, kissing her chin. "But you know it, don't you?"

Emily breathed deeply. This wasn't what she'd intended. Her sexual experience was more limited than Sean could possibly imagine. But how could she tell him that after the performance she'd put on for him tonight?

He stopped ranging his hands over her back. The zipper was now opened all the way and his hands were inside the suit, spread wide over her bottom. She couldn't make herself move.

"Something wrong, Emily? Am I doing something wrong? I'm a bit rusty, you know. That probably surprises you, but it's true."

She rested her forehead on his shoulder. There seemed nothing to say. He already had her pigeonholed as sexually experienced and ready for action.

"Emily—" he put a thumb under her chin and raised her face "—what is it? Did I turn you off somehow?"

Her mouth trembled. Holding his shoulders, she kicked aside the uncomfortably high sandals. Only the tight fit of the bodysuit kept it from falling away.

"Hey—" Sean tilted his face sideways, kissed the corner of her mouth quickly "—what is it?"

She tried to smile at him, but tears were welling in her eyes and as she lowered her lids, great drops ran down her cheeks.

"Emily, Emily," he said in a voice that sounded as if he, too, was perilously close to tears, "what's happened to us here? What is all this?"

How did you tell a man you thought you'd fallen in love for the first time and you were scared to death?

He shook her gently. "I'm sorry if I came on too strong. You look...oh, Emily, what did you expect when you already knew I was crazy about you and you put on an outfit like this?"

She moved closer into his arms. "I knew what I was doing. I wanted to. I don't know if we can have much together, Sean, but I'd like us to be together at least once."

He became rigid. "What's that supposed to mean?"

She wasn't being fair, at least not now. The day would come when he'd be grateful to move on and somehow she had to force herself to feel the same. "I don't mean anything," she said. "Kiss me, Sean."

He only hesitated a fraction of a moment before his lips descended on hers, moving slowly back and forth, his tongue caressing the softness just inside her mouth. No pressure, no force, just a languorous deepening, a joining that drew her closer and closer until she strained against him, running her fingers into his hair, opening his mouth wide with hers, meeting his tongue, challenging.

Sean was not a man to avoid a challenge.

He kissed her until her mouth was sore. Then he moved to her ear and blew, nipped the lobe, kissed along her cheekbone, back to her mouth again, tilting her face up.

"Emily," he said after a long time. "I don't want to make love to you here."

She shook her head, disoriented.

"I don't want to make love to you at all until you're ready," he continued.

"I am ready, Sean," she whispered. "I just—" her voice broke and she clung to him, burying her face in his shoulder.

"Yes, love?" he asked softly. "You just what?"

"I'm not exactly what I seem."

He laughed and lifted her in his arms, carried her through the child's room, across the hall, through the sitting room and stopped beside the great Jacobean bed with its heavy tapestries.

She kept her arms tightly around his neck. "I don't think you know what I mean."

"Oh, but I think I do. And I'm the one who's really afraid, not you. Or at least, I'm as much afraid as you are, Emily. You haven't had a lot of men in your life, have you?"

Her whole body seemed to turn crimson. "No."

He lowered her to the bed and released the drapes on the far side and the bottom of the bed. "There haven't been a lot of women in mine, despite my reputation." He shrugged. "And I'm grateful, for both our sakes."

Emily watched the heavy damask fabric swish closed and wanted, more than she'd ever wanted anything, to lie with this man in this marvelous bed.

She wished the stupid bodysuit would disappear. She looked down at it. "I may disappoint you."

"No, you won't. Loving, in the physical sense, is like any other important thing in life, it gets better with practice. This thing is lovely." He touched the sequins over her right breast and she shivered, closed her eyes. He spread his hand, pushed the breast higher. "Would you mind if I helped you out of the suit? I'd like to feel your skin."

Her being fell away, the nerves, the muscles and sinew. With no embarrassment, she put her hand between his legs. He was hard, straining inside his pants. Without saying a word, she undid the fastener at his waist and slid the zipper down.

All he said was "Lady," and in feverish haste she pushed him away, the bodysuit hampering, but not stopping her from dragging off his jacket and the ridiculous suspenders, from pulling his tie away, getting rid of the shirt and, finally, taking off the striped pants, his socks and shoes.

He stood before her, unsmiling, watching her reaction. He must know he was a beautiful man, beautifully made, wide at the shoulder, narrow at the waist and slim through the hip, that his legs were long, strong and well shaped. The hair on his chest and stomach was heavier and darker than she would have expected from his blond hair. The same dark hair was on his legs. Inside she melted, felt an unaccustomed weakening, a slight shrinking beneath his masculinity and she loved it. Too often men failed to make her feel feminine. Not so Sean Townsend. Every inch of the man was perfect for her and she wanted him.

She stood up, her arms at her sides.

Sean kissed her again, slowly, smoothed back her hair, let his hands carry their caress down her back, over her buttocks and back up. Very slowly he brushed aside the thin nylon with its patches of sequins from her breasts. He looked down, then deliberately, he kissed a nipple, sucked, long and slow, while he gently covered and smoothed her other breast with his palm. Too soon he moved his mouth, dragging his tongue into the deep dip between her breasts. But he only searched out the other nipple and began again the gentle nipping, suckling motions.

Emily arched back and felt only Sean, his tongue, his mouth, his hands, the exquisite aching her body had become. Together they fell onto the bed and he pulled a pillow beneath her head. He worked the bodysuit away, inch by inch, wiggling it over her hips, kissing, kissing down, over her thighs to her knees, past her calves, until, finally, he pulled the silken fabric from her feet with a last, tickling kiss to the arch of each foot. She giggled but quickly became silent. He was kissing a return path over her body.

"Sean," she said, but weakly. She had taken no precautions, but how did she say that?

He was easing over her and running his tongue down between her breasts until he reached the silkiness between her thighs. Then she cried out. All so new. All so wonderful. Her mind began to disconnect. Then a violent shudder came, and she pushed her hips against his mouth. He gave a low moan, a sound of joy. Oh, she'd known all this, she'd read, but she'd never felt. Blackness, almost lassitude, yet determination. She couldn't let this stop now, couldn't bear it. She moaned and Sean held her hips tightly.

"It's okay," she heard him say. "Let go."

She did as he told her, and something inside her exploded, and instantly he was soothing her, telling her everything was fine.

Her thoughts cleared just a little. She should please him, too. Awkwardly, she tried to change positions, to move lower over his body. He stopped her and positioned them so that one of his elbows rested each side of her head. "Not everything at once," he said.

But she saw the raised veins at his temples, the knotted muscles beside his mouth. And she knew that for both of them, this had not been enough.

He looked into her eyes and frowned. "Do you know what you want? Really want?"

She nodded.

"You want to make love?"

"You know I do."

He looked down at her for a moment then turned aside. She closed her eyes at the sound of foil tearing, but, at the same time, she silently thanked him for doing what should be done.

"Emily," he said and pulled her into his arms, "do you know how I feel about you?"

"You want to be with me," she said, praying he'd say at least that.

"I've wanted to be with you since I found you beside that dumb bank machine. I'm not sure I'll ever stop wanting to be with you. But it takes two, doesn't it?"

Emily parted her legs and urged him near. "I think we have to live for the moment sometimes. Right now we both want each other and I'd like to believe the wanting wasn't just sexual. And I'd like to not talk anymore."

They didn't talk, for a long time. Sean entered her body slowly. He stroked her insides carefully with the unyielding force of his need for release, pushing deep, drawing back, pushing again. He didn't speak words, only murmured soft sounds against her ear.

And the sensation mounted in Emily. She began to move, to meet him. Her breath shortened, then gained strength. The tightening increased, drawing him in, holding him, and the wanting to hold him grew unbearable. It was happening, that thing they wrote about, the thing some women said was impossible, he was drawing her with him to a peak she would want to climb higher and higher.

She began to pant. The little noises she made, whatever words she spoke, she didn't really hear, knew she would never remember.

Sean rose over her, his knees straddling her hips. He'd lowered the lamplight but she saw the heavy rise and fall of his chest. He still moved inside her, but so slowly, so gently. "Are you ready?" he asked.

Emily tossed her head sideways. She wasn't sure what he meant. "Don't stop," was all she could say.

"You're ready?" He moved steadily above her.

Emily let out a long breath. "Make love to me, Sean."

He fell on top of her and later she couldn't reconstruct the moments that followed.

There was the mounting pressure, so strong her head seemed to burst. The glorious burning inside her turned to a throbbing, ecstatic ache, then contracted as if to keep Sean within her.

She heard him cry out, felt the dampness of his skin on hers, and treasured their joining, the sense of their two bodies becoming one. After their cries of ecstasy, when she fell back, he thrust again, once, twice, before he lay still.

He pressed his face against her shoulder, kissed the bone there and said, simply, "Thank you."

Emily closed her eyes and rolled her head away.

He was silent a moment, then he put a hand beneath her cheek and urged her face toward his. "Wasn't that the right thing to say? I do thank you, Emily. Nothing as good as this has happened to me since…" He buried his face in the pillow.

Her heart turned. "I know. I understand and I'm glad. It's all okay. Everything's okay. But, stupid as it sounds, all this is still a bit new to me. I was even engaged once—" She stopped abruptly and turned her head away. She couldn't be with him if she couldn't be honest.

"I can tell," he said gently. "You haven't had a whole lot of experience. Surely you don't think I mind that? I'd take you any way I could get you, my love, but the way you are is perfect. Whoever you were engaged to was either a fool or as young as you must have been. Probably the latter.''

Emily thought about Charles, about the way they'd grown up together, their awkward first moves toward becoming more than just friends. She snuggled closer to Sean. ''It was the latter,'' she said, and felt a flush of loyalty for Charles. ''We knew each other from when we were kids and we never did manage to think of each other as anything but buddies.''

Sean laughed softly against her hair. ''I'm glad—for me. Sorry for him. Are you sorry for him?''

''Not anymore. We've both grown up a lot since then.'' She hoped Charles had really grown up a lot.

''Emily, will you stay with me tonight?''

''Well, I really should go—'' She felt his penis stir and the answering leap inside her body. ''Yes, I'll stay,'' she said and rolled on top of him. She kissed his lips then sat back on his hips while he strained upward to kiss her breasts. When he leaned back on the pillows and pulled her down, she spoke against his mouth. ''Even if I wanted to go home, I couldn't. And I don't want to.''

Chapter Twelve

Emily closed the office door carefully behind her. Joe was seated at the scuffed desk, his head bent over a pile of papers. He showed no sign of having heard her come in.

She tiptoed across the room and set a bag of doughnuts and two large Styrofoam cups of coffee in front of him. "Good morning, partner."

"Mmm." He continued to add up columns of figures.

"Sorry I'm late."

Joe looked up. "Who's late?"

"I am. It's almost eleven."

"So you finally showed you're human." He pressed his hands together. "Praise be. It gets tough trying to keep up with a saint."

Emily blushed and sat on the desk. He must know she hadn't come home last night. Should she just come out and say she'd been with Sean? "Have some coffee while it's hot. And a doughnut." Why should she tell Joe who she'd been with? He didn't tell her his private business and she didn't want him to.

"Yeah, thanks," Joe said. He gave her his full attention while he pulled the lid off his cup. "So what's Mr. Golden throwing our way next?"

For a moment she didn't understand. She took the lid off her own cup slowly. "Don't you like Sean, Joe?"

He flipped a hand back and forth. "I like him, I don't like him. What does it matter as long as he goes on giving us the kind of business success is made of?"

Emily didn't want the coffee anymore. "I thought you liked him. You always act as if you do when he's around."

Joe paused, his teeth sunk into a powdered doughnut. He took the bite and chewed, reaching for a napkin. "I'm not with you, Em," he said around the food and swallowed. "The guy's a client; of course I'm nice around him."

"But you don't like him?"

The rest of the doughnut disappeared in two large bites and Joe wiped his mouth and hands. "I get it. *You* like him."

"Yes, I do like him."

He crumpled his napkin into a ball, swiveled his chair and made an over-the-shoulder throw into a can standing by the bathroom door. "How's that?" He smiled at Emily. "Not bad, huh? The old man's not losing his touch?"

She stared at him and moved to a chair, taking her rapidly cooling coffee with her.

Joe stopped grinning. "Okay, okay. I'm sorry. It's just father Moreno going into his protective act, okay? Sure, I know you like him. Hell, Emily, I know you're crazy about him. And I know you spent last night with him. I just want what's best for you. And getting hurt by a guy like that will not be the best for you, baby."

"Don't call me baby."

"Yeah, okay, I won't call you baby. Am I forgiven?"

"How do you know I spent the night with Sean?"

"I'm not a complete fool. And neither is he. I've seen the way he looks at you and in that getup you had on last night..." He gave a low whistle. "Bab—I mean, Emily, that was some number. You have been hiding a lot of your assets. But last night I knew the two of you were heading in one direction—Sean Townsend's bed."

"I don't like the way you're talking."

"I'm telling it like it is." His face hardened. "From that first day at his house, I've watched Sean Townsend looking at you like you were a gourmet dinner he'd like to get his teeth into."

"Charming."

"I'm just a plain, hard-working man and I know the score. Townsend has wanted you for a long time and I guess last night he got what he wanted."

Emily's cheeks throbbed. "You make it sound so cheap. I would never say things like this to you."

"You don't have to worry about some dolly screwing up my life and leaving me in pieces. You're different, Em." His voice had softened. "You're gentle and quiet. Do you know, I've never seen you go out on a date?"

She took a sip of coffee and made a face. It was cold. "What is all this? Where are you leading? Am I supposed to say I won't see him again, because if that's what you want, forget it." She hadn't intended to say that but now she had she meant every word. Not only would she see Sean again, she'd find a way to tell him the truth about herself. The rest would be up to him.

Joe had got up and was now leaning against the front of the desk. "I'm not telling you to stay away from Sean. I don't have the right to, anyway. What I am telling you is to remember that men like him can have whatever they want. And usually, once they get it, they move on. Don't fall in love with the guy, Emily."

"Are you an expert on falling in love, too? You surprise me."

"I'm not an expert on falling in love. I've never been in love and don't intend to be. I've seen what it can do, though, and take it from me, it's not worth it."

"What made you so hard, Joe?" She felt suddenly, achingly sad for this man who had come to mean so much to her. "You've got a lot to give to the right woman. Why make a decision to be on your own forever? And what about kids?" She'd seen him with children in parks and playing ball on Overland Avenue. He always had great rapport with them.

"My father used my mother up," he said very quietly, flexing his fingers steadily. "She loved him and he used her all up. She had seven kids and he never brought in enough money and she tried to do whatever she could to keep us all going. When she was forty-three, she died and the old man moved on to someone else. I never heard him mention my mother's name." He looked up at her, his eyes dark and hard. "I mean as in never. *Hey, you. Your ma. Ma. My old lady*. She wasn't anyone to him but a thing to use. Her name was Mary."

He was quiet for a moment before he continued, "I've got an older brother and an older sister. I was third in line. They both left home the minute they could find bus fare. And they both married and they've ended up like my folks, nothing. Kids? Yeah, I'm kind of sorry about that. I might have liked some, but you make trade-offs. End of lecture, Em. I don't believe in love. I don't think it exists. What you and I have, a good solid friendship with nothing physical, is about as good as it gets between a man and a woman."

"Oh, Joe." She wanted to hold him but knew he wouldn't let her. She wanted to tell him he was wrong, but this wasn't the time. All she did dare say was, "You don't have to worry about me. I've had my knocks, too, and I'm not going to let anyone hurt me." And while she said the words she knew she could be so very wrong.

"Good," he said, all business again. "Back to my original question. Did Sean mention any future work for us?"

Emily still felt as if she'd been punched. "No," she said almost under her breath. "But I'm sure he will. And he isn't our only client, Joe. We have two weddings this month and that retirement party for... what's the man's name?"

"Leavitt. Look, Em, I don't want to harp on this, but Sean's stuff has brought in more money than anything else we've done. We do need to keep going with him."

Irritation made her jaw tighten. "We will keep up with Sean, I promise. And after last night, which, by the way, was a big success, I think we'll be getting a lot more business through referrals."

Joe smiled broadly. "Yeah, you're right. And those people have the big bucks. We're going places, Emily Smith, you and I are really going places."

She smiled, too, but another thought came, a disturbing thought. Joe was into being alone for life on a personal level, but he needed her and he didn't want to risk her getting so involved with a man that she might give up the business. She'd never really considered the possibility, but she supposed it could happen.

"Joe—"

A rap at the door and Sean's head sticking into the room stopped Emily from finishing her sentence. "Hi, you two," he said and came all the way in. With only a glance at Emily, he pushed a package into her hands and turned to Joe. "This is something extra, Joe. Just to say thanks for the fantastic job you and Emily did last night." He handed him an envelope.

Joe opened it slowly and pulled out a check. Emily saw the slackening of his jaw before he raised his brows at Sean. "We didn't send you the bill yet." He reached around and selected a piece of paper from the desk. "You don't owe us half this much. What would you like us to do? We can give you credit if you like, or make a refund."

"No, no," Sean said, shaking his head. He put the invoice into the breast pocket of his jacket. "You didn't hear me. My phone has been ringing off the hook all morning. I even made the gossip columns—with no snide comments attached. That check is to say thanks for a great effort. The bill is separate. Thanks for everything, Joe."

Joe looked from Sean to the check in his hand. "Well...thank you, Sean. Emily and I both thank you." He laughed and Emily glanced at him sharply. The laugh was different, awkward.

"You're welcome."

"Hey." Joe checked his watch. "I hate to grab and run, but I just remembered I promised to catch Larry for lunch." He didn't quite meet Emily's eyes. "We're going to eat over at Chin-Chin's. I think he's going to end up working with us pretty full-time for a while." To Sean he added, "Larry Young was at your place last night. The tall thin guy. He's a would-be actor and Emily and I feel kind of responsible for making sure he doesn't starve."

Then he left, still saying something about Larry and Chin-Chin's and Emily sat quite still in her chair.

"Open it."

She fingered the package in her lap. Sean's presence overwhelmed her. She couldn't be more aware of him if he had touched her, but her mind was still partly on Joe.

"Emily?" Sean stood beside her, a hand massaging the back of her neck. As she raised her face, he bent to kiss her mouth softly and her stomach pulled in sharply.

Spangled gold ribbon sparkled against deep blue paper. She slid the wrappings away and opened the box. Inside lay another, smaller box of black velvet. Emily picked it out and opened it. Inside lay a pair of earrings.

"I can't accept these," she said simply and began to close the box.

Sean's strong fingers, easing her own aside, stopped her. He took the earrings from the box and put them in her hand. "Yes, you can take them. I want you to have them."

"And you always get what you want," she said, and opened her hand. The large diamond studs glittered.

"Not always," Sean said. His voice wasn't quite as steady now, not quite as sure. "Pretty rarely lately. In fact, only once for a very long time as far as I can remember."

For an instant their gaze met in total understanding before Emily turned the earrings over. "These cost a fortune."

"They're worth what they cost. And you're worth something far more special, but I didn't have that much time and I wanted to see you. We hardly had time to talk at all this morning.''

She looked directly at him then. They'd awakened at eight when a light tap at the door announced Sean's breakfast. He'd told Sekowsky he wouldn't be eating this morning and turned his full attention on Emily. She, not he, had been the one to say, at almost ten, that they couldn't stay in bed all day making love, that they both had jobs to do.

"What are you thinking?" Sean asked. "If you don't like the earrings they can always be changed. We can go do it right now."

"They are the most beautiful earrings I've ever seen. Thank you." She slipped out the ones she was wearing and put on the diamonds. "How do they look?"

"Wonderful."

"Do you still want to know what I was thinking?"

Sean went down on his haunches beside her. "Let's have it."

"I was thinking about you and me, about making love last night, and this morning. And I was thinking all kinds of things nice women don't think about when they're supposed to be working."

He stroked her cheek with the backs of his fingers, pulled her face to his and kissed her full and strong on the lips. Somehow in the next seconds, he got to his knees and pulled her into his arms. Her mouth opened wider against his, and she made a small sound when he pulled up her sweatshirt and slid a hand inside her bra.

Emily pushed her fingers into his hair. Reason was slipping away. It took a strength she hadn't known she had to move a hand to his shoulder, to press two fingers over his mouth and wait until he opened his eyes.

"Emily, we're going to have to do something about this." His voice was thick but didn't protest when she eased his hand from her breast and straightened her shirt.

"We will," she told him. "But I don't think it had better be here, do you?"

They laughed together and he got up and pulled her to her feet. "I've got to see you tonight."

Emily sighed. "Tonight we've got a rehearsal dinner."

"Damn. Okay, tomorrow night then."

"Tomorrow I'm free. Thanks for understanding about tonight."

"Ooh, I don't want to understand, but I guess I don't have a choice, either." While he spoke he searched through his pockets. "Here." He handed her a card. "I knew I was forgetting something. I want you to come to this with me."

Emily read and reread. She felt a constriction in her throat and her skin became very cold.

"Friday's a bit soon, but, knowing you, you'll be able to arrive looking like the star of the show even if you decide to come in jeans. Do you have a fur?"

She shook her head numbly.

"Will you let me buy you one? You'd look terrific in sable. Long. Floor-length. If it's hot you can always wear it over your shoulders."

"I can't come."

He didn't answer at once. Then he held her arms until she looked up. "Why? Do you have a job? Joe could manage without you for once, couldn't he? I want to show you off, Emily. And you'd enjoy it, I know you would. Movie people are fun to watch."

A movie opening. Searchlights. Cameras. Television shots of arriving limousines. Close-ups of smiling, opulently dressed guests. Close-ups that would be beamed all over the country for curious people to see. Curious people like her parents, and Charles . . . and the ever-present gossipmongers. "And here we have Mr. Sean Townsend, the industrialist. He's escorting, ah, a Miss Emily Smith. We don't seem to know who she is, but something tells me we will." And they would, they'd find out and she wasn't ready for that.

"No! Forget it. I hate that kind of thing. All those people. The cameras...I can't do it, Sean." She must calm down. She was making too much of this. "I'm sorry. It's a wonderful invitation, but I just don't do well in that kind of setting. I don't belong."

Sean knew that something was wrong, very wrong. Her body was shaking. What did she mean, she didn't do well around a lot of people? Last night there had been plenty of people and she had done very well. Her response to the invitation didn't make sense.

But the opening didn't matter. And he could figure out what had just happened later. The main thing was to keep moving ahead. Instinct warned him not to give her too much time to think. She thought she didn't belong with the kind of people who went to a movie opening? He was forced to spend a good deal of time with people like that. She must learn to feel relaxed with them, and with his help she'd manage just fine. Only he had to move fast, not let her start to slip away again.

She was quiet now. The trembling had stopped, but she seemed drained.

"I understand," Sean said. He had an idea. "And I don't blame you. Those things can be pretty overwhelming. Look, forget I ever suggested it. We'll just go for a run tomorrow night, then have pizza, maybe. How does that sound?"

"Great." She smiled up at him and smoothed the lapels of his jacket. "I'm sorry about the other."

"Don't be." His plan was going to work. "But how about a couple of days away? A little cruise. I keep my boat down at Marina del Rey. We could take off on Friday and come back on Sunday."

"But you'll miss the opening."

"I don't want to go either. Forget that. How about the trip?"

"My work—"

"That's exactly why I suggested waiting until Friday. All you'll miss is Friday."

"We're busiest on the weekends."

A scuffle outside the door almost made him panic. "Of course, of course, I wasn't thinking. But couldn't we work it out? Maybe we should leave tomorrow. I can get away."

The door opened and Emily moved away from him. He saw her open her mouth and inhale shallowly.

"Is Emily taking up half your day, Sean?" Joe said. The tall man, Larry, was with him.

"Sean was just leaving," Emily said, keeping her eyes on the floor.

"I need your help, Joe," Sean said with sudden inspiration. He nodded at the other man, "Hi, Larry. Nice to see you again."

Larry muttered a response and closed the door.

"What can I do for you, Sean?" Joe asked.

This had to work. And he had to be careful. "I want to take a few people out on my boat for a couple of days. And I want to leave tomorrow. I've got a skipper and a good cook, but I'd like Emily to come along and make sure I keep up the standards my friends are beginning to expect from a Townsend event." He chuckled.

Joe was looking at Emily. "Sounds good to me. How about you, Em?"

She continued to count the little chips in the linoleum. "I told Sean there's work to be done here."

"And you don't think I can handle it?"

Sean felt his shoulders loosen up a little. Joe Moreno had smelled money again and he was about to become Sean's most useful accomplice of the moment.

"Of course you can handle things, Joe." Emily looked from Sean to Joe and back to Sean. "A few people? How many?"

He knew he'd turned red. "No more than it takes to make a perfect time."

"Emily will be glad to do it for you, won't you, Emily?" Joe said and Sean noticed, with distaste, the forceful edge in his voice.

Emily smiled too brightly. "Yes, certainly. I'll be glad to do it for you, Sean."

Chapter Thirteen

Sean dropped his bag. "When do you intend to talk to me?" He switched Emily's bag from one shoulder to the other, and picked up his own again. She was already yards ahead of him on the dock.

He ran to catch up. "Come on, Emily. Sulking doesn't become you."

Her chin lifted and she sniffed. "I'm not sulking, Sean. Just feeling a bit quiet. Smell that air? Isn't it wonderful?"

"Yes, it is. But you are sulking."

"No, I'm not."

"You think I pulled a fast one on you with Joe yesterday."

"Didn't you?"

"Turn left here. I did kind of, but I was a desperate man."

"I talked when you picked me up this morning."

"Sure you did. That's exactly what you did. You said, 'Good morning, Sean,' then you clammed up. That was a pretty long ride down here with someone beside you who doesn't say anything."

"Well, I'm talking now. How much farther is it?"

"Not far. Keep going."

He fell behind a step, enjoying the way her lithe body moved. She wore a blue-and-white striped T-shirt and white cotton pants. Blue rope-soled sandals completed her out-fit. Just right. She would always choose the ideal clothes for any occasion and she would also look elegant in whatever she wore. Warm satisfaction filled him. He'd been right from the beginning, Emily was the woman for him—in every way.

His gaze moved from her hips up her back, just in time to meet her eyes as she looked over her shoulder. She raised one brow. "Am I appropriately dressed?"

"Of course. Why do you ask?"

"You were checking me out. Or did I imagine that?"

She turned away again and he grinned. "I'm normal, that's all. Of course I was checking you out. And you pass."

He heard her mumble something and he smothered a laugh. The day was perfect, warm, the sky almost blind-ingly blue, with wispy clouds being swept along by a brisk breeze that would do wonderful things to the *Serena*'s sails. The scent Emily had mentioned was a heady concoction of salt and creosote and hyacinths growing in tubs.

"There she is," he said. "At the end."

Emily halted. "The black ketch?"

She knows her boats he thought, feeling surprised. "Yup. What do you think?"

"That she's a knockout. What did you say she was called?"

"I didn't. We weren't talking this morning, remember?"

She smiled at him, one of the smiles that wrinkled her straight nose. "I was a bit of a witch, but I'm over it now. Tell me her name."

"*Serena*." For years he hadn't even thought about the name. Now he did and frowned. "We named her after our daughter."

"I . . . I didn't know you had a daughter."

He could see the consternation in her face. Why had he felt compelled to tell her, at this moment? "We . . . I don't.

We lost her when Margaret was six months pregnant and we'd already decided that if the baby was a girl we'd call her Serena. When we bought the boat it seemed natural to name it after the baby. Come on, this stuff's getting heavy.''

Talking about it didn't hurt anymore. He was surprised at that, but then, he hadn't talked about it for a very long time and he was bound to have become increasingly reconciled to all that had happened.

Emily wanted to ask him more. How had his wife died? Had she had other pregnancies? What caused the miscarriage? And most of all she longed to ask if Sean still grieved for Margaret. He'd said he missed her, but it was possible to miss someone and yet be over the grief. She asked nothing, only put her arm through his. Side by side, they walked the final yards to his beautiful boat.

"Why a black boat?" she asked as they crossed the gangplank. The tide was in and the boat's glistening hull rode high beside the dock.

"When I was a kid my dad had a black boat. A little one. He always said he'd get a ketch one day and that it would be black. He never quite got around to buying one.''

"So you did. She's about fifty feet? What a beauty.''

"Fifty-two. You've spent time on boats, haven't you?''

In her mind, she saw the vacation house at Cape Cod, and then Charles on the deck of his father's 135-foot motor yacht. Charles was smiling, his brown hair whipped flat to the side of his head.

"Emily?''

"Oh, I used to be around the water a lot when I was a kid and most of the people we knew had boats.'' She would ease into the rest, the whole story. She'd already decided that in these two days, she would tell Sean everything about herself.

They went aboard and immediately a burly man, probably in his mid-fifties, Emily decided, approached and introduced himself as Cabrini. This, Sean explained, was his skipper. Later, she'd meet the man's wife, who was deck hand and cook.

Cabrini enveloped Emily's hand inside callused fingers, gave one brief shake and left.

"He's not what I'd expected," Emily whispered.

Sean shrugged and put an arm around her waist, shepherding her toward open doors leading below. "I should dress him up in whites, huh? With a few brass buttons?"

"No, I don't care what he wears, I just didn't expect him to look like a fisherman, that's all." She clattered down metal steps, taking in gleaming brass and softly shining teak as she went.

"He *is* a fisherman. He works for me whenever I need him, but he's out fishing most of the time. He's also a fantastic seaman. These are your quarters."

He pushed open a door and stood back, waving her into a cabin that looked like a room in a luxury hotel.

Emily stood on the threshold, suddenly feeling awkward. She met Sean's watchful eyes and crossed her arms tightly. "It's lovely." Pale blue predominated—the spread on the double bed, the deep-piled carpet, the small bathroom, which had touches of gray and pink. "It doesn't look as if it's ever used."

"It hasn't been for a long time." Sean lifted her bag onto the bed. "I've been too busy to organize trips lately and for the first year or so after Margaret died I didn't feel like coming here, anyway. I'm sure you understand."

Her feet made no sound as she crossed the rug to stand close beside him. "Are you over Margaret?" The question had to be asked.

He smiled at her and looked away. For a moment he was silent. His fingernails made a scraping sound as he ran them back and forth along the zipper of her bag. Then he said, "Yes. Yes, I am. The answer's more complicated than just yes, of course, and we'll talk about it. I need to talk and you need to hear and this is going to be the perfect time and place for it."

The perfect time and place. Emily took a shaky breath. *Please*, she prayed, *let him accept me for what I am and let him believe that my side of the story is the true one.*

Somewhere beneath them, engines rumbled and the boat vibrated a little.

"I guess we're off," Sean said. "As soon as you're ready, meet me on deck. I think Cabrini will put us under sail pretty fast and you're going to love the way this thing moves then."

He left quickly and Emily stared at the closed door for a few seconds before she pushed her bag aside and stretched out on the bed.

Her need for Sean was growing, expanding, filling her. When he was physically near she had to quell the urge to touch him constantly. When he wasn't with her, she still felt him. Today he seemed different. Despite his jokes about her silence on the drive, he hadn't said much either and the usual traces of humor that turned up the corners of his mouth and crinkled his eyes were missing. He was serious, somber even. And he'd started letting her into the deeper parts of him, confiding in her. She turned on her side and chewed a knuckle, trying to sort out exactly what Sean was trying to accomplish.

Trust.

She curled up her knees. He was giving her his trust because, contrary to Joe's theory, she wasn't someone he only intended to play with for a while then leave. He wanted her in his life.

Emily got up. She put away the few clothes she'd brought with her and changed into shorts. Her hand was on her comb when she decided that doing anything to her hair would be pointless.

Outside her door she paused. A door faced her. Another to the right, this one double, spanned the width of the corridor. This must be Sean's cabin. Emily started up, grabbing a railing as the boat swayed. The separate sleeping quarters hadn't surprised her. With other people around, Sean was the kind of man who'd be careful not to cause her any possible embarrassment.

Emily stepped into the sunlight and wind, and into Sean's waiting arms. He held her tightly against him, rested his chin on top of her head and she closed her eyes. She passed her hands up his chest and around his neck and they kissed, long and soft.

He tangled his fingers in her hair and the old, sweet funny smile was back. "Do you suppose there are enough of us to have a perfect time?"

She pinched his ribs through his navy polo shirt. "We'll see. If conversation lags too often we may have to invite Cabrini and his wife to join us."

"Wendy!" Sean slapped a hand to his forehead. "She'll kill me. I was supposed to bring you at once. Brunch is served and she doesn't like anything to *spoil*, as she puts it."

They ate on a white-linen-covered table beneath an awning on the gently swaying afterdeck. Brunch was fragile crêpes with a delicate sweet cheese sauce and strawberries, croissants that had to be fresh from the oven, a huge bowl of fresh fruits, champagne and orange juice. Emily, having been favored with a thin smile from Cabrini's tanned and sinewy little wife, Wendy, ate everything set before her with gusto.

Throughout the day, the boat slipped through the water under sail. Sean and Emily lay side by side on chaises, holding hands, talking little, not needing to do more.

By midafternoon the fresh air and warmth made Emily sleepy and she rested her head on Sean's shoulder.

He stroked her face and neck. "Glad you came?"

"Mmm."

"We should talk, Emily."

She opened her eyes but kept her head where it was.

"You agree?" he persisted.

"Yes." Where would she begin?

"I think I'd rather go below."

Emily got up at once. Her heart began to pound. She went below without looking back at Sean and didn't pause until she stood in front of her cabin door. Then she felt foolish and turned. "Where do you want to go, Sean? The salon?"

He frowned, and walked past her and opened the double doors at the end of the corridor. "In here. There's a sitting area and we won't be interrupted."

For a dull, weakening moment she wondered if he already knew about her. *They wouldn't be interrupted.* He made it sound as if they were to go through some sort of inquisition where privacy was essential.

The sitting area, on the far side of a king-sized bed, was furnished with a gray corduroy couch and two love seats. The bed extended from the aft bulkhead and was low, covered by a thick gray quilt. Burgundy drapes in gathered panels were evenly spaced along the teak-paneled walls and held in place above and below by continuous brass rods.

Emily settled herself in the corner of a love seat. The cushions around her were soft but she couldn't relax.

"Comfortable there?"

Sean stood over her.

"Very."

"Can I get you a drink?"

"Nothing, thanks. But you have one."

He sat on the edge of the couch so that their knees almost touched. Sean also wore shorts and beside Emily's light tan his legs were golden brown.

"You look uptight."

She felt like a rubber band about to snap. "I'm okay. You seem so serious, that's all."

"Sorry. I guess this is pretty serious to me. I've got a lot of things I want to say to you, to ask you, and they aren't things I've had a whole lot of practice talking about."

"I know what you mean."

He held her hand until she looked into his eyes. "I think we understand each other very well. Do you know... no, you don't know. Emily, that first night, in the basement of the ABC building, something happened to me that I would have said wasn't possible.''

Her heart was thudding harder. She felt sick. Everything was so right, should be so right, yet she could end up losing this man she loved within the next few minutes.

''Okay,'' Sean was saying. ''Just listen. You don't have to say anything.

''After you went home in that taxi I spent the rest of the night roaming around my house looking at your card. I was counting off the seconds till I could call you. Emily, I knew it was weird, that it's not supposed to happen, but I fell in love with you the minute I saw you.'' He squeezed her hand and laughed awkwardly. ''I kept trying to convince myself I was temporarily unhinged and that when I saw you in normal surroundings you'd be ordinary, and maybe even ugly. Only you weren't—aren't. And with every day since then I've loved you more. Does this all sound as dumb to you as it does to me?''

She shook her head.

''Emily—'' he raised her hand to his mouth and kissed the backs of her fingers ''—do you . . . love me?''

Wordlessly, she reached across the space between them and clasped her hands behind his neck. His face was so close she saw the dark flecks in his eyes. ''I love you, Sean,'' she said. ''For a long time I tried not to, but I can't help it.''

He rested his forehead on hers. ''Thank God for that. I thought you did, but you seem to hold back. Emily, there's no need for us to wait. Let's get married. Just do it. The only person I have to consider is my mother in Florida and she can be up here in a few hours. You've never said much about your folks. Will they come? We could head back in tomorrow morning and call. We could go tonight, if you like.''

"I'm not sure..." She couldn't get enough air. "You come from such a different world from mine. I'm not sure I can be what you need."

"You don't know what world I come from, Emily, not really. We'll be fine together, the best, you'll see."

He wasn't giving her time to think, and what she had to say needed a lot of thought. "When I was a kid...when I was growing up, I didn't always get along with my folks. I haven't seen them for years."

"Then maybe this is the time to try to heal some of that up?" Sean suggested quietly. He moved beside her on the love seat and pulled her into his arms.

"I've changed," she said. "I was a bit wild when I was younger. I got into some trouble."

"Sure, sure you did. I can imagine." He loosened her unconscious grip on his shirt. "Relax, will you? I don't give a damn about whether or not you were a teenage rebel or if your parents had to ground you every other week. Listen to me. Sure, I seem to have it all, and I do, I suppose. But my grandparents came over from Ireland on a boat and they traveled steerage, my love. I'm the product of a rags-to-riches story. My grandparents had one kid, my dad. They worked like crazy to give him a start and they did. Then my dad built on what he had. He was one smart guy and he could make money like no one else I've ever met. He could smell a good deal and he seems to have passed that little trick on to me. I was also the only child and what I inherited was considerable. I landed into an already very successful operation. I was lucky.

"My mother came from a solid middle-class family. Her father began working in the rag trade in New York. He pushed racks of clothes through the streets. By the time he retired he had his own factory manufacturing stud closures, snaps, hooks and eyes and eventually zippers, that kind of thing. And when he died and my mother's older brother took over, Mom didn't do so badly in the inheritance department either. We aren't old, well-polished money, Emily, just some of the lucky ones whose hard work paid off.''

Emily pressed her face against his chest, loving the smell of him, the hardness of his flesh. He could tell her every little detail about his past, and she wanted to hear, but nothing, not one word he said, was making her part easier. He thought she was worried about the difference in their financial pictures. If only he knew. Oh, if only he did know and understand.

He was quiet for a while and when she still didn't speak he held her face and kissed her lips softly. ''As long as we love each other, Emily, we'll have it all.''

There was a tap on the door.

Sean called, ''Come in,'' and made no attempt to move away from Emily.

She stiffened in his arms as Wendy Cabrini put her head around the door. The woman's face remained expressionless. ''I wondered what time you'd be wanting dinner, Mr. Townsend?''

Sean stood up and brought Emily with him, keeping his arm firmly around her waist. ''Wendy, how long have we known each other?''

Wendy opened the door wider until she stood just inside the cabin. ''About ten years, I reckon.''

''Would you vouch for me? Give me a reference, I mean?''

A hint of color rose over weathered cheeks. ''Say you're okay, you mean?'' She frowned.

''Exactly. You see, I'm in love with this lady and she's in love with me, but I have to convince her I'm honorable or I'm never going to get her to agree to marry me.''

At any other time Emily would have laughed. A battery of expressions crossed Wendy Cabrini's face, ending with a wry smile.

Wendy centered her attention on Emily. ''He's trustworthy, miss. A bit of a fraud, with his jokes and so on, I mean, but a good man. He's got a lot to give.'' And here she cleared her throat and looked down. "He's been on his own too long and...and Mrs. Townsend, the first Mrs. Townsend, that is, wouldn't have wanted that. Anyway," she began retreating, "if I were you I'd say yes. And I was going to let you know we'd dropped anchor for the night, Mr. Townsend. Perhaps you'd prefer something light for dinner. I'll leave cold cuts and cheeses in the refrigerator, so just get it when you feel like it. Oh, and should I ice some champagne?"

"Yes," Sean said promptly. "You do that, Wendy. And thanks."

The woman left and Sean turned Emily toward him. "I've been pretty lucky with most of the people in my life. The Cabrinis were a real find."

"Sean, we haven't said it all, have we?"

"No."

"We're going to have to."

"Yes. You want to know about Margaret, don't you?"

Strangely, she'd almost forgotten Margaret. She already felt she knew and would have liked the woman. But she said, "Yes."

"It wasn't so complicated, really," Sean said. "Just wonderful for a while, for as long as God gave her to me, then so sad when she died I thought I was going to die too. She lost Serena because her uterus was too small, only we didn't know that until too late. The baby should have made it, but her lungs weren't developed enough. Anyway, afterward Margaret had a lot of problems and about a year later she had to have a hysterectomy. That hurt a lot because we both wanted children."

"Why didn't you adopt?"

"We would have, but then there were more problems and it turned out Margaret had ovarian cancer. She fought a damn good fight, wow, she had guts, but the time came when we knew she wasn't going to make it."

Emily blinked back tears. "How long ago did she die?"

"Four years. Four and a half, now."

She hugged him. "I wish I'd met her."

Sean made a small, choking noise and she looked up at him anxiously. Tears coursed down his face, but he was smiling. "Only you would say a thing like that. How does one guy manage to meet two wonderful women in his lifetime?"

She rubbed the wetness from his cheeks with her knuckles. "I'm not Margaret, Sean. I don't think I can measure up."

"You will. And you'll marry me, won't you?"

"When I was in college I was a real . . . Sean, I had a way of taking on whatever cause seemed the most impossible."

He held her tighter, then lifted her in his arms. "That's exactly what I would expect from you. You're one determined lady and I like that."

"But I hurt my folks because . . ."

"Shhhh." He kissed her mouth closed and set her on the edge of the bed. "I had my problems too, Emily. I always had to live up to what my father called 'the respectability' he'd worked for. Mom and Dad were really into respectability, and having their one and only son and heir thrown in the county jail for driving without a license and while drunk didn't do a whole lot for my popularity rating for a while. I was fifteen the first time. The second time I was nineteen. At least I had the license then, but the rest of the story was the same. Finally, after not being able to drive for a year, I got the message. Convincing my folks I'd cleaned up my act took a lot longer than that but eventually they believed I really wanted to straighten up and fly right. I don't think you've tried hard enough with your mother and father. Do they know about your business?"

She shook her head. He was kissing her neck, easing the T-shirt higher over her midriff.

"I didn't think so. Wait till they see what their little rebel has accomplished. They'll be putty in your hands. And, of course, there'll be the old Townsend charm to back you up."

He didn't have any idea what she'd been trying to lead up to and at this moment the timing for telling him was all wrong. But it would be all right, it would. They loved each other too much not to overcome *anything*. She would know the right moment to tell him the whole truth and then there would be no more secrets between them.

"Don't you think I'm right?"

"Yes, probably."

Crossing his arms, he pulled off his shirt and tossed it aside. Emily kissed him, his mouth, his jaw and neck, a collarbone, each flat hair-roughened nipple. She passed her mouth over him fiercely, holding his waist, digging her fingers into muscle.

"Wait," he said hoarsely. Swiftly, he pulled the T-shirt over her head and kissed the soft swell of flesh above a lacy bra. "I love you, love you," he said against her skin and eased the straps from her shoulders. His tongue worked the fabric beneath her nipples and heat and longing surged through her veins.

"I want us to sleep here, tonight," he said, raising his head, looking at her eyes, her hair, her mouth. "Then tomorrow we'll go home and start making arrangements."

"Yes," she said and knew she was agreeing to become his wife.

He closed his eyes and his lips came together in a trembling line. First he just held her crushed against him, then he eased her away and reached behind her to undo the bra. Her breasts felt heavy and pulsing. She helped him remove the rest of her clothes and his, and they threw back the quilt and slipped between cool, burgundy sheets.

They loved feverishly at first, with a passion that drove them wildly. Later they came together languorously, with the intensely arousing abandon of lovers who knew how to please and be pleased.

Around midnight, when the moon sent a single shaft of light through a porthole, across the tangle of sheets on the bed and their entwined bodies, Emily awoke and found Sean looking down at her, his chin propped on one fist.

"Hi," she said sleepily. "Did you just wake up?"

"Uh-uh. I haven't been to sleep."

Emily rolled toward him and slipped an arm around his waist. "I don't believe you."

He cradled the back of her head and pulled her nearer. "I was thinking."

"Mmm. About what?"

"You do love me, don't you? We are going to get married?"

Her mind cleared. A tinge of fear started then faded. It would be all right. How could she doubt everything would work out when she knew how much she meant to him?

"Yes," she said, "to both."

His laughter rumbled beneath his cheek. "Good, that's settled. Now I can sleep. You didn't exactly say that before."

"I didn't?"

"No, Mrs. Townsend-to-be, you didn't. Emily Townsend, I like the sound of that, don't you? Unless you want to keep your own name, that is." She heard a hint of anxiety enter his voice.

"Townsend is a lovely name. Mrs. Townsend sounds great. Go to sleep, Sean."

"Yes, ma'am." He turned her over and curled around her back, cupping one of her breasts. "Now everything's settled I'll definitely sleep."

Emily lay very still. Soon she heard his breathing become slow and regular. He was sleeping. She expected to watch the night sky turn to dawn.

Tomorrow, when they got home, she'd make him listen to her story and she'd make him understand and accept.

She was cold but didn't dare risk waking Sean by reaching for the covers.

Surely she could make him understand.

Yet she kept thinking of something he'd said.

His family was into respectability.

Chapter Fourteen

Cabrini hadn't grumbled when Sean roused him at two in the morning and asked him to weigh anchor and head in. He uttered not a word when Sean used the ship-to-shore radio, choosing to send his message to Frank Horton rather than a member of his own household. But there had been a suspicion of a glint in the old skipper's usually expressionless eyes when Sean turned to leave the bridge. Cabrini had smiled at him then. Obviously, Wendy had recounted their earlier conversation and what he'd said over the radio had filled in any gaps in her story.

Now it was almost six. They hadn't covered a large distance yesterday and within an hour or so Marina del Rey should be in sight. He'd better wake Emily. This day promised to be busy and she would need some time to get ready for all he had planned.

He looked down at her for a long time. He was never going to get tired of looking at her. The sheet was pulled up to her chin and wound about her long, slender body. She sighed and turned, throwing one arm over her head, letting the other hang from the side of the bed.

Sean sat beside her, lifting the hanging hand and holding it between his own. "Emily," he said softly. When she didn't stir, he kicked off his shoes and stretched out beside her, nuzzling her neck, pulling down the sheet a little to plant small kisses across her shoulders and the tops of her breasts.

Her fingers in his hair, pulling his face up, stopped him. She gave him a sleepy, droopy-eyed stare, then rolled him over and kissed his mouth.

Within seconds Sean felt his arousal, full and strong and he closed his mouth tightly, breathing through his nose, while he pushed Emily away and held her straying hands over her head. The sheet was now draped around her hips and he kissed each breast, smiled when she arched toward him and tried to free her hands.

"We're about an hour from Marina del Rey," he said in a thick voice that didn't sound like his own. "I think we'd better stop while I still can."

Emily became still. "What? How can we be?" She squinted at the porthole. "When did we weigh anchor?"

"Around two."

"Why?"

"Because I'm an impatient man. I looked at you sleeping there and decided I didn't want to spend many nights without having you beside me from now on. So I hauled Cabrini out of his bunk and we started in."

He had let go of her wrists and she pulled the covers up again. "We're going to rush right into this, Sean? You're sure?"

"I've never been more sure of anything. By my figuring, we should be able to get married within a couple of weeks, three at the most. But there's a fair amount to be done and we've got to get started."

She looked panicky. He'd seen that in her before and it worried him. He still believed that sweeping her along fast was the best way to get over any misgivings she had, but he was going to have to be careful not to overwhelm her.

"Get dressed, Emily," he said, smiling reassuringly. "I've put Frank Horton onto some preliminary stuff. He's a rock and so is his wife."

"Who's Frank Horton?" Emily's voice was small and shaky.

"My vice president. Actually, he's almost the other half of Townsend Alarms. I don't often make a move without talking to Frank about it."

"Sean, it's only six in the morning. Didn't this Frank Horton think it was funny, you calling him so early."

"I called him at two, and once he stopped calling me names he told me how glad he was for us."

She pulled her knees to her chest and pushed a hand into her hair. "What was he supposed to do at two in the morning?"

"Call my mother in Miami, then get back to me with her answer."

"Answer to what?"

"How soon she could get here."

"So when we get back, Frank will have spoken to your mother." Her eyes were huge, so dark they were more black than blue.

"He already spoke to her and called me back. I'd have had him contact your folks, but I don't know where they live or anything and I thought you might rather do that yourself."

She scrambled to the edge of the bed, letting the sheet slip away. With difficulty, he kept his attention on her face. "I should send another message and ask Frank to call them, if you like."

"No, no thank you. I'll do that myself in my own way." He saw her swallow. "I told you we haven't spoken for a while, several years actually. I'm going to need to ease into this with them."

"But they will be happy for you? They will want to come?"

"Well..." Her shoulders came up, then she gave him a tight little smile. "I think they'll be happy."

"Where do they live?"

"Ah...Boston."

He nodded, laughing, "I knew there was something I should be catching about your accent. Boston, of course."

"Sean, when will your mother come out here?"

"She'll arrive at—" he checked his watch "—oh, late this afternoon, I guess. Her travel agent was going to get her on the first available flight and then her housekeeper will let me know." His stomach made turns. The excitement he felt was a crazy, intoxicating thing. "Mother sent you her love and said she's looking forward to meeting you at dinner tonight. Now, lady, move it."

"ARE YOU SURE you know what you're doing?" Larry, almost a fixture in the office these days, wrung his hands together. "I mean, I saw the guy at that murder party and he seems...solid? Is he solid?"

"He's solid," Emily said but she looked at Joe who stood with his back to her, staring up toward the high little window behind the desk.

Larry began to pace. "Why didn't you let on that you were really serious about someone?"

"Hey." She looked at him, frowning, irritation growing. "Let's get one or two things straight here. One, you aren't my father or my keeper. Neither is he." She pointed at Joe's ramrod-straight back. Joe had said nothing since she walked in and made her announcement. "Two, nothing stays the same. It's been a lot of fun sharing part of my life with you two, but we all know we're going to move on in our different ways. We want that, don't we?"

"I guess," Larry said, his face almost haggard.

Emily couldn't understand the intensity of his reaction. "Don't you want to become a famous actor? When that happens and you get an offer to perform with the Royal Shakespeare Company in England, won't you go? And if you met a woman you wanted to marry, wouldn't that be just as much your decision to make as it's mine to marry Sean?"

He let out a gusty sigh. "Yes, on all counts. It's just that I kind of worry about you. I guess I always will even though you probably don't need my concern. In a way you became the sister I left behind. Look, be happy, okay. That's all I want for you."

"I'll try."

"You won't have to try so hard, will you, Emily?" Joe turned as he spoke and his face was set in hard lines.

Emily took a step backward. "Probably not. I'm marrying a man I love."

"A rich man. A man who'll give you the easy life without you having to work for it. Boy, I bet you can hardly wait to brush our dust behind you."

Now she understood. Before she'd only guessed, but now she knew without any doubt that Joe believed he needed her to carry on the business and assumed that her marriage meant she'd be dropping out.

"Joe," she began with far more patience than she felt, "I won't be able to give as much time to the business as I have, but I'm not dropping out immediately. I wouldn't do that to you."

His laugh was mirthless. "Don't do me any favors. Anyway, I can't see Mr. Golden putting up with his wife carrying trays of hors d'oeuvres at his friends' homes. Leading games for their kids' birthday parties."

"Damn it, Joe. You call Sean Mr. Golden one more time and so help me—"

"You'll do what?"

This day had been more than she could cope with and it wasn't over. She wasn't taking any more from Joe Moreno. "I came in here to announce my engagement. I expected a little enthusiasm. Instead I get Larry's worry, worry act. And all you can think of is whether or not you're going to lose out. Larry I understand. I truly believe he cares what happens to me. But not you, Joe. We're friends and I hope we always will be. But there are sides of you that aren't so sweet."

"And you're perfect?"

"Hey, you two—"

Emily cut Larry off, "I'm not perfect. Who is? But I don't deserve this. I'm *not* abandoning the Occasion People. Got it? I'll just have to cut back the hours I put in here. Larry's ready to take on more. It should all work out."

As she finished speaking she knew she was wrong. Larry wasn't the answer to the problems that would arise once she was partly out of the business. They'd have to find someone else with skills similar to her own. And the time would come when she'd be unable to remain involved at all, when Sean needed her more for other things, like taking care of their children...

"I'm leaving," she said abruptly. Obviously, there would be no opportunity for her to have a private talk with Sean before they met his mother for dinner. There was shopping to do, a dress to be bought. She didn't have anything suitable to wear.

"Emily," Larry said. He put an arm around her and hugged her quickly. "I'm glad for you. And so's Joe, aren't you, Joe?"

Good old Larry. Always the peacemaker, Emily thought.

Joe managed an unconvincing smile. "Sure, I'm glad for you. You took me by surprise, that's all. Anything I can do to help, let me know. Like give away the bride or something."

Emily's heart softened instantly and she covered the distance between them in two rapid steps. "Thanks, friend. There may be something very important you can do, like hold my hand if I get the jitters. I haven't had... any experience at this type of thing." She'd almost said that she hadn't had *much* experience. "Anyway, could you two hold the fort for the rest of the day so I can buy something better than the rags I've got in my closet? I think I should be presentable the first time I meet my mother-in-law-to-be, don't you?"

The two men murmured assent and Emily grabbed her purse. Outside the door she paused, waiting to hear if Larry and Joe would immediately start talking, but there was only silence. She still had hurdles to cross with those two.

EMILY HAD BEEN to Jimmy's before, to discuss party arrangements for a client. Tonight, on the drive from Overland Avenue, she had insisted on sitting in the Jensen's narrow back seat while Gladys Townsend sat beside Sean. As they swung into the restaurant's narrow forecourt off Moreno Drive, Emily wished she were behind the wheel of her beloved little Fiat and on her way to do something as simple as arrange someone else's party.

Sean put the car in park, but left the engine idling. He got out, nodded to the valet, and came around to open the passenger door. His mother, a spry, tanned, carefully coiffed gray-haired woman, took his hand and got out of the car easily. Sean reached in to help Emily and she gripped him so tightly, she was ashamed. He'd feel the moisture on her palm and know she was terrified.

He leaned into the car and kissed her cheek. "Cool it," he whispered. "She's as nervous as you are and you're going to get along fine." He shook her hand firmly, then supported her elbow as she got out.

"I don't remember this place, Sean," Gladys Townsend was saying. "Are you sure it's all right?"

Sean threw up his hands in an exasperated gesture. "Women! You're all the same. You worry and worry. You told me to choose the place, Mother, and I did. Jimmy's is first class. Take it from me."

Emily considered backing him up but changed her mind. She didn't know how much Gladys had been told about the Occasion People, or how she might feel about the subject.

The maître d' showed them to a secluded table in a sunken area of the restaurant. Emily liked the heavy use of green, in carpets, plush chairseats, and the profusion of plants. Voices around them rose and ebbed, and there was soft music, but the sounds didn't intrude.

Gladys Townsend smoothed the skirt of her simple black suit and put her little purse on the table. "This is nice, Sean. I think I even remember coming here, but it must have been a long time ago."

"Dad probably brought you."

Emily half heard the conversation between mother and son. The midnight-blue Halston dress she wore was backless, the bodice a triangle of silk caught into a wide band around her throat, wrapped about her waist and disappearing at the center of the back into the waistband of a slim skirt. Looking at Gladys Townsend's understated suit, Emily was convinced her own choice for the evening had been a mistake, too flashy, provocative even. She must remember to sit straight. The low cut beneath her arms would reveal the sides of her breasts if she weren't careful. A bra had been out of the question. Yes, she'd made a mistake. She should never have listened to the salesperson who convinced her the dress was perfect. Her breasts were too full for a braless anything. How could she have been so stupid? What would Sean's mother think?

"Are you okay, Emily?"

She started at the sound of Sean speaking her name. "Fine. Wonderful." Crumpling her napkin in her lap, she smiled winningly at Gladys Townsend. "You must be so tired, Mrs. Townsend. This impetuous son of yours never seems to wear down and he expects everyone else to have his kind of energy."

Instantly, she blushed. Would the woman think she was making some sexual innuendo?

"He's like his father, thank God. But I'm not tired. I'm too excited to be tired. I knew this would happen one day but I was beginning to wonder just how long it would take. Please call me Gladys, Emily. I'd like that if you're comfortable with it."

Emily felt as if every muscle in her body had relaxed at the same time. Relief made her want to laugh. "Gladys," she said. "Thank you, I'd like to call you that. But can I ask you something?"

She felt Sean staring at her hard but didn't look at him. "How do you feel about Sean and me getting married so quickly? I mean, are you comfortable with the rush or would you rather have a little more time to get to know me?"

Sean lifted her hand on top of the table and held it tightly. He said to his mother, "Do you see why I fell for this woman? She doesn't know how to be anything but direct. She reminds me of you in a way, Mom, honest to a fault. I bet that's the type of thing you'd have said to Dad's folks."

Gladys chuckled. "I was eighteen when I met your father. The day I first saw his parents he warned me they were demanding and would ask a lot of questions. I never got a chance to ask any. They didn't even wait for answers to their own before they piled on more. I was terrified." She turned to Emily, "But to answer your question, Sean isn't a child. He's a man and I trust his taste, in all things. Knowing what he sees in you physically doesn't take a crystal ball. You're absolutely beautiful. I don't know you as a person yet, but I'm sure he does and that you're worth knowing. I'm happy to take all the time it takes to become your friend and it seems to me that I have the best chance of making a good job of getting close to you with you as Sean's wife."

Emily couldn't reply. She searched for a Kleenex and couldn't find one. Sean handed her his handkerchief and they all laughed when Gladys did manage to produce a tissue from her minuscule purse. She waved it in the air, moisture glistening in her eyes. "I always come prepared."

They ate slowly, drank little, talked in spurts punctuated by long silences. Sean sent a hundred glances in Emily's direction, all of them carrying a love so deep she ached with happiness.

When the waiter brought liqueurs, Gladys put her hand on Sean's wrist as he was about to drink. "There's something I'd like to do, if you'll let me."

Emily looked from one to the other, suddenly feeling like an outsider.

Slowly, Gladys pulled off the magnificent sapphire and diamond ring from the fourth finger of her left hand. She handed the ring to Sean who stared at it. His face had paled beneath his tan.

"You know what I want you to do, Sean?"

He nodded. "Are you sure?"

"I've never been more sure. This is all I need now." Gladys touched her simple platinum wedding band. "I always loved my engagement ring and I'll love it even more when it's on your wife's hand. It'll go with those eyes of hers."

Sean looked into Emily's face. She had never seen him so serious. He reached for her hand and she let him slide on the ring.

"It's beautiful." Turning her hand, she held it up for Gladys to see. "Thank you. I don't know what else to say."

Gladys dabbed at the corners of her eyes. "Your face says it all," she said. "And so does Sean's. I'm so glad he's found you. Now—" she pushed the Kleenex back into her purse "—let's get serious. I've already spoken to Frank Horton's wife. Sean, she's a woman after my own heart, a doer. And, of course, Sekowsky's always armed for battle; Zig too. We're going to pull off an engagement party tomorrow night. Everything's in motion and it's my party. I don't mean *my* party, just that I'm giving it."

Emily opened her mouth to protest but Sean was faster. "Tomorrow, mother? We weren't even thinking of having an engagement party, but tomorrow? That's not possible."

"You watch me," Gladys said, folding her hands on the tablecloth. "Will you be married at the house?"

"I'm not sure," Sean said.

Emily's mind was still reeling. An engagement party. And she hadn't even told Sean who he was really getting ready to marry.

"What do you think, Emily?" Sean asked tentatively.

"I . . . I'd like to be married in church."

His delighted smile swept away some of her misgivings. "Me, too. I guess we never discussed things like that."

"We haven't discussed a lot of things, Sean," Emily said and her throat seemed to close completely.

"Well, you'll have about three weeks to discuss whatever you want to discuss," Gladys interjected. "It'll take at least that long to arrange a church wedding. But between today and tomorrow night none of us will have time to discuss much of anything."

"Like mother, like son," Emily said and immediately made a wry face. "Sorry, I just meant you're both impetuous and determined."

"We certainly are," Gladys agreed. "Sean tells me your parents live in Boston and that you aren't close, so I decided to go ahead with this. You don't mind, do you?"

What could she say? "I don't mind. I think it's lovely of you."

"Well, that's that, then. And now I am tired."

Outside, the fresh air, laced with a sprinkling of rain, felt good. Emily raised her face to the sky while they waited for the car to be brought.

She watched a couple leave the restaurant and almost dropped her purse. Instead, she clutched it to her chest.

Flattened against a wall, just far enough away for her not to be able to see his face, was a tall man in dark clothing, a cap pulled so low on his head that his face was a shadow. Him.

Emily glanced back at Sean, then at the man. He could just be passing . . . he wasn't just passing by. He was watching them. She took a step in his direction and he immediately moved, turning away, pulling up the collar on his coat or jacket, she couldn't make out clearly.

"Here we go." The car had arrived and Sean's hand closed on her elbow to steer her into the back seat.

Once inside, she craned around to look for the man. He'd gone.

Sean and his mother got into the the car and they pulled smoothly onto the main highway.

Emily looked back and saw nothing but darkness in the alley beside Jimmy's.

"I'll drop you off first, Emily," Sean said. "Then I'll pick you up in time for the party tomorrow. What time *is* this party, mother?" There was laughter in his voice.

"Eight. And it'll be long and lavish," Gladys responded matter-of-factly.

Emily didn't feel like laughing. What if that crazy man who was following her decided Sean was a threat to whatever he had in mind? She had become this stranger's obsession, that was certain.

She huddled down in the seat. Before the party she'd make sure to talk to Sean . . . about a lot of things.

Chapter Fifteen

Emily didn't get her quiet moments with Sean before the engagement party.

At six forty-five she left her bedroom and walked, carrying black moiré pumps, into the living room. Larry's and Joe's reactions were unexpected and they made her start.

"Wow." Larry had been drinking Coke and he held his glass in midair.

Joe gave a low whistle. "I'd better check our bank account, lady. You didn't get that number at the Salvation Army thrift shop."

"Thank you." Emily was too nervous to smile. "I'll take *both* comments as compliments. And you don't have to check the bank balance, Joe. Remember, I don't spend much normally."

He would have no way of knowing that her "little black nothing" from C. Notti in Beverly Hills cost more than she took out of the business in a year.

"By the way—" she gave each man a slow once-over "—where are you two going? Tuxes? Larry, this is a new side of you—Larry the fashion plate." He wore very formal evening dress, a three-piece suit with satin lapels and a shirt with a wing collar. His tie was the one nonconformist touch. Large and blindingly crimson against a plain-fronted white shirt, it made her smile. "I love the tie, Larry."

He looked self-conscious. "I thought it ... *did* something for me."

"It does." She went to stand close to him. In an angular, fine-boned way, Larry was a very attractive man.

"You'd better hope his tie doesn't whistle and do wheelies."

Emily hadn't forgotten Joe. She knew he was there and that he also wore a beautifully cut evening suit, but with a black tie and a black satin cummerbund that accentuated his narrow waist. She also hadn't quite forgotten some of the barbs he'd thrown at her the day before and a suggestion of awkwardness had remained between them ever since. She turned to him.

A vaguely wounded expression made his dark eyes opaque. "Oh, Joe." She couldn't stay angry with him. Dropping her shoes, she went to embrace him. "You look marvelous. I really appreciate the send-off. But you'd both better have somewhere spectacular to go tonight, with someone wonderful. You're both too good to waste."

Joe held her loosely by the shoulders. "I don't think I've ever seen you in black before. You look sexy as hell. But I guess you know that."

Uneasiness crept up her spine. She hadn't imagined it, there was something different about Joe. "Thanks again," she said evenly.

"Emily, Gladys Townsend called."

She heard discomfort in Larry's voice. He was unnerved by Joe's behavior too. "She did? When?"

"Just after you left this morning. She said Sean knew you would want Joe and me at the party this evening." He smiled and looked at the toes of his patent shoes. "She insisted Sean was right, so we accepted and headed for the closest tux rental place. Don't worry, the tie's tame. I got it because I liked it, but there's a black one, too, so I'll change it if it'll make you feel better."

"I love the one you're wearing. And I'm glad you're both coming. I should have thought of it myself, but I think I'm walking around in a kind of daze." She felt ashamed for forgetting Joe and Larry. "Sean was coming to get me, but Gladys wants to send a limousine. More romantic, she says, with Sean waiting for me at the house. I think she's having more fun with this than any of us."

"She sounds decent," Larry said.

Joe mumbled something indistinct, then smiled brightly and said, "She's probably okay, Em. And you're going to need her with the kind of scene you're getting into. I'm sure she'll keep you straight in the etiquette department."

Emily wrinkled her nose. "I'm trying not to think too much about Sean's social life," she said and added impulsively, "let's all go in the limousine. The intrepid trio. You two have seen me through a lot, and I sure need some support tonight. Will you come with me?"

Larry and Joe looked at each other and Joe grinned suddenly, the old, wicked smile she loved. "I think we'll pass. We'd look like a couple of overgrown bridesmaids. But don't worry, kiddo. We won't cut out until we hear your car coming. Okay if we use the Fiat?"

"Keys are on the desk," Emily said.

How many times had she dressed for a party, a ball, some big bash at her parents' club? In all the years of being "part of the crowd," she had never felt the fear she felt tonight. When she had left Boston it had been with the unspoken resolve never to reenter any kind of social whirlpool, yet here she was, poised over that rushing water again and she couldn't step back, not when stepping back would mean she had to leave Sean.

She took a slow breath. A long-sleeved beaded-lace overlay reached the waistline of her strapless silk dress. The skirt was slim, mid-calf-length. At each ankle of her black hose a line of minute jet beads started, ending just below the hem of the dress.

"You look lovely, Emily."

Larry's voice startled her. She smoothed her skirt. "Thank you. I'm scared." Somehow she was going to have

to control her nerves and stop jumping every time someone spoke.

"It shows," he said gently. "But it's sweet. You aren't
like the people here, Emily, not tough and glittery. Sean
Townsend isn't just a lucky man. He's got a good eye for
something worth having."

She couldn't say anything for a moment. If she did, she'd
cry.

"He's right," Joe said. "And I think I hear the limo.
Thank God. We'll all be bawling if we stay here much
longer. See you later." He left the room, swinging her car
keys on an index finger and with Larry close behind.

The next half-hour was a blur for Emily. Seated in the
sleek black car she tried to order her thoughts and failed
completely. She fingered her earrings, the diamonds Sean
had given her, and looked at the beautiful sapphire ring,
still so foreign. Her fingers were long, slender and well-
kept, and she'd gotten into the habit of filing her nails
short. But tonight she wished they were long enough to
paint.

Too soon the car turned up Sunset Plaza Drive. Hardly
noticing the incline, Emily moved to the edge of the big,
lonely seat and held herself in place by gripping the leather
strap above the door. The car's tinted windows made the
houses, flowers and trees they passed seem smoky and dis-
torted.

The gates to Sean's house stood open. Cars were parked
outside and in every available space beside the driveway and
around the house.

Now was not the time to throw up. Emily swallowed
hard. Of course, Gladys was a showwoman in her own way.
She'd arranged for the guests to arrive first so that she,
Emily, would enter with Sean. She closed her eyes and remembered one of Grandmother James's instructions. *Always enter a room as if everyone else is waiting for you and
you're glad they are. You are beautiful and charming and
good. Whenever you feel unsure, repeat those words.* Em-

ily wasn't adept at patting her own back, but as the car swept to a halt in front of the curved white steps leading to the front door, she whispered, "You are beautiful and charming and good." Then she added, "And you are loved by the man you love." She picked up her purse and smiled.

The chauffeur didn't move.

Emily looked through the window and saw that rather than the crush of people she'd half expected on the steps, only one figure stood there.

Sean walked quickly down to the driveway, pulling his white shirtcuffs below the sleeves of his dinner jacket. He paused there, and even through the darkened glass, Emily saw his expression, a mixture of apprehension and anticipation. She took yet another deep breath. She loved him for that, too, that he was, beneath his self-assured manner, still a vulnerable man.

He opened the door and bent toward her. His appraisal was quick, his smile instant and wonderfully wide. Emily looked at his mouth and thought of the first time she'd noticed how beautiful it was, in that dark scary complex, in the middle of the night, how long ago? A long time, or was it only yesterday? Nothing seemed real.

"Are you ready, sweetheart?" he asked softly.

"I think so."

He helped her from the car, but stood between her and the house as if shielding her. "Mother has really gone all out, Emily." Gently, he kissed her cheek, then lifted the hand that bore his ring. "I know you aren't into being the center of things, but tonight is definitely your night and, darling, you look the part. I'm so proud of you. If it seems too much just hold on to me. Okay?"

"Okay. I'll do that." She moved far enough away to take in his stark white tucked shirt and black tie, the perfect fit of his suit. "Sean, I am *terrified*. So I hope you don't bruise easily."

He put her hand between his upper arm and his chest, covered her fingers with his own and said, "Let's do it.

You'll recognize a lot of the people. Jean Horton and Zig worked pretty much with the list from the murder party. There are a lot of additions, of course, old friends of the family, and so on." They mounted the steps. "This is definitely my mother's show, too, but she means well."

"I like her," Emily said as they entered the foyer.

Anything else she might have said was forgotten. The applause was sporadic at first, then slowly built to a sharply echoing roar.

Sean walked firmly to the center of the Italian marble floor and waited for the noise to subside. His fingers were intertwined with Emily's now, so tightly they hurt but she hardly noticed. All about them was a haze of brilliant color—the women's dresses and the flowers everywhere—contrasting sharply with the austere black and white of the men's clothes.

Gladys Townsend hurried forward, beaming, and stood beside Emily. She waved for silence. "People," she said in a loud voice, "People!" And Emily was reminded of a theatrical production with the producer calling his cast to order.

A hush fell, broken by the rustle of expensive fabrics.

"People," Gladys repeated. "Sean and Emily and I wanted to share this evening with you. Of course, you all know why we're here and later we'll have the good old-fashioned toasts, but before we even start our party I want to present my son, Sean Townsend, and Emily Smith, the future Emily Townsend."

She reached up to kiss Emily, then Sean, and the applause broke out again, louder this time, and from then on the evening became a magical time with Emily feeling suspended in a shimmering bubble with Sean. They floated amidst groups of smiling, admiring people. She was kissed by men and women she didn't know and liked it. Sean's arm was constantly around her shoulders. They drank champagne, ate nameless delicacies that appeared in front of them on silver trays, and moved on.

Once Emily saw Joe deep in conversation with a very young woman whose hair was an overwhelming dark mass about her pale face. They walked slowly out to the terrace and Emily didn't see them again. *Be happy for me, Joe*, she wanted to say, but then an elderly man, quite bald, with a vulpine face, blocked her view of the doors and she was forced to concentrate on more small talk about things she didn't understand. This was Jacques Gaultier, once a competitor of Charles Townsend, now the clearly disgruntled first runner-up to Charles Townsend's son in the security systems business.

"Ah!" Emily said suddenly, "Charles, of course."

Sean inclined his head to her. "What, darling?"

She blushed. But she needn't have felt embarrassed. Gaultier was more interested in her cleavage, shadowy beneath the lace overblouse, than in anything she said. She leaned to whisper in Sean's ear. "*Charles*. Sorry about that. I never knew your father's name was Charles." She thought briefly of another Charles, but only briefly.

"So?" Sean whispered back.

"Just something silly. On the desk in the room you had carved your initials. SCT. I meant to ask you what the C was for, now I think I know."

"Brilliant." He kissed her lips as if there weren't a hundred people milling around them.

Emily refocused on Gaultier with difficulty. His thoughts were almost visible and they had little to do with business. At the moment his libido was working overtime.

"There you are, Jacques." A florid, breathless woman, tastefully dressed in a dark blue dress that made the best of her overly ample figure, descended upon them. "Monopolizing Sean with business, as usual, I suppose. I'm Yvonne Gaultier." She smiled at Emily and said to Sean, "She's lovely, dear. But that doesn't surprise me. You always had good taste."

Gaultier scowled. "Yvonne, we should circulate."

"Has he been pumping you about the latest in the trade?" Yvonne giggled and looked surprisingly young when she did. "He tried Frank Horton and didn't get anywhere, as usual. But he's convinced you're on to something new and wonderful—"

"Congratulations to both of you," Gaultier broke in and shepherded his wife none too gently away.

Emily looked questioningly at Sean. "What was all that about?"

He grinned. "Word travels fast in my business, just like any other. Frank and I are working on something a bit different for us—security systems for penal institutions—and we've had to make some enquiries in areas that are bound to give away what we're after before too long. Good old Jacques has gotten wind of what we're doing, I expect."

"Sounds fascinating." She clasped his arm. His telling her of what must be a highly classified business project warmed Emily. She looked past his shoulder and pressed his arm harder. "Sean, look at Red."

He turned around and laughed. "If you weren't here she'd have a good shot at holding all the male attention in the room, wouldn't she?"

"Yes, but that's not what I mean. Look who she's with."

Sean frowned. "Do I know him? He looks familiar, but I don't think...did they come together? That awful tie's the same color as her dress."

"They didn't come together." Emily slipped her arms beneath Sean's and they swayed to the music that had been playing in the background all evening. "That's Larry Young, my housemate."

"Not for long."

"No," she agreed, "not for long. But, Sean, they're positively all over each other." Larry and Red were also dancing, Red in a strapless knock-'em-dead red taffeta dress. This was a side of Larry that Emily had never seen before and she loved it.

Sean swung her around so that he could see again. "Hmmm. Didn't you say he was the quiet type? Usually either working or reading lines for some part or other?"

"It's true."

"He doesn't seem to need any practice for the part he's into now."

"Sean," Emily said, pulling away to see his face. "You sound as if you don't approve. She couldn't meet a nicer man than Larry and don't worry, he doesn't have a cent, so she probably won't see him again after tonight."

"Don't bet on it. He'll probably drop one of his glass slippers on the steps when he rushes out of here, correctly deducing that Red was always a soft touch for underdogs."

Emily thought about that for a moment. "Sounds good to me. They've got a lot in common. Theater, I mean. They might be good for each other. By the way, I forgot to say how much I like Frank Horton and Jean."

"They like you. But I knew they would."

"Sean! Emily! Over here, look over here."

At the sound of Glady's raised voice they stopped dancing and turned.

A flashbulb went off, then another and another. Sean shook his head and held Emily closer. "That mother of mine. I might have guessed she really intended to make this an *event*."

Sean felt Emily twist in his arms. She strained around as if she intended to continue dancing. He looked at the row of photographers, then her. She was white. A gleam of perspiration stood out on her brow.

"Hey," he whispered urgently. "Turn around, will you, honey? They just want a few shots for the local rags and I expect mother's decided on a photo or two for posterity."

She didn't move. He shook her gently and put his mouth to her ear. "What *is* it, Emily, for God's sake? Everyone's looking at us. *Please*."

Slowly, her fingers digging painfully into his back through his jacket and shirt, she faced the cameras again.

"Smile," he said through gritted teeth.

More flashes. He saw the bright emblem of a national television station on the side of one camera and wondered how his mother had managed that. Then he saw the camera pan the room and remembered that he and Emily were far from being the best-known people in this room. He looked for Red and was pleased to see that Larry was nowhere in sight but that she was center front, leaning on the arm of one of Hollywood's *in* producers and smiling her best ingenue smile.

"Red's really on tonight," he said to Emily.

She didn't reply. He glanced at her and his gut suddenly felt heavy. Emily was smiling, that is, her mouth was fixed in a turned-up-at-the-corners position. But she stared straight ahead, her eyes glassy and where his hand rested on her shoulder he felt a steady tremor and a clamminess.

This wasn't her scene. Center stage was the one place she didn't want to be. Intense love for this gentle woman, the urge to protect her, overwhelmed Sean. "That's it," he shouted over the din. "That's it, fellas, and ladies. Thanks for coming." He tried to move toward the paparazzi, but Emily remained rooted where she was. His control broke. "Emily, knock it off, huh? Cooperate with me for a few seconds and I'll get these buzzards out of here. It's just their job and you'll have to get used to a photo now and then, maybe a few questions. It goes with the territory. Help me through this, will you?"

She stirred and met his eyes as if seeing him for the first time. Then she nodded and aimed a dazzling smile at the pushiest of the camera people.

He relaxed a little. A woman with a notebook forced herself in front of them. "Ms., ah, Smith?" She didn't wait for Emily to reply. "Could you tell us something about yourself? Sean's an old friend." She grinned at him and

Sean couldn't remember ever having seen her before. "Are you new in Los Angeles, Emily? May I call you Emily?"

"I've lived here for some years." The clarity of Emily's reply was a pleasant surprise to Sean. "And I mean to live here for good now."

He smiled at her and squeezed her arm. She'd be all right.

The woman asked several more questions and Emily answered each one in a steady voice.

An older reporter, a man, elbowed his way beside the woman. "What did you do before you came to L.A., Ms. Smith? Where are you from?"

Emily didn't answer.

"Are you from Boston?" the man persisted. "You sound as if you're from Boston."

"Emily is from Boston," Sean interjected, then added firmly, "and that's all you have to know, folks. We'll be sending announcements to the appropriate columns. Help yourselves to champagne on the way out."

The voice he used announced that the picture-taking and question-and-answer session was over, and the camera people and reporters melted into the crowd. The music, which had been lowered, became loud again.

"Sorry, darling," he said to Emily. "Want to dance some more?"

"Yes." She leaned heavily against him, her face beneath his chin, and he knew her eyes were closed. "Forgive me for being such a wimp about that," she said, "but I have a thing about cameras, Sean. I hate the things."

"Good."

"What?" She looked up at him sharply. "Why good?"

"Because it means I'll never have to worry about some movie magnate sweeping you away because you decided you want to become a star. And the way you look, my love, that would not be unlikely. In fact, I'm going to have to be constantly on guard."

"No, you're not. Sean, can we go somewhere quiet, for a while, just the two of us?"

There was nothing he'd like more than to be somewhere, anywhere, alone with Emily, but he couldn't do that to his mother, or to all these people. "When everyone leaves, darling. Can you hold out until then?"

"I don't . . . I really need to talk to you, Sean."

"Emily! Sean!" Gladys Townsend's voice rang out again. "Toasts, darlings."

Emily felt as if she were moving through deep water, her arms and legs dragging. The toasts were made, endless toasts, to Emily and Sean, to people who made toasts. More champagne was brought, and then a beautiful pale pink cake shaped like a heart with satellite hearts, encrusted on all sides with crystallized strawberries.

Then the music swelled yet again and the crowd spread out. Emily went into Sean's arms and noticed he was beginning to look almost as tired as she felt.

They swayed together, until Emily couldn't contain her desperation any longer. "Sean, take me out of here," she said and stopped moving.

"Just a little while . . . oh, no. Mother strikes again. Will you look at this?"

Emily looked in the direction Sean indicated and saw a winding procession of mimes threading a path through the guests. Her body felt boneless. She didn't know how much more tension she could bear. She *must* talk to Sean.

A man in classic white-face, his hair oiled into spikes, two vertical black lines sweeping from his cheekbones through each eye to his brow, sprang in front of her and crouched. *Hold on*, she told herself. She was strong, she could make it, and when this madness was over she'd refuse to let Sean leave her until he knew the whole truth about her.

"He's good," Sean said quietly and she concentrated on the mime.

He hunched over, then gradually, incredibly slowly, straightened, feeling his way up an invisible wall in front of Emily. Once on tiptoe, he pivoted, working, hand over hand, until he had delineated the imaginary box that surrounded him and returned to face Emily once more. She felt trembling begin and willed herself to be still. She was in a box too, but she'd get out, and soon.

"He wants you to copy him." Sean dropped his hand from her shoulders and she felt naked and alone.

Emily raised her hands until they were inches from the mime's, palms facing palms and she began to follow his motions, gaining confidence as she went, down, up, around, feeling the non-existent corners, and back to face him. The man bowed and retreated while Sean and those guests who had seen what happened applauded.

"Isn't this a crazy party?" Sean asked, as they stood side by side, watching the mimes work the room.

Gladys Townsend came and put a hand through Sean's elbow. "Aren't they wonderful? What made you think of mimes, darling?"

"Me?" Sean asked. "Come on, mother. You know I didn't arrange any of this, including the media."

"Well, I plead guilty there. The publicity will be good for the firm and anyway, mothers are entitled to show off their children a little. But honestly, Sean, I don't know a thing about the mimes."

Emily felt Sean stand straighter. She looked at his face. The cigarette smoke in the room was getting too strong for her; she had to squint. "What's wrong, Sean?"

"If mother didn't arrange for the mimes and neither did I, who did? Sekowsky and Zig had enough to do with getting the flowers and the food together. They wouldn't think of entertainment, not this kind, anyway."

"Well, someone must have," Gladys said, her face smoothly unconcerned.

"But, I want—"

Sekowsky, tapping Sean's arm, stopped him in mid-sentence. "Mr. Sean, do you have a key to your wing?" she asked in a low voice. "The door must have swung closed with the key inside and there isn't a spare on the servants' board."

Sean felt through his pockets. "I'm not sure I put them...we're in luck." He produced a key ring and handed it to the housekeeper. "You know which one it is."

As soon as Sekowsky had left, Sean returned to the subject of the mimes and who had arranged for them to come. Emily barely stopped herself from announcing that she didn't care.

Gladys, looking as fresh as when the party had begun, shrugged and said, "I expect one of those incorrigible friends of yours sent them, Sean. As a gift."

"Maybe." Sean's puzzled expression cleared a little. "Yes, I bet that's it. Someone like Red."

A yell soared over the general babble. Emily scanned the room but no one else seemed to have noticed the cry. Everyone was watching as the mimes retreated, twirling, somersaulting and finally joining hands as they rushed into the night. Surely the guests would also start to leave soon.

The yell came again, this time wildly, and conversation lulled.

"What is it, Sean?" Emily said. "Something's wrong."

"Stay here. Mother, you stay too." He set off running toward his own wing, which had been opened for the evening to make more bathrooms available and more space for coats.

People gradually filtered into the big foyer with its soaring ceiling. Emily and Gladys went, too, and were met by Sean, white-faced and stiff-backed.

"I'm going to need all the help I can get," he said in a low voice. "Someone deliberately locked the door to my wing, then robbed us. Sekowsky discovered it just now. The paintings and special pieces are gone. But they took all the guests' stuff that was on my bed. Mostly furs, I think. I've called the police."

Bodies were pressing in on them. "I'm going to have to keep this lot under control until the police get here. Help me, please. No one should leave."

"I HOPE THEY ALL have insurance," Gladys said. Several hours had passed, the police had left and, finally, the last of the guests.

Sean sat on a couch in the little sitting room off his bedroom. He checked his watch. "Three o'clock. Jeez, it feels like it's got to be five at least. This has been the longest night of my life." Emily sat beside him and he rubbed the back of her hand. "The best and the worst night of my life."

Gladys, looking suddenly frail, sat on the edge of a small Victorian chair. "Notice what they didn't take?"

"No." Sean's voice was listless and Emily wished she could just hold him and make him forget what had happened.

"They knew their stuff," Gladys said, with a mirthless laugh. "They didn't take my fake screen."

Sean laughed too. "That's about all they didn't take. Anything that could be easily moved through the doors of my bedroom to the terrace is gone. I can't believe it. My games table. The paintings. My entire collection of Empire Waterford, it goes on and on. And they must have done it so fast. In and out. The bastards even took rugs."

"You have insurance," Gladys murmured.

"It won't replace the irreplaceable." Sean stood up and the couch bounced beneath Emily. "Come on, sweetheart. You've had enough for one night. We all have. Go to bed, Mom; I'll run Emily home." He tried to smile. "At least no one was hurt. It'll take me a few days, but I'll get over it. And I don't have time to sulk."

"No, you don't," Gladys agreed, getting to her feet. "We have a wedding to arrange."

EMILY SPENT THE NIGHT alone in the little house on Overland Avenue. Sean kissed her passionately in the car, clung
to her, but she felt his exhaustion and preoccupation and
said she thought the sooner he got back home and slept, the
better. He seemed grateful for the suggestion and the Jensen roared away as soon as she'd stepped inside the house.

She lay awake during early morning hours, the evening's events playing over and over in her mind. Occasionally she'd think about Larry, who, like Joe, failed to return
home. Surely Larry hadn't ended the night with Red. The
combination seemed so unlikely.

Sean.

So much for him to cope with so quickly. His friends and
acquaintances had been understanding, sympathetic. He
was not to worry. Insurance would take care of their losses
and furs could always be replaced. But Emily knew there
would be no replacing some of the things he'd treasured.
On top of that, he would have to know before they got
married—and he'd made it clear that he intended to go
ahead with their plans at once—he'd have to know that she
was not exactly the woman he'd thought her to be.

She watched pale light enter her bedroom, casting gray
shadows on the wall. Dawn was nearing, and finally giving
way to exhaustion, she slept.

The distant sound of the doorbell barely penetrated her
brain, but she heard it. Then she heard it again and again.
Whoever was there must be leaning against the button. She
sat up, wondering if she'd only imagined that she'd been
sleeping, but the room was brighter now and the clock beside her bed showed six-thirty.

The bell rang on and on.

Joe or Larry must be locked out. The new lock was a
good one and she'd probably shot home the new dead bolt
too. Without bothering to put on slippers, she stumbled
from the room, pulling on her white, embroidered cotton
robe. Her head was so fuzzy she rubbed at her eyes as if she
might somehow clear her brain.

"Coming," she said, fumbling with the bolt far too long. Finally she got it undone and opened the door.

The morning air hit her squarely in the face and she shuddered. "I forgot the . . ." She shot out a hand, beating away what faced her.

Sean, not Larry or Joe, stood on the doorstep. He held a newspaper in front of him, arranged to show a picture of her at his side at last night's party.

She read the words above the front-page spread: AND THE LADY SAID SHE WAS FROM BOSTON.

Sean folded the paper, pushed her hand aside and stepped into the hall. "There may be no point, but for what it's worth I think we should talk, *Sidonie*."

Chapter Sixteen

He would say what he had to say quickly. If he faltered, looked at her, really looked at her, he'd cave in and they'd both suffer. Sean didn't believe Emily, or Sidonie?—what was he supposed to call her?—had set out to deceive him. But she hadn't had the courage to tell him the truth about herself and leave him to decide what he did or didn't believe. That meant she didn't love him enough to trust him, and she had to if there was ever going to be anything more between them.

She was standing behind him in the shabby little sitting room with its mismatched furniture. Once he'd found it touching that she could be happy here. That angered him now. She'd been playing a game. The spoiled rich girl pretending to be something she wasn't while he made a fool of himself by telling her about new money and old money and how his was new. He'd told her about his grandparents and parents, the way they'd worked for what they had. And all the time she must have been laughing. The James money was so old it was probably coated with mildew and people of their kind never discussed money anyway, unless they were complaining about a supposed lack of it.

"Sidonie James," he said and walked behind the couch to stare unseeingly through the window. "It's kind of a nice name. What should I call you?"

"Emily."

Her voice cracked on the word.

Sean rocked onto his toes. "Why?" His head ached.

"Because that's who I am now, who I've been since I left Boston. I don't think of myself as Sidonie anymore."

God, she sounded as if she was going to cry. He felt as if *he* would cry. "Did you think there was even the remotest chance that we could get married and go through life without your real identity ever coming out?" Now he did look at her. "Or was that just another part of your little charade? The marriage? Did you ever intend to go through with marrying me?"

She nodded. Her face was scrubbed clean of last night's makeup and her pale skin had turned even paler, making her eyes appear huge and unblinking.

"Yes, what? Yes, you didn't think I'd ever find out you weren't who you said you were, or yes, you did intend to marry me?"

"Yes, I wanted to marry you," she whispered. Wrapping her robe tightly around her, she sat on a straight-backed chair. Her feet were bare and she placed them one on top of the other.

"But you didn't think you owed me the truth about all this?" He slapped the paper against his palm. This had been the first morning he remembered his coffee arriving without the newspaper. He'd almost had to pry the thing out of Sekowsky who had immediately started defending Emily. "Young people do things, Mr. Sean," she said as he started to read. "Then they grow up and all that silly stuff is behind them." Well, four and a half years ago, Sidonie James hadn't been so young that she'd been discounted as the possible cause of a man losing the things that mattered most in his life.

Emily hadn't replied to his last comment and when he looked at her he saw tears falling from her wide open eyes. That almost finished him. He turned his back on her again.

"I tried to tell you," she said and made a raw, choking sound.

"If you tried, why didn't you manage it? There have been enough opportunities."

"None of them seemed right, somehow."

"You didn't trust me." He threw the paper on the couch. "And you let me make a fool of myself over your little Miss Simplicity act. I'm not a a particularly proud man, Emily, but I am a man. No man likes to be treated like a fool."

"I didn't—"

"Yes, Emily, you did. Anyway, I can't spend any more time on this now. I've got more police reports to file and a lot of friends I should call."

She was sobbing now. He held his jaw rigid and narrowed his eyes against the tears he felt forming. Was she crying because he had found her out, or was she hurting, wanting him? How could he know? How could he believe anything she ever said again?

"Don't cry, please." He started for the door.

"Are you going to tell people we're not getting married?" She caught his hand as he passed and he stood still. "Are you? Is this the last time I'll see you, Sean?"

"I'm going to apologize to people who had things stolen at my house last night. I won't be discussing anything about you and me." He let out a draining sigh. "Can you believe it? You and I, and particularly all this stuff about you, made the front page. But some of the biggest celebrities in town lost enough furs to stock Bonwit's and that was only worth half a column on page nine."

"I'm sorry. But will I see you again?"

A few more seconds and he'd be taking her in his arms. He must not do that, not without knowing a whole lot more about this woman.

"We'll see each other again. We have a lot to settle." Reluctantly, he looked down at her. "You owe me a few things, like an apology for a start. If you can figure out a suitable apology for something like this, do it. Then I'd like you to put that fertile mind of yours to work on figuring out exactly what you do feel for me."

"I know what—"

"No, you don't." Pulling his hand from hers took more determination than he'd ever let her know. "If you did we wouldn't be having this conversation. I've got to go, Emily. Think about what I've said. Think about us."

She didn't try to stop him from leaving. After the front door closed she stayed where she was for a long time. The newspaper Sean had left lay crumpled on the couch. She didn't have to read what it said, she knew the words by heart, but she made herself get up, cross the room and pick it up.

Almost apathetically, she scanned the lines of print. Inset between columns was an old shot that was burned into her brain. So why did the woman in the picture look like someone she'd never known?

Sidonie James, the caption read, *photographed early this morning leaving the penthouse apartment of State Senate hopeful Mark Bates.* And beneath that the comment: *This was the photo taken of Miss James a few days before she disappeared from her Boston home over four years ago.* Then came the rest, all the innuendos, the false assumptions made because some political rival of Mark Bates, a man she'd hardly known, must have decided to gather enough dirt to make the road to Boston's State Senate a little less crowded.

Emily peered closely at the photo of herself looking startled, a suitcase held in both hands, with an equally shocked Mark Bates standing behind her in the doorway to his penthouse.

After a last long look at Sean's face, smiling proudly beside her in the photo taken last night, she threw the paper on the couch and crossed her arms. The old rage was burning again, the frustration, the exhausting sense of impotence that she'd been unable to make anyone who mattered believe that she hadn't been having an affair with Bates, a married man with four children. The press hadn't wanted to believe. Her friends had said they did, but the tempta-

tion to enjoy the scandal had been too great for them. Even
those partly responsible for her being at Bates's apartment,
where she'd hoped to get him to talk to her about stopping
the demolition of low-cost housing, even the most vocal of
those had become meek with nothing to say in her defense.

But what had hurt most of all had been her parents' reaction, their willingness to condemn without really listening to a word she had to say. *Their* daughter had disgraced
them. Once smeared, always smeared. Guilty or not, the
doubt would always remain. And wasn't Charles Hennessy a saint to agree to marry her regardless? And weren't
his parents saints to be so magnanimous when, after all,
they had no means of knowing how much truth had been
printed in the papers? On and on it went. Around and
around.

The combined James-Hennessy message had been: Give
up your little causes, Sidonie, if they really are what
brought about this mess, and disappear into the fold while
we can still hope to regain some respect. For two weeks
she'd thought about it. Then she made her decision. She
had done as suggested and disappeared—completely, as far
as her precious family were concerned.

Now she heard a key in the front door and whirled
around. Joe and Larry would soon know everything. But
she didn't want to face them now.

There was no escape. Footsteps sounded, then Joe stood
a few feet from her, still dressed in evening clothes that were
now badly rumpled. He was unshaven and looked as if he
hadn't slept in a week.

"Well, well, well," he said, slumping against the wall.
"Guess what I heard on the radio this morning?"

Emily pressed her fingers to her temples. Again. It was
all happening again.

"And all this time I thought I had a struggling soul mate
living with me. You might have told me, partner. I'd have
worried a whole lot less about money if I'd known I had a
real live heiress to rely on."

She stared at him. Someone else she'd failed to trust with the truth, but how could she have? "Joe, it wouldn't have worked if I'd told you who I was. When I answered your ad for a housemate all I was looking for was a place to disappear into."

"Yeah, I know. But you took it a lot farther, didn't you? You allowed me to give up my job and get into a business I couldn't have handled without you."

Slowly rising anger replaced the last traces of her tiredness. "I didn't *allow* you to do anything," she said icily. "The Occasion People was your idea. You told me you'd been thinking of something like this for years and all you needed was someone with a flair for knowing the right way to do things. I've been that person for you and we've done well. You've got a good start."

Joe dragged his already dangling tie from beneath his collar. "Okay, okay, I'll give you some of that. But what did you say just now? That I needed someone with flair and you were that person. I could never figure out how you understood all that stuff. Until this morning. You lived it, baby, didn't you? That's why you were so good at it."

She opened her mouth to tell him not to call her baby, but changed her mind. He was as angry as she was, and he did have some excuse to be. "Let's not argue about this. Why not look on the bright side? All this publicity is going to make the firm the most sought-after entertainment phenomenon in town for a while."

"Uh-uh."

"Why not? If you don't think it'll work with me as a part of it anymore, I understand. But that doesn't mean you can't be a success. Find someone else with very similar talents to mine and carry on." The guilt was sliding in again. "The business is in good shape, Joe. And I don't want anything from it. Look, use whatever I've got in the pot to make a little time, go slow for a while until you find the right person to work for you."

"And where are you going?" He rested his head against the wall and studied her narrowly. "The big question with the news people is, 'Will the little lady still marry the guy, or will he chuck her? And if he chucks her, is this the time she'll go running back to the family bosom?'"

"It's none of your damn business what I do." As soon as she'd said it, she covered her mouth and sat down once more. "I'm sorry. It's just that it all sounds so cold and mean and small. And I guess I'd hoped you might be a little bit worried about me, Joe. Not totally tied up with what's going to happen to you, but with me. We've been through a lot together."

"I don't even know you. Why would I worry about a woman I don't know?"

She had genuinely wounded him. "Joe," she said very softly, "you've known me better than almost anyone in my whole life. What difference does a name make? I had a lot of problems when I came to Los Angeles and all I wanted was to forget who I really was. In time I learned to think of myself as Emily Smith. As far as I'm concerned, I *am* Emily Smith."

He shrugged. "I've got to get this rented outfit back. The mess it's in, I'll probably have to buy the thing."

"Where were you all night?' she asked and immediately wished she hadn't.

His laughter made her cringe. "I've never made any secret of who or what I am. I was with a friend. Now, if you'll excuse me, I've got a lot to do."

Everyone had a lot to do—except her. All she had to do was wait for telephone calls from the press to start, for reporters to stake out the house, for the inevitable call from her parents, and maybe even Charles Hennessy.

Joe was still watching her and she met his eyes defiantly. "At least you know where you're going and what you're doing." Why couldn't he separate her, the woman he'd known, from the newspaper reports? "Joe, it's hard to explain how I feel. Hurt, I guess. You and I have made a good team. Why can't I carry on with you for a while? Sure, falling over reporters can get to be a pain, but I'm a big girl and the dust will settle. I don't know where I'm going from here. I suppose I'll just wait and see, like I had to all those years ago." She fell back and let the ceiling blur before her eyes. Emptiness was all she could see ahead. "Why can't I be left alone and allowed to get on with my life? What did I ever do to anyone else?"

"That seems to be a question that's up for grabs," Joe said tonelessly.

Emily leaped to her feet. "You can think what you like. I didn't do what they said I did and as long as I know it, the rest of you can go to hell! What I have to decide right now is what to do today, tomorrow. Do you want me to go on working with you until you find someone else?" Doing nothing, waiting, would be impossible.

"If I was staying I'd say yes, Emily."

"If?" She frowned, taking in what he was saying. "What do you mean, if? Where are you going?"

"I don't know yet. But I've had enough of being a glorified busboy—"

"You aren't a—"

"That's exactly what I am and I've had it. The whole ball of wax. The end. I'm moving on."

"But, but you can't. This house. Larry. For God's sake, Joe, the *business*. You can't give everything up."

He gave her a long stare that turned her stomach. "If Larry's so important to you, *you* think about his future. I'm selling up, buying some sort of rig and moving on. I've wanted to see Alaska for a long time. They say there's still big money to be made up there and I may give it a try."

She couldn't believe it. Joe, the guy who wanted a business and security. Joe, who wanted to be someone, was cutting out on the best thing he'd ever had. "You're reacting without thinking," she said desperately. "You've made a place for yourself here and in time you'll be a big success. I know you will."

"Decision's made. And you don't have to feel sorry. This was coming for me. I'm ready for a new challenge. We're paid up on rent through the end of the month. That's three weeks from now. You and Larry will both have gone wherever you're going by then. Or, if Larry wants to, he can try to find himself a couple of people to share this place. I can't worry about him, Emily. Don't hate me for that, it's just the way I am."

IN THE NEXT TWO DAYS Emily saw Joe twice. Each time he was polite but didn't want to talk.

Larry came and went, and surprised her with his lack of concern over his own future. His preoccupation seemed to be with her. What did she intend to do right now? He was persistent and sometimes short-tempered with her wishy-washy responses. She must know what she was going to do, he insisted. Had she heard from her family? No? Then why didn't she call them? And Sean? What about Sean? Emily began to avoid Larry.

As she had expected, reporters tried every avenue to get a story. And they showed no signs of backing off. She felt like a caged animal, the last of a species, only imprisoned behind walls rather than bars. She dared not ignore the phone in case Sean called.

Sean didn't call.

She heard nothing from her family.

On the second evening following the party, a silver Mercedes coupe drew up in front of the house. Larry ran down the short path, shrugging off reporters, and climbed into the passenger seat of the car. As it pulled away, Emily saw the license plate, RED ONE. She remembered what Sean had told her about Red VanEpson and underdogs. Larry would be just fine.

A few minutes after Larry left, Emily put on jeans, a plain T-shirt and running shoes and climbed out the kitchen window at the back of the house. She made it away without being seen. A taxi was cruising Pelham Avenue behind

Overland and within minutes, she was seated in the worn back seat heading for Sean's home. If he was out, she'd wait. If he was at the house, she would ask him to hear her out.

An irrational fear started inside her as the car neared the wrought-iron gates. He could simply refuse to let her in. She got out of the cab, paid the fare, and waited for the man to drive away. A witness to the humiliation of being spurned by Sean was more than she could countenance.

She needn't have worried. As soon as she announced her name the gates swung open and Sekowsky met her before she reached the steps to the front door.

"I'm so glad to see you, Emily," Sekowsky said, walking beside her toward the house. All trace of the reserve the woman had previously shown was gone. "He misses you."

Emily stopped. "He does? You're sure?" Her heart lightened a little.

Sekowsky's brown eyes slid away. "I'm sure. But he's not going to let down easily. He's going through the motions—the office, home, dinner, early to bed. And he says everything is okay, that everything is going to be fine. But he's not okay, Emily. He's all muddled up and I can't do a thing with him. Neither can Zig and even his mother's given up trying."

Emily had almost forgotten Gladys. "Is Mrs. Townsend here?" she asked tentatively.

"No." Sekowsky looked at her worn hands. "She said she had to go back to Miami to take care of some business. At least that's what she *said*."

"But you think there's more to it than that?" Emily looked closely into Sekowsky's face.

"I heard Mr. Sean tell her she should go," the woman said in a low voice. "He said there was nothing for her to do here now. But he did say there might be if things worked out," she added defiantly. "Go and see him. Make him understand whatever he has to understand."

"Where is he?"

"Back in that half-empty sitting room of his. He spends a lot of time roaming around looking at the spaces where his things used to be."

And she was one more space that he was trying to cope with. "Should you go and tell him I'm here?"

"I think you should just go and see him."

Emily did as Sekowsky suggested, walking silently in her soft-soled shoes, until she entered Sean's private wing and reached the closed door to his sitting room. Her heart was a leaping thing in her chest.

She knocked.

"Yes?"

The instinct for flight was strong but Emily opened the door, stepped inside and closed herself in with Sean.

Dressed in red-and-white striped Bermuda shorts and a short-sleeved purple shirt, unbuttoned and apparently unpressed, he lay flat on his back on the polished hardwood floor, a bedpillow under his head.

"Sean!" Emily was shocked. His hair stuck out in different directions and his feet were bare. "Are you sick?"

He turned his head to look at her, then closed his eyes. "I'm resting," he said. "And I never felt better. How are you?"

"Lousy," she replied honestly and stood over him. "Will you let me tell you a few things?"

A slight shake of his head turned her stomach. She breathed deeply. The little room was stuffy and she went to open the windows.

"Don't do that!"

Emily jumped. "Why? It's hot in here. You don't even have the air-conditioning on."

There was too much silence before he said, "I'm sorry. I'm being a boor. Open the windows if you want to. I don't like air-conditioning so there isn't any back here."

"I won't open them if—"

"Open the damn things, I said." He sat up.

"Yes, yes." The cranks that rotated the jalousies slipped ineffectually in her sweating palms. She shouldn't have come here.

"Let me do that."

Sean came and reached around her to turn the levers. He didn't touch her.

Emily's legs felt wobbly, and her arms, her whole body. "I should have called first, Sean. But I was afraid you might not speak to me if I did, or that you'd say you didn't want to see me."

He stayed where he was, at her side, looking at the early evening sky through the narrow gaps between slats of glass.

"Would you have told me not to come?" Emily turned to him.

"I don't know." His hands were in his pockets, the shirt hooked behind his wrists.

"That's what I thought." The sight of him, his closeness, light gilding the dark hair on his chest made Emily ache to lay her hands on him, ache to have him cover and surround her.

Sean slowly faced her. "You thought I wouldn't know whether or not I'd want to see you?"

"Yes."

"Have you wanted to see me?"

"Every minute of every hour, Sean. I've missed you so much."

"Mmmm." He patted her cheek absently, almost as if she were a child. "What have you been thinking about?"

"About you. And that I was wrong. I should have found a way to tell you everything. And I'm sorry, but it happened. It just happened. I didn't expect to get involved with you."

"Do people usually *expect* to get involved with each other?"

She felt the rapid rise and fall of her chest. "No. At least, I guess not."

He was watching her face intently now. "But we did get involved, very involved, and you still didn't let me completely inside your life."

"I was already too far in—"

"Too far in? You mean the lie was already too much in place to try to set it straight?"

His sigh hurt her.

"You muddle me up, Sean. I want to tell you exactly what happened in Boston."

"That's all you want to tell me? What happened in Boston?"

"Isn't that the problem? Really, Sean, isn't the stuff you read about me in the paper what's standing between us?"

"If you have to ask me, then you don't know what's standing between us, do you?"

She looked at the sapphire ring on her left hand. "Is there any way I can put all this right?"

"That's up to you."

"Without your help, I don't think I can." And she started to twist off the ring. "You should have this back."

He held her hand tightly, stopping her from removing the ring. "I still hope it's where it belongs," he said in a husky voice. "It will be if I can figure out exactly what I'm feeling right now."

"How long will that take?"

Sean pulled her into his arms and studied her face. "I don't know." He kissed her lips gently and looked at her mouth before he let his hands fall to his sides. "All I do know for sure is that there's something missing now. We have this grayness between us, an empty space that feels like I'm not sure I should try to cross it."

Emily raised a hand toward him, but he moved out of reach. "Would you like me to go?" she asked.

"Yes," he said, "I want to be alone."

She left him then, retraced her steps to the foyer and telephoned a cab.

When she put down the receiver, Sekowsky was standing in the doorway to the kitchen area. "Come and sit down while you wait," she said, a catch in her voice.

Emily shook her head and walked out into the night.

Chapter Seventeen

Emily decided the next move must be Sean's.

For twenty-four hours she clung to the resolution. Then she tried to call him.

Although it was almost six, Zig was still at the house. She asked Emily to wait, then came back on the line, "I'm sorry, Emily. I didn't realize he'd gone out for a while. Why don't you call back in an hour."

"Thanks, I'll do that." She hung up. There was no way of knowing if Zig had taken the initiative in suggesting another call, or if Sean, and Emily knew he must be there, had decided to buy another hour of thinking time.

She shuffled aimlessly through papers on the desk, unsure what to do next. At least there had been an easing of tension with Joe. He had come to her this afternoon. At first he'd simply sat at the other end of the couch, saying nothing, his hands hanging between his knees. Then, in a rush, he'd asked her to forgive him for coming on so strong when he first found out about her. "I'm happy, Em," he had assured her with a serious glow in his eyes, "really, I am. I did need a change. I know that now. It's too bad you're going through so much rotten stuff, but it'll come right." Then he'd left, saying he would be in and out of the area for a while and that they'd always keep in touch, if that was what she wanted.

And while he'd talked, Joe had unknowingly made her decide to take her own fate in her hands and move forward.

For a few minutes after her failed attempt to reach Sean, she roamed the house. The telephone rang and she snatched it up. Another reporter. She hung up tiredly.

The telephone rang again. She answered, heard a reporter's voice and quickly replaced the receiver. Then, lifting it again, she slowly dialed a long distance number. She should have done this days ago.

"James' residence. Hello."

Her throat closed.

"Hello?"

"May I speak to Mr. or Mrs. James, please?" They wouldn't talk if they didn't know who was calling. "This is their daughter."

A few moments later she heard her father's voice. "Gordon James, here. Who is this?" Her parents had probably been getting their share of annoying calls in the past days and must be suspicious of every ring of the phone.

"Dad?" she said softly.

She almost expected him to hang up. Instead there was a brief pause before she heard him clear his throat. "Sidonie?"

Tears welled in her eyes. She should have expected to cry. "Yes. I thought I owed you a call, Dad. I'm sorry about all the fuss again. I guess you were right, huh? The press never forget a juicy story."

"Don't worry about us. We can take it. How are you?" Her father's voice sounded suspiciously uneven. She must be mistaken. Gordon James never showed any emotion.

"I'm fine, Dad."

"Good."

She didn't know what she should say next. Then she remembered. "How's mother?"

"Fine. Just fine."

"Good. Well, I guess—"

"That Sean Townsend looks like a nice fella."

They must have studied the photographs carefully.

"He is."

"Sidonie. We...we, ah...your mother, I'll call your mother. Is that all right?"

She sniffed. "Of course it's all right."

Emily heard her father ask someone to tell his wife that their daughter was on the line. The wait seemed interminable, then there was another click and Elizabeth James said faintly, "Sidonie?" Her father was still holding another phone and promptly filled in everything that had been said so far. Emily smiled. Some things never changed. Gordon James had always been a totally take-charge man.

"Why did you choose Emily?" her mother asked when she was given a chance to speak. "It's a pretty name, but... well, I suppose I can't think of you as anyone but Sidonie."

"I am Sidonie, Mother. You must understand why I've had to use another name. It doesn't change who I am."

"I suppose not. Sean sounds like a very nice man, dear. We're very happy about the engagement. We thought we shouldn't try to contact you until you...well, we've learned a lot about some things in the past few years, Sidonie. We didn't know how strong-minded you are, dear." There was a second's pause. "Not that we think that's a bad thing. Young people have to be strong in today's world."

Gordon James cleared his throat.

"Anyway," Elizabeth continued, "we knew we shouldn't be the ones to make the first contact. I am sorry the press has dragged everything up, dear, but you mustn't let that worry you. They *always* do that."

"I know, mother," Emily said. Tension was exhausting her and she sat on the floor setting the phone in front of her crossed legs. She buried the fingers of one hand in her hair. "I've missed you both, you know."

A loud sniff and yet another clearing of the throat followed before her parents chimed together that they'd missed her, too. Hesitantly, Elizabeth wanted to know if Emily would see them again, could they be a part of her wedding? Emily closed her eyes. Gordon spoke, evidently interpreting the silence as a drawing back on her part. "We won't interfere, Sidonie. But your mother and I would like to give you whatever kind of wedding you've decided to have. And we'd like to be there if that's all right."

"I'd like that, Dad," she said tiredly. "But I don't know exactly what's going to happen at the moment. The publicity has hit Sean pretty hard. He didn't know about me until the newspapers splashed it all over the place. I should have told him, but there never seemed to be a right time."

"Now you listen, young lady," he replied with what Emily recognized as his smooth-everything-over voice, "it'll be all right. Give him a bit of time to get used to the idea and he'll forget it, just like we have. By the way, Charles said you'd call."

Emily sat up straight. "How is Charles?"

"He's getting engaged himself soon and he said to give you his love."

Emily laughed and relaxed. "He really was sure I'd call."

"You were friends a long time, Sidonie," Elizabeth put in. "He knows you very well. Maybe that's where we all made our mistake, we should have encouraged you to remain friends instead of pushing for... for the other."

"Maybe," Emily agreed. "But that's history. Give him my love, too, will you?"

By the time they all hung up reluctantly, Emily had promised that it wouldn't be too long before they were reunited.

She was surprised to discover that more than an hour had passed since her first call to Sean. Another hour went by before she found the courage to try reaching him again.

This time Sekowsky answered. "He's gone out, Emily."

Emily didn't believe the housekeeper, but neither did she blame her. She thought rapidly and made a decision. Getting away was the answer. She wasn't ready to go home to her family, but where else was there to go? Then she remembered Joe's cabin in the San Gabriel Mountains. He'd taken Emily and Larry there once, early in the summer, when they'd all been suffering from the heat. And he'd always said she was welcome to go back whenever she pleased.

"I'm going away for a few days," she told Sekowsky. "When Sean—when he gets back, please tell him I called and that I'm going to Joe Moreno's cabin in the mountains. It's not far from the Crystal Lake Recreation Area."

"Is that in the San Gabriel Mountains?" Sekowsky asked.

"Yes," Emily replied. "It's not much of a drive from here but it's remote and being totally alone is what I need for a while."

"Emily," Sekowsky said carefully, "how would I reach you if I needed to?"

"You won't need to," Emily assured her, while she wished the truth were otherwise. "But the Crystal Lake people know how to contact the private cabins. There are a few scattered vacation places up there and the regulars know each one of them by the owner's name."

"I wish you wouldn't go now."

"Why should I stay, Mrs. Sekowsky? He doesn't want to see me. He won't even speak to me."

A gusty sigh was the woman's reply.

"I'll probably be talking to you," Emily said hurriedly, feeling that if she didn't leave soon she might lose her courage. "One more thing."

"Name it. Anything."

Emily pressed her lips together hard for an instant. The stinging was in her eyes again. "Would you tell Sean that I love him very much?"

She dropped the receiver into its cradle before Sekowsky could respond.

Gathering a small bag of her oldest clothes didn't take long. In a plastic carryall, she stacked a jar of instant coffee, some cereal and a box of powdered milk, a few pieces of fruit, a loaf of bread and some peanut butter. As a last thought she wrapped a container of dishsoap in a plastic bag and tucked it between the boxes.

Ready. Except for the note she must leave. The main thing was to make certain neither Joe nor Larry felt they should come after her.

Emily thought carefully, then wrote with haste, telling them where she was going, that she was okay, that they were not to worry.

Then she left, stopping once to fill the Fiat's gas tank, before heading east to the Angeles National Forest then north on San Gabriel Canyon Road toward Crystal Lake.

She passed the lights of the recreation area and headed higher into the mountains. In the dark she had to lean forward, peering over the dashboard to make out the route she'd only taken once before. The road to Joe's place was no more than a track and likely to be covered with scrub grass now that there'd been a little rain up here. Within a month there would be the first dustings of snow even this low.

Emily did almost miss the winding cut to Joe's cabin. She sensed more than saw it and turned right sharply, then crept along between the crowding trunks of trees.

A small clearing was ahead and she drove on, slower yet, and smiled when the moon suddenly appeared from behind some clouds and illuminated the cabin. It was a little two-roomed structure Joe had bought from an old man who had finally decided there was no gold to be found in these hills.

Armed with a flashlight, Emily got out of the car and reached behind her seat for her bags. She stopped, half in and half out of the car. There had been a noise. Slowly, she

straightened and trained her flashlight on the track leading
in from the main road. A light patter started in her chest,
then grew with the swelling sound of a car's engine.

Sean had come. She walked toward the trunk of the Fiat.
Sekowsky had told him where she was going and he'd followed her.

Headlights swayed around the last curve then aimed directly at Emily. She shaded her eyes and took another step.
He did want her. He'd come.

The engine was cut and the headlights switched off. Emily strained to make out the shape of the car. It wasn't the
Jensen. She heard a slam and a familiar tall figure pounded
toward her over the hard ground. The moon picked out
blond hair.

Not Sean.

For an instant she couldn't move. The patter in her chest
turned to a heavy beating that pulsed into her throat. Emily raked at her own hair. The man came closer. "Oh, God,
no," she whispered. Then she screamed, "No! Go away.
No!"

She would know that loose-limbed stride anywhere. She
had seen it often enough. How could she have been such a
fool as to forget the man who'd been following her, to allow him to trap her in this place where there was no escape?

Blindly, spinning away, she started to run. But it too late.
A hand grabbed at her shoulder and held her fast.

Tearing at the hand, she tried to stumble on. "Let me
go," she moaned. He was too strong.

"Emily, it's me, Larry. I'm sorry I shocked you."

Larry. There wasn't enough air in the whole night to allow her to speak. It couldn't be Larry. The breath she did
take seared all the way to her aching lungs.

"Come on," he continued. He found her hand and
started pulling her toward the car he'd driven. "I've really
messed up, but at least he's not here yet."

The beating was in her head now. All this time he'd watched and waited, tailed her, preyed on her and finally he had her completely alone. Her legs threatened to fold. "I'm not going anywhere with you."

"You have to," he insisted. "Trust me, please, and let's go. I was afraid I'd be too late. But we don't have much time."

Not much time before what? Before he raped her? Killed her? Panic fueled her strength and she clawed at him, struck for his eyes and missed. She shook so badly her jaws cramped. "What do you want from me? What kind of a crazy man are you?" Emily wrenched her hand free. Larry, the man she'd thought of as a gentle friend, had been deceiving her for weeks, following her for weeks. She'd *lived* with this twisted pervert.

"Calm down," he said in a harsh tone she'd never heard him use before. "Cooperate. I expected him to get here first. He should be here by now. Oh, my, that's it. He wanted me here, too. We've got to get away, now."

His arm shot around her shoulders and she grabbed his jacket, steeling herself to make a dash for it, into the trees if necessary. "Larry—" she attempted a soothing note "—we can talk things through. You just go on back to the house and I'll meet you there. Then we can talk."

Larry didn't reply for several seconds. He dropped his arm from her shoulders and stepped back. "You just figured it out," he said simply. "You know I was the man following you."

"But it's all right," she said in a rush. "We can talk about it. You go back, Larry, and wait for me."

"Oh, my God. You're scared to death of me."

Emily heard a sob break from her own throat.

"Damn, damn. I should never have gotten into it," Larry said harshly. "I should have known I'd foul it up. Look, yes I followed you, but no, I'm not a kook. And if you'll come with me, while we still have time to get away, I'll tell you the whole crummy story."

"No." She mustn't do anything stupid, like pass out. Her head felt lighter and lighter.

He sighed. "I've been living a double life too. Does that hit any kind of sympathetic chord? And I haven't hurt anyone and couldn't if I wanted to. Emily, if I were a rapist who wanted your body or a murderer, wouldn't I have had enough chances to get it by now?"

She tried to think, but her brain wouldn't sort out everything he said.

"Emily, are you hearing me? Yes, I am the man who followed you, but not to do you any harm, quite the reverse. Think, I'm making sense. I could have gotten at you on any one of a million occasions without leaving home, right?"

"Right," she agreed slowly, "but why have you been following me?"

"There isn't time for that now."

"I'm not moving from here until you tell me."

"We *have* to get out of here," Larry pleaded. He looked over his shoulder. "I found your note, but he'd already seen it. Emily, *please*, come with me now."

She nodded past him at the car he'd driven. "Where did you get that?"

"From Red," he said impatiently. "We don't have time for this now. Come on!"

"Larry," she said patiently, "until you make some sense I go nowhere. You said you read my note so you know why I'm here. I'm just getting away for a while."

"Yes. I also know my first hunch was the right one. You had nothing to do with it, did you?"

"You could be talking Chinese, my friend. I'm not understanding you."

"Damn. You're putting a noose around our necks." His hand, clamped around her arm, propelling her toward the cabin, shocked Emily into silence. He hurried her up the two steps to the narrow porch and the front door.

He bent down and picked up the hemp mat, then swore, something Emily had never heard him do before. "Now what, Larry?"

"The key's not here," he responded, and with a wild charge that left Emily gaping, he rushed the door and succeeded in smashing a hole with his shoulder.

"Larry," she whispered, "Joe's going to be furious."

He ignored her and reached inside to unlock the door. There was no electricity and he grabbed Emily's flashlight. "Now are you getting the message?" He swung the beam left and right, then slowly brought it to rest on one area after another.

"Oh, no." Emily took back the flashlight and toured the main room of the cabin. "Oh, Larry, no. The police said—"

"That whoever robbed Sean Townsend knew what he wanted, where each item was, and had figured out a plan to get the stuff out quickly. Well, you have three possible choices for your criminal."

She lifted the flashlight beam high enough to see his eyes. "Three. Yes, of course. Three people who knew Sean's house and had access to it. And the same three people who knew about this place."

"You didn't do it, Emily, did you? Why would you when you already have a fortune of your own and you were marrying Sean anyway?"

Emily wanted desperately to sit down. She sank to the rough wooden floor. "Where were you later that night, Larry? I saw you with Red earlier, then there was all the photo stuff and I lost track of things a bit. But you weren't with Red then."

"No, I wasn't. Turn off the flashlight. We may need the batteries and I don't want anyone to know we're in here."

She turned it off. "You didn't . . ." the words trailed off and she waved a limp arm in the darkness.

"No, I didn't. You don't have to believe me, but I swear I didn't."

"I do believe you." She felt the conviction so strongly, she reached to find Larry's arm and squeeze.

"That leaves only one candidate," he said quietly. "Emily, listen closely and take in what I say fast. I got home and saw your note. I could tell it had already been read because it was all crumpled and there was a beer can beside it. The only person in the house who drinks beer is Joe. He read your note, knew you were coming here and would find Sean's stuff. Joe isn't going to risk having you blow the whistle on him."

"Joe?" she whispered. "I can't believe it."

"Just listen. He could have taken the note so I wouldn't read it and come after you. In theory no one would be any the wiser. Sidonie James, alias Emily Smith, does another flit. What else is new?"

She felt sick enough to vomit. "He would kill me and no one would know?"

"Correct. Only he decided to wait. You know why?" He didn't wait for an answer. "Because he's suspected I know he pulled the robbery and tonight he decided to get rid of me, too. I'm like you—my absence isn't likely to be taken very seriously by anyone. Red's car would be a problem, but he'd work that out. I wouldn't even make the papers in a missing persons column because no one would report me missing. Now, can we go? He's not going to be far behind me, I know it."

Still there was something missing in the story. And he hadn't explained a lot of things she needed to know before she could completely trust him. "When did you know Joe had done this?"

"Emily, you're going to get us killed, lady. I knew the night of your engagement party. Let's go."

Emily peered into the gloom, trying to make out Larry's face. "You knew, but you didn't go to the police? I'm not getting much of this."

She heard him make a frustrated grunt, then he lowered his long body to the floor in front of her.

He sighed. "We're going to regret not getting the hell out of here while we can. But you won't go until I explain, will you?"

Although he couldn't see, she shook her head.

"The fastest way through this is to explain all about me first. Emily, I didn't come to Joe's house by chance exactly. Oh, the ad for a housemate was useful, because it got me closer to you and made my job easier. But it was an opening I didn't expect."

"What are you trying to tell me?"

His shoes made a scraping sound as he must have crossed his legs. "I promise you, you'd be better off trusting me and talking this through in the car, driving *away* from here."

Pressure swelled in her head. She wanted to go, but she'd made too many mistakes. "Keep talking."

"Yes, okay." But he remained silent.

"Larry?"

"Everything I've told you about myself is true. Almost everything. My folks. Where I come from. Wanting to be an actor, everything."

"But something's not true?"

She could barely see him lean forward. "Okay," he said, "here goes. After I got to L.A. I couldn't make ends meet with the kind of part-time jobs I was getting so I signed on with a detective agency—"

"Oh, sure, Larry. You're a detective." She was tired and scared.

"No, not a detective, just a not very adept tail who earns extra money snooping after people for a bunch of private eyes. The truth is, that a lot of people love you. Your parents love you so much that they had you traced and when they found out where you lived I got the job of following you around to make sure you were okay."

She began to shake. "You mean you reported my movements to my parents." That explained why, when she'd called them earlier, they hadn't asked where she lived. They already knew.

"No," Larry said in a patient tone, "I've never spoken to your parents. Before the newspaper spreads I didn't even know you weren't Emily Smith, rebel offspring of ordinary doting Mom and Pop. I'm a peon who follows orders. One of the guys I work for passes on the information. And although you're too rattled to accept it now, all your folks wanted was to make sure you were okay."

"Were you watching me before I moved in with Joe?"

"When you lived in the apartment in Santa Monica, yes. I was watching you."

"I never saw you."

"You never went anywhere. You didn't have a job. The running track was right where I could see you from my window in the next building. All you did was go to the grocery store and run and stay home. It wasn't until you moved to Joe's that you really became a problem." He laughed mirthlessly. "And I had actually congratulated myself that my job would be even easier."

Emily absorbed what he said. "All right. Forget all that for a moment. How did you know for sure that Joe stole Sean's things and brought them here, and why haven't you gone to the police?"

"Are you sure I can't tell you this while we drive?"

"Absolutely sure."

"Hell! I met Red at your engagement party and, wonder of wonders, she seemed as interested in me as I was in her. Then the cameras arrived and she wasn't anywhere around. Instead she was hanging on the arm of some producer so that she'd get her face front center for whatever publicity was going. I felt lousy, so I went outside and sat in your Fiat to calm down. That's when I saw that the truck was missing."

"The truck?" She squinted toward him.

"When we were on our way to the party, Joe suggested we stop by your office and get the truck. He would drive it and we'd both have wheels in case one of us wanted to leave early. When I went out to the Fiat, the truck was gone."

"I saw Joe leave earlier, with a girl, Larry. They must have gone for a drive."

"Wrong. *I'd* seen Joe a couple of minutes before I went outside and he was headed for the bathroom, I thought."

Emily frowned. "He could have moved the truck."

"That's what I wondered about," Larry said. "But I was worried so I went looking for Joe, but the door to Sean's wing was locked—that's where he was headed when I last saw him—so I assumed he wasn't in there. I was going to give up but I wasn't comfortable somehow so I kept looking and finally went outside. Guess what I found?"

"I can hardly wait."

"Your very own Occasion People truck parked behind the terrace outside Sean's suite."

Emily clutched at him. "And Joe was loading things?" She stared around the shadowed room. "These things, into the truck?"

"Correct."

"And you didn't call the police?"

"I couldn't."

"Why, Larry?"

He loosened her fingers and held her hand. "Because, my silly lady, while I lived with you and watched over you I got to like you. You were a friend to me. And when I saw that truck being loaded up I couldn't be sure you didn't know anything about it. For these last three wild days I told myself you couldn't possibly have done something like this just to hurt your folks again, because that would be hurting Sean and I was sure you loved him. But I couldn't be certain. And until I was, I was damned if I'd blow the whistle on you."

"Oh, Larry." She went limp and began to cry. "Why didn't you just come out and ask me?"

"Doesn't what's happened to you in the last few days answer that one? Sometimes we go too far to know how to get out. And the easy way, like being honest, seems too easy. As soon as I saw your note tonight I knew you were clean.''

He pulled her to her feet and wrapped an arm around her shoulders. ''We're the only people, as far as I know, who can put the finger on Joe. We *have* to leave.''

''He wouldn't do—''

''He would and he will. I'd bet everything I have—even though it isn't much—on Joe Moreno's ability to make absolutely certain we aren't around to turn him in.''

''Why do you think he knows you're on to him?''

Larry took her hand again and started toward the door. ''When he left Sean's I followed him and saw him start up here. I figured he planned to hide the stuff here and get rid of it slowly. Once I knew where he was going, I went back to the party, by which time the police were there and people were being questioned. I slid in through the terrace doors and stood just inside. No one even seemed to notice me until about an hour later when Red came over. She'd already been questioned. She asked me where I'd been and I said down to the Strip for some cigarettes.''

''You don't smoke.''

''I know that. Red doesn't always pay a lot of attention when she's got other things on her mind. She's never noticed. But while I was standing there, I noticed Joe. He was outside the doors and I could tell he'd just arrived. He never said a word but I'm sure he'd heard my conversation with Red and knew I'd been gone. He just turned around and walked away. He heard what I said to Red and that blew everything. He *does* know I don't smoke. He couldn't have been sure how much I knew, if anything, but when we looked at each other there was something that passes between people when they don't trust each other.''

''Wouldn't he have expected you to go to the police and tried to shut you up right away?''

''I wondered about that and I think the answer's tied to the one I gave you about why *I* didn't go to the police. I believe he thought I'd wonder if you could be tied in and that because we're close he decided he probably had a little time."

"He took a gamble," Emily stated flatly.

"If he catches us here together it could pay off. I wish I'd taken the time to call the police before I left tonight."

Emily thought awhile. "There are two of us and one of him."

Larry gave a short laugh. "If you've got some idea of waiting in the dark and jumping Joe, forget it. First, he'll probably be armed, and second, even if he's not, he could still finish us both at the same time."

"What if we meet him coming—"

A steady rumbling sound made Emily stop. The sound got closer. They'd waited too long.

"Stay where you are," Larry whispered. He dropped to the floor and crawled to the door then back. "Get down. Hide. We'll have to try to get out without him seeing us and hope we can make it away. He's under the trees to our right. No headlights. I can see the truck because its white."

A scream rose in Emily's throat but she choked it down and sank to her knees. "Is there a back way out?"

"Not that I remember."

"Okay." Emily took a deep breath, and another. "We will jump him. Find something heavy and...what's that?" They heard an engine noise again, then it stopped.

"He's out there watching, deciding how to make his move. He probably turned around so he can get away faster."

Emily was frantically pawing through a pile of fur coats. "Something heavy that's not worth a fortune," she muttered, feeling around.

"Who cares how much—"

The door swung open. Emily crouched, one of the coats in her hands. They hadn't even bothered to close and bolt the door properly.

He entered, tall, broad-shouldered. For a moment he stood still and she saw his head move from side to side, scanning the room. To her left, a small sound let her know where Larry was.

The man took another step.

"Jump, Larry!" Emily yelled and at the same instant she leaped at the figure, catching the coat squarely over his head and torso and clinging to his back with her legs wrapped around his waist.

He struggled, but his arms were trapped.

"Grab him," Emily managed to gasp. "Quickly."

Larry was behind her then, throwing his weight against the man's legs and they all fell, grunting, to the floor.

Emily panted, but she held fast to the writhing body inside the coat. "Get on top of him," she ordered Larry. "I'll find the flashlight. If he moves, I hit him, and that thing is heavy." Why hadn't she thought of the flashlight immediately?

While she felt around, Larry stayed on top of the now unmoving bundle.

Her fingers closed on the flashlight. "Turn him over," she said and kicked at a leg until she connected hard. There was a muffled and very satisfying "Ouch," and Emily kicked again, saying, "Over, you!"

She trained the beam on the fur-swathed head. Larry maneuvered himself and the unresisting man until his own knees were securely pinning the other's arms.

"Did you really think we'd just let you come in here and kill us?" Emily parted the coat, then shone the flashlight on the face inside.

"I wasn't really thinking about killing anybody," Sean said, blinking and trying to turn his head, "until now."

Chapter Eighteen

"Oh, hell, Emily, it's Sean," Larry said. He continued to stare down into Sean's lit face.

She knelt beside the two men. "We thought you were Joe." Relief made her giggly. Shaking started in her legs and spread all over her body. Her teeth wouldn't stay together. "He... he stole your things and brought them up here. See?" She waved her spare arm. "He locked your rooms while he loaded all this stuff in the truck, then he put them up here. We weren't supposed to find—"

"For God's sake, Larry, will you get your bony knees off my biceps?" Sean broke in, "and turn off the damn flashlight, Emily."

Larry swore under his breath as he shot to his feet. Sean sat up, shrugging free of the coat. "Where is Joe? I saw the truck outside and your car, Emily, and Red's." He glanced around. "Is Red here too?"

He sounded bemused and Emily's giggles erupted into jerky laughter. "Larry borrowed Red's car," she managed. "And we don't—"

Sean took the flashlight, and Emily almost fell forward. He steadied her. "What's going on here?" He swept the flashlight beam over the room. "Joe stole my things? Why?" His hand, tightening on Emily's arm, hurt. "I don't understand one bit of this."

Emily took a deep, calming breath. She never remembered becoming hysterical over anything, but the way she felt right now suggested the first time could easily be at hand.

"We don't understand it all either, Sean," Larry said. "But I don't think we have many more seconds to find out. I think Joe is sitting out—"

A deafening crash drowned out anything else Larry might have said. The door smashed against the wall and behind a massive flashlight beam loomed the giant flickering shadow of a man. "You don't have any more seconds. Get up slowly, Townsend," Joe ordered. "And drop that flashlight."

Sean must have made a move toward Joe because there was a rush of air and Emily heard flesh and bone connect and a grunt, then there was a clatter and her flashlight spun across the floor.

"Joe, please—" Emily began.

"Shut up. This is your fault." The light moved, to the right, then behind them. A hand smacked her between her shoulder blades and sent her sprawling, face-first, onto the rough floor.

"You son of a bitch, Moreno. I'm going to—"

"Do nothing," Joe cut Sean off. "I've got a gun, golden boy, and you'd better believe I'll use it if I have to. You forced me into this, you and my *partner*. Now, I'm going to make sure you take a very long time to get to the police with your little story. Get outside."

Emily had gotten as far as her hands and knees when she felt Sean's arm around her waist, lifting. "Hang on, sweetheart," he whispered. "It's okay."

"Shut up!" Joe shoved Sean, making him stagger but he quickly regained his balance. "Larry, go first. Too bad you couldn't have minded your own business the other night. You could have gone right on being a nothing, but you had to interfere."

Larry went silently ahead of them into the cool air. Sean kept an arm around Emily and they felt their way down the steps from the porch.

"Get to the truck." Joe jabbed something hard into Emily's back. She winced and couldn't hold back a little cry.

"Leave her alone." Sean swung around and Emily saw moonlight flash on the darkly gleaming barrel of a gun as it connected with the side of his head. He fell to his knees, hunched over, and she dropped beside him.

"Sean, Sean," she whispered. "Don't argue with him. He's gone mad. He's going to kill us all if we don't do as he says."

"He's going to kill us anyway if we don't think of something," Sean muttered, his face close to hers. Larry bent over them and rested a hand on Sean's back.

"Look, you three," Joe's voice softened persuasively, "I didn't want it this way; it just happened. Emily forced my hand. But it'll be okay. I'm going to drive you far enough away to give me a good head start. By the time you make it back I'll have split, but you'll be okay. So cooperate, huh? Make it easy on us all."

"Sure." Sean got up, finding Emily's hand and squeezing it. "Whatever you say, Joe."

He shepherded them to the back of the truck and opened one door. "Get in," he said. "And in case you've got any ideas, these doors will be locked—on the outside—and there are no windows. So just sit tight and there won't be any trouble."

Larry was first inside and he helped Emily scramble up, followed by Sean. The door clanged shut and a bar fell into place, closing them into thick darkness.

Almost immediately the truck's engine roared and the vehicle bumped over rough ground. Emily knew Joe was driving back down the track to the road, then, as they were thrown against the left side of the bare interior, she figured their route must be to the north, where the terrain got higher and rougher and people were even fewer than around the cabin.

Every turn sent them sliding across the metal floor of the truck. Sean tried to cushion Emily and he felt Larry do the same, but there was nothing to hold onto. Blood had run down the side of Sean's head, congealing along his cheek and jaw.

The truck made another abrupt turn. "How far?" Emily asked abruptly. "How far have we gone? What will he do to us?"

Larry muttered something unintelligible and Sean decided he liked this quiet man whom Red had evidently decided to take under her wing.

"He isn't going to leave us anywhere alive," he said, hating the way Emily stiffened against him. "He's going to take us to the remotest place he can find, kill us, then go back and get rid of the cars. Then he'll move his haul on to a place where he feels safer and start fencing it."

Emily's long, slender fingers twined with his. "People don't get away with things like that. He'll—" They slid halfway across the floor, then were thrown against the back doors in a tangled heap.

"Damn him!" Larry yelled. "Joe, damn you!"

Sean scrambled to find Larry's face and pressed a hand over his mouth. "You won't say a word, do you understand? Not a word. When he opens the back of this truck one of two things will happen. The first and worst, he'll shoot us all where we are, then drag us out and throw us over some cliff. If that's what he's decided we might as well help him pull the trigger. It's my guess he won't want to dirty up the inside of his truck." Emily made a sound but he pressed on. "I think he'll get us outside and then finish us. Only he's not going to do it without a fight."

"The bastard—"

"Larry," Sean said warningly. "We've got to keep our heads and save our energy. Don't talk, just follow his orders like you've lost your nerve. And when I give the signal, spread out. Just start moving steadily away from me so he can't keep us all in his sight at one time.''

"Then what?''

He never got to answer Emily's question. The truck ground to a halt. Joe left the engine running and Sean moved back from the doors, pulling Emily with him. Larry was on his other side. He braced himself for the impact that could come and felt the others do the same. His deduction about Joe not killing them in here could be very wrong. The engine could have been left running to make the getaway quicker, or to cover the sound of gunfire.

The bar scraped from its hooks and a handle was wrenched up.

"Okay," Sean murmured. "Are you both with me?''

"You've got it," Larry said.

"Got it," Emily echoed.

The cold air that rushed in when the door swung open cut through their clothes.

"Out.'' Joe spoke from the blackness outside. He had the flashlight on again and was only a moving hulk against a backdrop Sean couldn't make out.

All he could think of for the moment was that they had one more slim chance to stay alive. He was last out of the truck and stood slightly apart from Emily and Larry, waiting for Joe's next move.

The door to the truck swung shut and Sean's spine jolted. Joe had swept the beam of light away and there was nothing but the sound of wind scuffling dust eddies across the land, the scent of pine and the interminable darkness. Clouds had hidden the moon again, the white truck's pale outline the only relief from endless blackness.

"Joe," Emily said, willing her voice to be steady. "I'm sorry if I did something to upset you.''

His laugh curled her insides. "*Upset* me? You didn't upset me, you fool. Warm beer upsets me. Losing a pool game upsets me. You messed with my life plans, baby, and that's the one thing nobody does and gets away with.''

She felt unnaturally calm. Sean stood behind her, a little distance away. She could feel him there. The uneven breathing she heard to her left had to be Larry. "There's always a way out of a situation, Joe," she said persuasively. "We can all come out of this winners."

"*I'll* come out of it a winner, baby."

Sean was right; Joe was going to kill them. She had a sudden idea. "Look, if you want that stuff back in the cabin, I'm sure Sean will give it to you. How about him signing a statement saying what you took is a gift. Then you go your way and we go ours and we'll forget it."

"Emily," Larry said in a tired voice, "don't waste your breath."

A movement she couldn't see sent Larry sprawling at her feet.

"Shut your damn, mewling mouth, Young," Joe yelled. "You should have stayed with your go-nowhere scripts, *loser*. Then at least you could have spread your misery out a bit longer."

Emily helped Larry up. He remained doubled over holding his middle.

"Leave him alone," Emily said, peering in the darkness until she made out Joe. "Whatever I've done to you, or supposedly have done to you, is none of his fault."

Why didn't Sean say something, *do* something?

"I don't want to hear any more from you, *Sidonie James*. If I'd known who you were before I pulled this job I'd have figured a way to make money a lot easier. I'm sure mommie and daddy dear would have paid good money to know where their only little girl was."

"Knock it off," Larry said.

Emily stood between him and Joe. "You said this was my fault. Why?"

"Because you let me down. I was doing okay. A little here, a little there, all good stuff that brought good prices and I thought I had time to plan the big one."

The dampness on her skin turned icy. "You mean you've been systematically robbing our clients?"

"Big deal. No one noticed. Move closer together—all of you!"

Emily stood her ground. "How did I interfere with your plans?"

He laughed again. "You don't catch on fast, do you? I wanted you to get buddy-buddy with Mr. Golden here, but not too buddy-buddy. I didn't want you to marry the guy, you little fool. I didn't want you to cut out or do anything so fast I didn't have time to plan cleaning him out and getting the hell away without any hitches. But you had to push it, didn't you? You ended up giving me one lousy day to plan the whole thing. And if Larry boy hadn't decided to turn into a snoop I might have pulled it off."

"I'd have found Sean's things when I got to your cabin," Emily reminded him quietly.

"Yeah. I'd have had one dippy broad to deal with instead of a crowd, plus a fleet of cars. You've dropped out before, Emily, who'd be surprised if you did it again after all the stuff in the papers. They're already writing that you and Sean are estranged. It would still have worked for me."

The soft play of fingers across her back brought a cry to Emily's lips. She turned it into a cough. "Did you arrange for the mimes, Joe? I guess you must have. That was clever."

"Yeah. You don't have to be born rich to have brains, baby."

She hated him. How could she ever have thought he was her friend?

"I always knew you had brains, Joe. That's why we did so well in business."

Sean was close behind Emily and Larry now. "Two taps," he murmured, "and you run, Larry left, Emily right."

"What did you say?" Joe demanded and the beam fell fully on them.

Sean pushed a hand into each of their backs and as she ran, Emily sensed him dropping to the ground. "Go!" he shouted. "Keep running! Go!"

A shot rang out. Emily stopped and turned. There was only silence. She wanted to call Sean's name but knew she could kill them all if she didn't follow his instructions exactly.

The next sound she heard was the jarring thud of flesh on flesh, then another shot, and another. Emily strained to see but there was nothing but the shapes of scrubby bushes and rocks close by. She heard men scuffling, grunts and a noise that could only be bone hitting rock. Joe and Sean were fighting—for their lives and for hers and Larry's.

She started picking her way back in the direction she'd come. The moon appeared again and she scanned the area. She had run farther than she'd realized. Where was the truck?

Emily took a step and slipped. Her right ankle scraped rock. She couldn't stop the scream. The shrub she grabbed halted her fall.

"Emily!" Sean's voice came from some distance away. Thank God he was still alive.

"I'm okay," she called. "Where are you?"

He didn't answer. She glanced to her right and her stomach shot upward—her leg extended over the edge of a sheer drop. She scrambled up, started to run and crashed into Larry.

He grabbed and held her. "I hear them," he said. His breath came in ragged sobs. "Over there." He pointed. "But I can't see them. Stay here, Emily, I've got to help Sean."

"Wait, Larry!" By interfering he might help, or he might finish whatever chance they had.

"For what?" As soon as he'd spoken a scream fractured the night. "Oh, God."

"Help me! Help me!" Sean's voice cried out.

Emily and Larry ran toward the voice.

"Careful," he yelled. "Come slowly. Get down on your hands and knees. He's gone over the edge."

Emily knelt and her shin hit something—Joe's flashlight. She turned it on and swept the ground until she saw Sean. He lay stretched on his stomach, his head and shoulders out of sight.

"Quickly," Emily urged Larry. "Joe's gone over."

At the edge of the great cleft in the rock, Emily flattened herself beside Sean with Larry on his other side.

"I'm losing him," Sean said. "He's slipping. Hold me, Larry."

The light picked out Joe's pale face below. His terrified eyes stared and his mouth was open, although he made no sound. Sean held him by one hand while he swung, his other arm flailing, trying to grab anything.

"Joe," Emily called, "hold on. It'll be all right." She set down the flashlight, lay on the ground and extended her own arms. Joe's eyes focused on her and he grabbed.

Their fingers brushed.

"Joe!" Emily screamed. "Try again."

The next scream wasn't Emily's. It was a terrible sound she would never forget, a shrill, piercing sound that grew fainter and fainter, until she could hear it no more. She buried her face in her hands.

"I couldn't hold him," Sean said, and he was crying. He moved closer and pulled her into his arms.

When the moon broke completely from the clouds it shone on three figures clutching each other. They didn't see the moon or each other, only felt the beating of their own hearts and heard their whispers of grief and gratitude.

A FAINT BREEZE rippled the surface of Sean's pool and gentled the heat of a glaring noon sun.

Emily watched the blue water and tried to relax, but the events of the night and the early morning hours crowded in. The drive to Crystal Lake Recreation Area to call the police. Questions. The horror of having to return to the place where Joe died. More questions. Back to the cabin. Then the drive to Los Angeles escorted by city police. And still more questions. "Go home and take a break for a few hours," they'd been told an hour ago. Emily felt almost as if she were a criminal out on brief parole.

Mrs. Sekowsky approached from the house and placed a tray of coffee and sandwiches on the wrought-iron table between Sean and Emily. "Is there anything else I can do for you?" Lines of fatigue scored her face.

"No, thanks, Sekowsky," Sean said. "The police will be calling when they're ready to question us again. Don't let it worry you. It's just routine stuff now."

Emily rubbed her aching eyes but managed to smile at Sekowsky. "I thank you, too. Did Larry get to sleep?"

Sekowsky chuckled. "He passed out in Mr. Sean's old room. I tried to take him coffee but I was too late. He didn't even close the door...or take off his clothes." She set off for the house, her steps less brisk than usual.

"This has been tough on a lot of people," Sean said. He stretched an arm across the table and Emily held his hand.

"Yes, a lot of people." She glanced at his exhausted face. Someone at the police station had washed away the blood but a bluish welt, raw in the center, stood out above his temple. He'd refused to see a doctor. The reflective expression in his eyes let her know Joe was on his mind. She thought about him, too, and looked away. She mustn't keep thinking about Joe, not until she could separate heart and mind. "I wonder if Larry and Red can really get something going," she said.

Sean twined their fingers together. "I hope so. The guy's got spunk and he's a lot stronger than I thought. Emotionally as well as physically. Red needs that."

"Mmm. They'll make an interesting couple."

"We'll make an interesting couple."

Emily eased her hand from his and made much of pouring coffee.

"Emily? Did you hear me? We're going to make a fantastic team."

A jumpy feeling started within her, a trembling in her limbs. "I feel filthy. If you don't mind, I'd like to have this coffee and go home for a long bath."

She'd set a cup beside him, but he covered her hand on the table before she could withdraw. "Don't avoid me, please. And I thought your home was supposed to be with me from now on."

"The last time I saw you...before tonight, I mean...you wanted to be alone."

"I was being unreasonable—"

"No, you weren't. I became a problem to you. I'm still a problem, probably more so. Why did you decide to come after me?" She already knew why.

"Sekowsky passed on your message, word for word. You said you loved me. You called several times while I sulked around wondering if you were going to hurt me even more. And still you could leave a message like that."

"I meant it. It's not so hard to say what you mean."

"Some of us don't do so well in that department. But I'm not going to let you down again, sweetheart."

Remaining sensible wasn't going to be easy. "You think that now. How will you feel when the media go after me again—and they will. And your friends, Sean, what about them? I want to be with you, but I don't think I could stand seeing you suffer the kind of ridicule that's likely to follow me around—and you if we're together."

Sean got up and dragged his chair until he could sit facing Emily. "I'm not a fool. Look at me and hear what I'm saying. You're right, there will be some talk, but anyone who doesn't like you and see the kind of person you really are can get lost. Understand?"

"Yes, but there are a lot of things that need to be said."

He leaned forward and pulled her head onto his shoulder. "Not now. Later maybe, but not now."

Emily rested her fists on his knees and looked at him. "Before all the newspaper garbage you believed in me. Then you were shaken up and I don't blame you. You didn't know if you could trust me or not."

"I do now."

"Probably. Yes, I think you do. But I should have been able to tell you about myself before you found out from someone else."

"It's not important anymore. I understand and I intend to forget the whole thing. God help any smartass reporter who tries to get near you."

Emily touched his stubbly cheek. "Thanks. You may want to change your mind on that."

"Never."

"Hear me out, Sean. This is important." She took a long breath. "Mark Bates was divorced after that little scandal broke. He never went anywhere in politics and he lost his family at the same time. The press said it was my fault."

His eyes, when they met hers, were bright with anger. "Mark Bates had a reputation for sleeping around. He should never have put his neck out and tried for another office. And from what I read, he and his wife were already separated. The end. I don't want to talk about it."

"Why? Because you think I was just one of many women with him and so it wasn't any more my fault than theirs?"

Sean frowned. "I didn't mean that. I meant that I believe you and it doesn't matter to me what anyone else thinks."

"There may be times when you really have to remind yourself you said that. But I *was* only a pawn in what happened to Mark Bates."

"Yes—"

"Please let me finish. I tried and tried to see the man at his office and when I failed, I decided to get into his penthouse somehow and wait for him. After all, I figured, he was bound to be impressed by my ingenuity."

"Why did you go to see him?"

"I was working with a group who were protesting the demolition of some low-income housing. Developers were planning on putting up a shopping mall. Old, old story, Sean, with all the usual trimmings. And I was young enough to think I could make a difference." She bit her bottom lip, remembering how idealistic she'd been. "That's kind of sad, isn't it?"

Sean held out a hand and she placed hers on top. "It's sad if we stop believing we can make a difference in the world."

"The night I went to Mark Bates's penthouse I knew he was out. I carried an overnight case. Walked right through the front door and told the security man I was Mr. Bates's niece from Cleveland, his sister's daughter, and that I wanted to surprise him.

"I should have known everything went too smoothly. When Bates did come he listened but said he couldn't help and by the time he showed me out the press were there. They'd gotten a tip-off. Someone was just waiting for the chance to set Bates up and I was even better than any dream they'd had. The innocent daughter of an old Boston family and engaged to the heir of another considerable fortune. Later I tried to find that security man but he'd left town."

Sean nodded. Absently, he turned the glimmering sapphire on her ring finger around and around. "Rotten old world, huh? But look at it this way, you got a crash course in life and you're still loving and giving."

Emily bowed her head. "I do believe you love me and want me, but I think we should wait until the dust settles before we decide what to do next."

"No way." Sean gave a short laugh. "I've decided and you already agreed. We're getting married. Have you finished your story?"

When she looked at him, he smiled, leaned forward and kissed her lightly. "You have finished. Good. And you're not backing out on me?"

Was it lack of sleep that made her light-headed? Emily didn't think so. "I could never back out on you."

"So you're game? We go ahead . . . together?"

"Together, Sean. But it won't be—"

"Easy. I know. We'll deal with whatever comes and you'll be surprised how fast a new focus for gossip comes along. Then you'll be one more matronly has-been."

"What?"

Sean caught the fist she waved at him. "One more wife and mother. Gorgeous, of course, but not newsworthy."

"Thanks a lot. We've agreed on the wife bit, and I'll go along with children too, in time. But I have thought that I'd like to build some sort of career for myself. In fact, I'm thinking of going into the party business. I've been told I have a flair for that sort of thing."

"Mmm." Sean screwed up his face in concentration. "You think you'll like it?"

"I know I will. How about you? Maybe Townsend of Townsend Alarms would be embarrassed to have a wife who worked."

"Nothing you do could embarrass me." The serious set of Sean's features showed he meant what he said. "I come from people who like to build and create things. You and I have that in common too."

Warmth, a mixture of love and respect, surged inside Emily. "You know how to say the right things, sir. I'm glad you understand that as wonderful as you are, I may enjoy doing something besides bask in your delectable shadow."

Sean feigned affront. "Dozens of women would kill for the chance."

"I'm sure they would," Emily said. "But they won't get the chance, I'll see to that."

"Good," Sean said, "very good."

ATTRACTIVE, SPACE SAVING BOOK RACK

Display your most prized novels on this handsome and sturdy book rack. The hand-rubbed walnut finish will blend into your library decor with quiet elegance, providing a practical organizer for your favorite hard-or soft-covered books.

Only $9.95

Approximately 16" x 8" when assembled

Assembles in seconds!

To order, rush your name, address and zip code, along with a check or money order for $10.70* ($9.95 plus 75¢ postage and handling) payable to *Harlequin Reader Service*:

Harlequin Reader Service
Book Rack Offer
901 Fuhrmann Blvd.
P.O. Box 1396
Buffalo, NY 14269-1396

Offer not available in Canada.

*New York and Iowa residents add appropriate sales tax.

BKR-1A

MAIL-IN-OFFER
---- OFFER CERTIFICATE ----

I have enclosed the required number of proofs of purchase from any specially marked "Gifts From The Heart" Harlequin romance book, plus cash register receipts and a check or money order payable to Harlequin Gifts From The Heart Offer, to cover postage and handling.

002

CHECK ONE		ITEM	# OF PROOFS OF PURCHASE	POSTAGE & HANDLING FEE
	01	Brass Picture Frame	2	$ 1.00
	02	Heart-Shaped Candle Holders with Candles	3	$ 1.00
	03	Heart-Shaped Keepsake Box	4	$ 1.00
	04	Gold-Plated Heart Pendant	5	$ 1.00
	05	Collectors' Doll Limited quantities available	12	$ 2.75

NAME _____

STREET ADDRESS _____ APT. # _____

CITY _____ STATE _____ ZIP _____

Mail this certificate, designated number of proofs of purchase (inside back page) and check or money order for postage and handling to:

Gifts From The Heart, P.O. Box 4814
Reidsville, N. Carolina 27322-4814

NOTE THIS IMPORTANT OFFER'S TERMS

Requests must be postmarked by May 31, 1988. Only proofs of purchase from specially marked "Gifts From The Heart" Harlequin books will be accepted. This certificate plus cash register receipts and a check or money order to cover postage and handling must accompany your request and may not be reproduced in any manner. Offer void where prohibited, taxed or restricted by law. LIMIT ONE REQUEST PER NAME, FAMILY, GROUP, ORGANIZATION OR ADDRESS. Please allow up to 8 weeks after receipt of order for shipment. Offer only good in the U.S.A. Hurry—Limited quantities of collectors' doll available. Collectors' dolls will be mailed to first 15,000 qualifying submitters. All other submitters will receive 12 free previously unpublished Harlequin books and a postage & handling refund.

OFFER-1RR

Take 4 best-selling love stories FREE
Plus get a FREE surprise gift!

from *Harlequin*

FREE BY MAIL With proofs of purchase plus postage and handling

A. Hand-polished solid brass picture frame 1-5/8″ × 1-3/8″ with 2 proofs of purchase.

B. Individually handworked, pair of heart-shaped glass candle holders (2″ diameter), 6″ candles included, with 3 proofs of purchase.

C. Heart-shaped porcelain keepsake box (1″ high) with delicate flower motif with 4 proofs of purchase.

D. Radiant gold-plated heart pendant on 16″ chain with complimentary satin pouch with 5 proofs of purchase.

E. Beautiful collectors' doll with genuine porcelain face, hands and feet, and a charming heart appliqué on dress with 12 proofs of purchase. Limited quantities available. See offer terms.

HERE IS HOW TO GET YOUR FREE GIFTS

Send us the required number of proofs of purchase (below) of specially marked "Gifts From The Heart" Harlequin books and cash register receipts with the Offer Certificate (available in the back pages) properly completed, plus a check or money order (do not send cash) payable to Harlequin Gifts From The Heart Offer. We'll RUSH you your specified gift. Hurry—Limited quantities of collectors' doll available. See offer terms.

403R

ONE PROOF OF PURCHASE

To collect your free gift by mail you must include the necessary number of proofs of purchase with order certificate.